JUNIPER WILES

Other books by Charles de Lint

JUNIPER WILES

CHARLES DE LINT

TRISKELL
PRESS

TRISKELL PRESS
P.O. Box 9480
Ottawa, ON
Canada K1G 3V2
www.charlesdelint.com

Cover design by MaryAnn Harris

"Fair Helena" by Arthur Rackham (1908)

Digital image licensed by Publitek, Inc., Fotosearch Stock Photography

ISBN 978-1-989741-01-6

This is a work of fiction. Names, places, businesses, characters and incidents are either the product of the author's imagination or are used in a fictitious manner. Any resemblance to actual persons living or dead, actual events or locales is purely coincidental.

*for Julie, Kenny
and especially Nora*

INTRODUCTION

Many urban-fantasy novels are told via a first-person narrative, and often feature mythological beings, romance, and female protagonists who are involved in law enforcement or vigilantism.
   - Wikipedia

I might add, those protagonists are usually a witch, vampire, a kind of were-creature, or someone who hunts the same.

From time to time I've seen myself cited as the "father of urban fantasy," and while I may not quite agree, that's a conversation for another time. What strikes me as particularly odd about being described that way is how different today's urban fantasy is from my own work, especially my novels set in Newford.

Now, don't get me wrong: I really like some urban fantasy— Melissa F. Olson and Patricia Briggs being among my favourite authors, the sort that when a new book of theirs arrives it takes precedence over all other reading.

I just hadn't written that kind of novel myself, but the novel you hold in your hands could loosely fit today's definition of urban fantasy. And it kind of snuck up on me, as stories tend to do.

After I finished *The Wind in His Heart*, I passed it over to MaryAnn to do her magic. Many of you know *The Wind* is a long book that took around seven years to write, and I knew it would take

MaryAnn a while to do her edit. So, as always when I finish a project, I opened a fresh file and started writing something new. I got about a page and a half into it when I realized I was more interested in a little throwaway part of the story (the mention of a TV series called *Nora Constantine*) than the actual story itself, and that it might work as my take on a modern urban fantasy.

So I opened yet another file and, by the time a good year or so had gone by, and MaryAnn had finished her edit of *The Wind in His Heart,* I had three short novels about a character named Juniper Wiles who played Nora in the TV series. Since then I've written another one and a half, plus a new novel that MaryAnn is currently editing.

I wrote these for fun, with no idea whether they'd be entertaining for anybody else. That's how I write all my fiction—to entertain myself during the first draft process. Rewriting and proofing the book in hand, I found myself still enjoying the antics of Juniper and her friends, so I've decided to send the tale out into the world.

~

This first Juniper Wiles story is set some fifteen years after the end of *Widdershins* (2006), which was the last time we visited with Jilly and her friends.

Ottawa, Spring 2021

I believe in kindness.
Also in mischief.
—Mary Oliver

1

MONDAY

"Do you ever get tired of being famous?" I ask Jilly.

She looks away from her canvas and laughs. "I'm not famous."

"Oh come on. Prints of your work are everywhere now. Not to mention the calendars, cards, mugs—"

"Okay. Maybe my work's pretty well known these days, but not me, personally. I can walk down the street and nobody gives me a second glance, except to wonder how someone my age can still be gadding about looking so scruffy."

~

WHEN I FIRST MOVED BACK TO Newford I didn't have a clue what I wanted to do with my life. I just knew it wasn't going to involve TV, films, or even theatre. I'd taken on a number of film roles and TV guest spots after *Nora Constantine* ended, and had offers beyond appearances at conventions to reprise Nora for photo ops, but at some point it was like a switch got turned off in my head and I just couldn't do it anymore. I liked the work. I just didn't like everything that went with it. A-listers can afford a buffer between themselves and all that extraneous crap, but I was never even close to being an A-lister and still had a fair amount of the crap. I just didn't want to play the game anymore.

Or maybe I just got sick of L.A.

All I knew at the time was that I had to get out. Leaving the West Coast to come home seemed like the perfect option. I'd been homesick for years. For one thing, Newford has actual weather.

Of course the old saying is true. You can't really go home again, mostly because home isn't there anymore. It resembles the nostalgic place in your head, but too many of the specifics have changed or disappeared.

But there are constants. Crowsea's always going to be boho cool. My brother Tam will still be playing in a half-dozen popular local bands, with no great ambition to make it big outside the city. And Jilly Coppercorn will still be doing her faerie paintings, except now—instead of eking out a living—she's famous for them.

I still remember going to one of her workshops at the Arts Court years ago, before I got "discovered" and the Nora gig drew me away. She reminded me of an elf with her crazy hair and those sapphire eyes. All she needed was the pointy ears. Tam and I used to hang out there all the time. He spent every chance he had learning any instrument he could get his hands on. I dabbled, trying everything. A little music, a little drama, a little writing. But I loved painting and drawing the most, so it's kind of weird that I became an actor.

I tried to keep up with my visual art when I first got to L.A., but life became too busy and I didn't find enough subject matter to hold my interest. I like the sun and surf, and even L.A.'s seedy streets as much as anybody—hello, Venice Beach—and managed to fill a couple of sketchbooks. But one day I set them aside and never picked them up again.

I wanted to paint seasons. I wanted Crowsea's streets, the Old Market, the oaks on Stanton Street. I wanted the characters that people Newford's streets in all their varied eccentricities.

⁓

THE ARTS COURT was the first place I went after I left my bags at the house I shared with Tam. I didn't know if Jilly'd still be volunteering there. She was lively and vibrant back in the day, if a bit of a raggedy old hippie to my teenage eyes. Over thirty? Might as well move into the retirement home. But when I found her in a side room off the main court surrounded by a gaggle of kids, she was still full of life and enthusiasm.

In fact, she seemed exactly the same, which didn't make a whole lot of sense. Doing the math, I figured she should be at least twice my age, but she looked like she only had a few years on me, as though she had my family's youthful genes on turbo charge.

"You don't look remotely old," I told her once. "What's your secret?"

"I spend a lot of time in Faerieland. It keeps me young."

At the time I thought she was kidding.

~

SHE LEANS CLOSER to her canvas to study some detail, then looks over at me again.

"What's got you talking about fame?" she asks.

I shrug. "Just some random guy in the coffee shop who insisted I was the real Nora Constantine."

Jilly smiles. "The famous kick-ass detective."

I groan. "I played her years ago. And it's not funny."

"Come on, now. It's cute, and a little sweet. It means your work touched him."

"He wanted me to take on a case."

"Really? What sort of a case?"

"I didn't ask and I shut him down before he could tell me."

She still seems to be smiling, but there's a quizzical look on her brow, so I know she's not happy with my answer.

"What?" I say.

"You catch more bees with honey than with vinegar."

"Except I wasn't trying to catch anything."

She nods as if she agrees, but says, "Creating art also creates an obligation. Our private lives should be private, but we should also make room to accept the appreciation of people who love and support our work. Without them, we'd still create, but most of our days would be spent scrabbling to make a living."

"I understand that. Nora and her fans let me live a modest life without having to work, and I totally appreciate it. It's just the fervour

of some of them that makes me uncomfortable—you know, the ones
that can't separate the real me from the work."

"Yes, well," Jilly says. "I know I'm a constant disappointment to
the faerie community because I'm nothing like the elegant faerie
princess they envision. They expect gowns, tiaras and long flowing
hair. Instead they get me."

"You're everything I'd want you to be."

She laughs. "You're too kind," she says, putting on an airy voice as
she waves away my comment. Unfortunately she uses the hand
holding her paintbrush, and a small constellation of cerulean blue
paint sprays out across the studio floor. Fortunately, it just blends in
with the older dried spills and splatters, and misses the two of us.

We're in the Grumbling Greenhouse Studio, a glassed-in structure
set against the rear of her house, which they all refer to as
Bramleyhaugh, after its original owner. The space had once been an
actual greenhouse, subsequently transformed into an artist's studio
back when Jilly and her friend Sophie were first attending Butler U. A
few years ago the property had been left to the pair of them by their
old art professor Bramley Dapple. Once they moved in, the house
underwent a transformation from a professor's residence, which
seemed to be more a library with a bit of living space, to an artists'
colony full of painters, writers and musicians.

On several occasions Jilly's said there's plenty of room for Tam and
me to move in, but as much as I like the people living there, and spend
a fair amount of time with them, neither Tam nor I can do the
commune thing. That's how we grew up. It's why we have hippie
names like Juniper and Tamarack. But it's a great place to hang out,
and I love working in the studio with Jilly and Sophie and whatever
other artists happen to drop by.

This afternoon it's just the two of us, but I'm sure the studio will
be crowded come evening. FaerieFest, the summer festival that
celebrates all things mythic and musical, is less than a week away and
everybody is helping Jilly with her final preparations, if not working
on their own magical art. I'm doing things like framing paintings and
organizing prints, while Jilly puts the finishing touches on various
paintings.

I've been trying to get her to sign prints all afternoon, but she
insists she has to work on the paintings. The truth is, she doesn't like
signing prints and I don't feel like arguing with her. The only people

who can get Jilly to do something she doesn't want are her husband Geordie or Sophie, and they'll both be here tonight.

FaerieFest is the reason for Jilly's current popularity. No, scratch that. Her art's the reason, but the festival is what brought her the attention of her legion of fans who've embraced not only her and her art, but also the work of that core group of friends Jilly calls her family of choice. They enthusiastically support Sophie's painting, Wendy and Saskia's poetry, Mona's comics, Geordie's music, and especially her brother-in-law Christy's writing.

"They treat us like superstars," Wendy told me the first time I went with them. "You'll see. We're like paragons for the three days of the festival. It's so weird."

Jilly wears what she always does—jeans and a baggy shirt, or maybe she'll switch it around with a T-shirt and some kind of baggy pants—but Wendy, Mona, Saskia and I always dress up. Sophie doesn't have to. She always looks like she just stepped out of a Pre-Raphaelite painting, so it doesn't matter what she's wearing, she fits right in.

The guys make a half-assed attempt with their leather vests and pirate shirts with puffy sleeves, but you wouldn't catch any of them with a pair of elf ears or wings. Personally, I like having pointy ears and especially the decorative wings. They make me feel like I can fly. Only Mona's boyfriend, Lyle, makes a real effort, matching his outfit to hers. If she goes as a mermaid, he's Poseidon. If she's Titania, he's Oberon. If she's a May Queen, he's a Green Man. You get the picture.

"I wonder," Jilly says as we wipe up the worst of her paint spill, "what sort of a case your—excuse me—Nora's admirer had in mind."

I roll my eyes. "You're still fixating on that?"

"I'm not fixating. I just find it intriguing."

"Well, we could always go back to the Half Kaffe Café and see if he's still there. Then you could ask him yourself."

Jilly grins. "What a brilliant idea."

"No, it's not. The FaerieFest is in less than a week and there's still a ton of stuff to do."

Jilly stands up. Walking over to her easel, she drops her brush into a glass jar full of muddied turpentine and lays a piece of plastic wrap over her palette. There's some paint on her hands, which she wipes off on her jeans where it fits right in with a half dozen other smears.

"Faeries spend too much money," she says. "The less we bring, the more they'll save. Now come on. Doesn't a latte sound tempting?"

She heads for the door, knowing full well that I'll follow.
Sophie's going to kill me.

~

A LIGHT RAIN starts up halfway along our walk from Stanton Street to
the Half Kaffe Café. When we step inside, Jilly shakes her head like a
dog, water spraying from her curly hair. Luckily, we're not near any
customers, but I have to wipe my face.

"Whoops," Jilly says with a giggle. "Sorry about that." She looks
around, eyes bright with interest. "Is he here?"

I shake my head.

"Go claim a table," she says, "and I'll grab us our coffees." She
catches my arm as I start to go and presses a crumpled ball of paper
and a pencil into my hand. "You should do a sketch of the boy."

"I wouldn't know where to start. He looked like anybody."

"Oh pish. You'll be surprised what you can remember if you put
your mind to it."

"But—"

"Just do the best you can," she says and sails off to the end of the
line at the counter.

I sit at a table by the window. Smoothing the paper out, I stare
down at its creased lines without a clue how to begin.

Jilly returns, lattes in hand, and eyes the blank paper in front of
me. "Nothing?"

I shrug.

She sits across from me and pushes one of the tall mugs over
to me.

She takes a long sip of her coffee, then licks the foam off her upper
lip. "Yum, I'm so glad you suggested this."

I'm mid-sip myself and almost spit it out as I choke back a laugh.

"Okay, start with the obvious," Jilly says with a grin. "Did he have
a face?"

"What kind of a question is that? Of course he had a face."

"Here," she says.

She plucks the pencil from my hand and sketches an oval on the
paper. With a few deft lines she adds the suggestion of eyes, nose,
mouth, ears. She turns it around so that I can see what she's done.

"Now we've got a face," she says.

"Which is completely nondescript."

"True. So think of a detail."

"I'm honestly coming up blank. I was annoyed." Then I remember locking eyes with him and I remember his features a little more.

"Okay." She scoots her chair around so that we can both look at her sketch. "Were his eyebrows thin?" She adds a fine set of eyebrows above the suggestion of the eyes. "Or thick?"

She starts to darken them. I stop her before she does much more.

"They were a little like that. Maybe."

"That's good. Now how about his nose? Slender? Wide? A bird's beak? Ski slope?"

As she continues to coach me, I find myself remembering more and more detail. Sometimes I take the pencil and make a little change, but mostly it's her drawing and asking questions. After about half an hour I stop her.

"Holy crap," I say. "That looks exactly like him." I give her a suspicious look. "How'd you do that?"

"Oh, it's just this gift I have."

"No, seriously."

"Magic?"

I give her a hard stare and she pats my hand.

"Okay," she says. "The truth is, I used to have this fascination with police sketch artists—you know, the way they can often get a pretty accurate representation of someone they've never actually seen. So I used to get my friends to take a picture of somebody at a bus stop or something, and then they'd sit with me and describe the person while I tried to draw what I could from their descriptions and corrections. At some point they'd be satisfied and we'd compare my drawing with the picture they took."

I've come to discover that only Jilly would do something like that for the fun of it.

"And obviously you got good at it," I say.

She nods. "But it took a long time."

She stands up and we take the drawing to the counter to show it to the barista during a lull in customers. His name tag says "Jason," but I've been here often enough to know that the baristas wear random tags, so who knows what his real name is. This Jason is the usual hipster you'll find in a coffee shop. Slender in his tight jeans, short-sleeved shirt buttoned at the collar, hair short on the sides, long on top, the almost-beard that you can tell has been perfectly trimmed to that length, glasses, moustache.

"Jason," Jilly says as she holds up her drawing. "Do you know this guy?"

"Sure," he says, taking the drawing to have a closer look. "That's Ethan. He's in here all the time." As he hands the drawing back he adds, "That's a good likeness."

Jilly turns to give me a grin before she asks the barista, "What's his last name?"

"Sorry, I wouldn't know. We only write first names on the cups."

"Well, when he comes in again could you give us a call?" Jilly takes a Half Kaffe Café business card and writes her phone number on the back as she speaks. "He's a person of interest in an investigation we're conducting."

I roll my eyes.

"Are you guys cops?" the barista asks.

It's plain he doesn't believe it, and who can blame him?

But then he takes a closer look at me.

"Wait, I know you," he says. "I've been trying to figure it out every time you've come in. You're Nora Constantine. My sister loves that show of yours." He frowns. "Except..."

"It's fiction," I fill in for him. "I know."

"Fiction, schmiction," Jilly says.

The barista looks from her to me, obviously confused, and I still can't blame him.

"So, what's going on?" he asks.

"My friend—" I jerk a thumb in Jilly's direction "—thinks we've suddenly become private eyes. Like in the show."

He nods. "And Ethan..."

"I was probably a little rude to him earlier today, so I wanted a chance to apologize."

"Cool. Hey, can we take a selfie? My sister's going to die when I post a picture of me with the real Nora Constantine."

Who, I want to say, we just established isn't real. But I manage to keep my mouth shut. Instead, I give him a high-wattage smile like you'd use in a headshot.

"Sure," I say to Jilly's obvious approval. "Why not?"

One selfie later, Jilly and I are out on the street. The rain's stopped, but the sky is still a lowering grey.

"I'm going to the animal shelter to borrow a dog," Jilly says. "Do you want to come?"

"Why would you want to borrow a dog?"

"To take him to St. John's Home for the Aged. The people there love a visit from a dog. I mean, who wouldn't?"

"What about those prints that need to be signed?"

"There's plenty of time for that."

She hooks her arm in mine and off we go to the shelter.

I LEARNED a long time ago that Jilly's idea of fun is to help people and interact with them. An outing with her might take you to the soup kitchen to prepare and serve a meal, to sort clothes and whatnots for a church bazaar, to the animal shelter to walk dogs or play with cats, to hang out at the Arts Court with the kids, or some combination thereof, which is what we're doing today.

I have to admit that an old folks' home is a lot more fun than I ever thought it could be. But this is the first time I've done it in the company of a couple of dogs. At the end of Jilly's leash is Bobo, a wiry terrier/toy poodle mix. At the end of mine is a large but calm golden retriever named James, which is weird because that was the name of my boyfriend in the last season of *Nora Constantine*.

The staff and the residents know Jilly, but that's not unusual. People seem to know her wherever she goes. It was the same at the animal shelter. Here, she's like a purposeful whirlwind as she darts around the common room, Bobo in tow, but at the same time she has a Zen peacefulness when she stops to chat with the old men and women. She knows them all by name, naturally, and enough of their personal histories to have meaningful, if short, conversations with each.

I was worried about Bobo. At the shelter and on the way here he exuded an unbridled energy that Jilly managed to mostly keep in check. But he's like a different dog now, following at Jilly's heels, leash dragging, a calm presence in the wake of Jilly's enthusiasm. By contrast, the formerly placid James tows me from one chair to the next, eager to greet each new face, then on to the next one. Thank heavens he never jumps up on any of the residents.

By the time we leave, the room is alight with smiles and I find that

I don't care about the prints waiting back at the studio any more than Jilly does.

As we near the shelter, Jilly's pace slows. I think I know what she's feeling. It's like we're putting the dogs back in jail, although the truth is, we've managed to break up the tedium of their day for a couple of hours so we shouldn't be feeling bad.

Jilly stops outside the door of the shelter and sits on her heels, right there on the sidewalk. Bobo leaps up onto her lap.

"You know," Jilly says, "I've been doing this for years, but it's only just occurred to me that I'm no longer living hand-to-mouth. I've got a house. I can have a dog."

"Are you sure about this?" I ask. To say that Jilly can be impetuous is like saying the sea is full of salt water. "It's a serious commitment."

"I know it is. I'll have to talk it over with Geordie."

I smile. Like he can say no to her.

"I wonder," she adds, standing up again and holding Bobo against her chest, "if they'll let him come home with me for the evening to meet everybody."

Which is how, a half hour later, we're walking back to the house, Bobo trotting beside Jilly. Every few steps he looks up into her face so adoringly that my heart just melts.

I feel a little pang—not for James, but for the idea of having a dog.

"I always wanted to have a dog," I find myself saying.

"What's stopping you?"

I shrug. "I don't know that I'd be the best pet owner. They're a big responsibility and they…" I don't want to say it in front of Bobo, which is weird, but I lower my voice. "They don't live long."

Jilly gives me a radiant smile. "Ah, but you'll never understand pure love the way you will when they are with you."

"You've had dogs before?"

"Not really. But I know what it's like to live your life and have every moment be precious."

She glances down at Bobo. "Everybody's going to love you," she says.

I smile. That dog's never going back to the shelter.

THE DEAL IS SEALED when we get to Bramleyhaugh. As soon as we walk through the door and Jilly lets him off his leash, Bobo goes racing down the hall to where he can hear people in the kitchen. I get there just in time to see him standing on his hind legs, front paws on Geordie's knees, wiggling his butt as Geordie strokes his head.

"And who's this?" Geordie asks, looking from Jilly to me.

"His name's Bobo," Jilly tells him. "I thought we could use some dog energy in the house if everybody agrees. Otherwise he has to go back to this little cage at the shelter and lie there all by himself on this thin ratty blanket in the scary dark and—"

Geordie cuts her off with a laugh. "I don't need the hard sell, Jilly. He can stay."

"You're sure?"

"We always had dogs when I was growing up. It's one of the things that kept me sane back then."

"What about everybody else?" Jilly asks the room in general.

There's a chorus of agreement in response.

Geordie smiles as the happy-go-lucky pup drops back to the floor and makes the rounds of everybody sitting at the table. He's joyous, tail up and wagging, until he gets to Mona's boyfriend Lyle. Just like that, his body language changes. Ears down, tail lowered, he stands quivering until Lyle slides down from his chair and confronts the pup on all fours. He whispers something in the pup's ears and Bobo perks up a little.

"That's right," Lyle says as he sits back on his legs. "You can be the boss of this house."

Bobo slaps his front paws on the floor, butt in the air, and barks.

Lyle ruffles the hair on top of the pup's head. "Don't let it go to your head." He stands up and returns to his chair.

I look at Jilly and say WTF with my eyebrows.

"Lyle's always been the top dog in this house," she tells me.

"Used to be," Mona adds and everybody laughs.

I've been hanging around with these people for years now, but I still don't get some of the jokes.

"It's because he's a werewolf," Jilly explains.

I shake my head. "As if."

Jilly just smiles. "Something smells amazing in here," she says, heading toward the pot on the stove. Wendy made a vegetable stew and there's still enough left for Jilly and me. As we eat, the conversation around the table bounces between books and music, social media and TV shows, politics and art. In other words, as much of a stew as what's in our bowls, and a typical evening here at Bramleyhaugh.

Before leaving for home I go to collect my backpack in the studio. Sophie's sitting at the long table that runs the length of one of the glass walls, sewing the binding on what I assume will be a new sketchbook. Some kind of fiddle music is playing softly, but I don't know enough about that kind of music to be able to name the band.

Sophie looks up with a smile when she hears me come in. "Hey, Juniper."

"Hey." I glance over at the untouched stack of prints and feel a pinprick of guilt. "I tried to get those signed," I tell her, "but what with one thing or another…"

Sophie waves off my failure. "Honestly, getting Jilly to do something she doesn't feel like doing is like herding cats."

"She says she's going to work at the soup kitchen tomorrow morning."

Sophie nods. "Maybe we can sit her down in the afternoon. I'll get Geordie and Amy to entertain her with some music while she's doing it."

~

Tam's sitting at the kitchen table when I get home. He's got his earbuds in and he's fingering chords, his right hand moving in a quick rhythm, though his pick isn't actually hitting the strings. He doesn't notice me until I put my backpack on the chair across from him.

"Hey," he says, pulling his earbuds off.

"Hey, yourself. What're you doing?"

The only light comes from a lamp in the shape of an old streetlight on the end of the counter. The air smells pleasantly of garlic, ginger and cilantro, so I know he made himself a stir-fry for dinner. Naturally, the dishes are still piled up in the sink.

"I'm just running over some accompaniment for Geordie's tunes— for the gig at the FaerieFest," he adds unnecessarily, because I'm the one who told Geordie about Tam when the band's regular guitarist had to bail.

I drop into a free chair. "Without actually playing your guitar."

He shrugs. "I didn't want to bug the neighbours, it being a school night and all."

"You know, it's been years since you lived in that little apartment. This place has thicker walls."

He shrugs. "Old habits." Closing the music app on his phone, he rests his forearms on the top of his guitar and leans forward. "What have you been up to today?"

"This and that. I went to the animal shelter with Jilly, and I'm pretty sure she's adopting a dog."

"I'm surprised she didn't get one sooner."

"That's exactly what Wendy said."

"Let me guess," he goes on. "It's young, small and full of energy."

I pull back, surprised. "How would you know that?"

"Come on. It's Jilly. Can you see her with some placid old retriever?"

I feel a twinge of guilt, thinking of James who's still at the shelter, so I decide to change the subject.

"Question. What do you feel you owe your fans?"

He smiles. "Is Greta trying to get you to do another of those conventions?"

Greta Swirsky's my agent. Even though I'm no longer working in the industry, all my residuals go through her and I'm happy to give her a percentage because without her, there wouldn't be a percentage to take in the first place and I'd be vying to wear the Jason name tag at the Half Kaffe Café.

"You're not answering the question," I say.

"I'm not sure I understand the question."

"The people who buy your music and come to your shows—when you're off stage should you still have to be the guy who was up there, or do you get to be Tam Wiles again? Your ordinary self."

Tam closes his eyes for a moment and drums his fingers lightly on the body of the guitar. "We are the same guy," he says. "It doesn't shut off." He gives me a considering look. "Why are you asking about this?"

So I tell him about the boy in the coffee shop and how extreme he was.

"Wow," he says when I'm done. "That's a whole new level of fan drama."

"I know. Over the top weird, right?"

"And tricky," he says. "The whole point of your craft is to portray a character that your fans can fully believe and invest in. But the person you're depicting isn't the real you. And to have someone actually believe that you're that fictitious character off-screen is…"

His voice trails off.

"Weird," I finish for him.

"You don't get a lot of that, do you? I mean, this extreme."

I shake my head. "So long as I don't listen to Greta."

2

TUESDAY

The next morning, as soon as I open the front door to Bramleyhaugh, Bobo comes racing from the back of the house barking his fool head off. He skids to a stop and dances around my legs until I give him a few pats. Mission accomplished, he races back the way he came.

I follow at a slower pace. There's no one in the kitchen, so I continue to the studio where I find Jilly sitting on the sofa studying her latest painting. I set my backpack on the floor and drop down beside her.

"Hey, Juniper," she says.

Bobo heads over to my pack, sniffs every inch of it, then jumps up on the sofa and settles between us with a sigh.

"Sorry, pal," I say, ruffling the fur on his neck. "No goodies for you in there." Then I look up and study the painting as well.

At first it seems like a landscape, some kind of a brambly hedge broken up by the trunk of a fat oak, with the suggestion of a big house rising up behind it. But looking closer, there's a whole community of tiny people living under the hedge. The detail is incredible.

"That's amazing," I say.

"Mmm."

"You don't like it?"

"I don't not like it. But it has no narrative. It's not saying anything to me."

"It says there are little people living under a hedge."

"Yes, it does say that. But how does it connect to us, the viewers? There's no way in and no final destination where the eye naturally rests. It's all just a busy clutter."

I see what she means. I get up to look at it from another angle and that's when I see this morning's edition of *The Newford Star*, half hidden under her palette. A familiar face looks out at me. It's obviously one of those images that newspapers pull from people's Facebook or Instagram pages. I pull the paper out to give it a closer look.

"Oh, that's an awful story," Jilly says. "I don't know why I look at the paper anymore."

"This is him," I say. "The boy from the café. Ethan."

And just like that my head takes me back to yesterday's encounter.

So it's not like I enjoy being snarky, but really. The boy standing on the other side of my table in the coffee shop should realize that, laptop open, earbuds in, me ignoring him—these are all clear signs that I'm preoccupied and don't want to engage in conversation. I suppose once he leaves I should make a "do not disturb" placard and prop it up on my table.

But he's unwavering in his mission.

"You're Nora Constantine," he says.

"No, I'm not."

He shakes his head. "You totally are."

"You know she's just a character, right? She's not real."

I could add that I'm only Juniper Wiles, the actor who played that part, but why bother? He's already waving a hand to show the irrelevance of actual facts.

"What are you doing in Newford?" he asks. "Are you working on a case?"

I blame the internet for keeping Nora Constantine alive, and my family for the genes that keep me looking like the twenty-year-old I was when I played that role ten years ago. But the gullibility of people like this guy, who can't tell the difference between reality and entertainment, that's all on them.

Nora Constantine was based on a series of books by Emma K. Rohlin about a feisty, red-haired, green-eyed, teenage detective, solving crimes in between her classes at a community college. The show was a minor success, running three seasons before it got cancelled. Once upon a time that would have been it, but between DVD sales, streaming services, and the limitless ability of people to download whatever the hell it is that they want from the internet, it's gained a huge cult following and a much longer life than anybody expected.

I haven't worked in film or TV for years now, but I still get calls from Greta about requests to appear at comic cons and the various permutations thereof. I used to call her back to turn them down, but I don't even bother anymore. She might think it's okay to charge fifty bucks to have your picture taken with some besotted fan, but I think it's reprehensible. My choice. Everybody else can do whatever the hell they want.

I can't lie. I love how the residuals from DVD and merch sales allow me to not have to think about where my next paycheque is coming from. So long as I keep my expenses reasonable and the money doesn't dry up, I can probably keep doing this for another ten years. But that doesn't mean I have to pretend to be Nora.

Except tell that to this guy.

"How much do you charge to take on a case?" he asks.

"A million dollars."

He laughs. "No, seriously."

"Seriously, I'm a real person, not a character in a book or TV show, and you need to leave."

"But—"

"Or seriously, I'm going to have the manager throw you out and bar you from ever coming back."

"You can't do that. This is my favourite coffee shop."

"Then you know what to do."

We lock gazes and I swear he stands there for a good half minute before comprehension finally dawns in his eyes. Turning, he stalks back to his table, shoulders stiff with anger. I return my attention to my screen and notice the time in the corner. So much for answering a few emails before I get to the studio. I sigh as I shut the laptop and drop it into my backpack where it rattles against my art supplies. Standing, I swing the pack to my shoulder and head for the door. I can feel the boy's gaze track me as I'm leaving, but I ignore him the way I wish he'd ignored me.

How much do you charge to take on a case?

What an idiot.

～

JILLY LEANS over to look at the picture. "There's a resemblance, isn't there?"

She's remembering the sketch she did, but I talked to him in the flesh. This is the same guy. They even give his full name in the caption. Ethan Law.

"Look," I say, pointing to the name. "It's definitely him."

Jilly frowns. "But the article says—"

"That he disappeared a week ago, which is impossible because I saw him yesterday." I continue to scan the article. "What? It says his body was found last night in Fitzhenry Park under some bushes. The coroner estimated he's been dead for several days. A jogger found him because her dog wouldn't come back to her. She walked over to get the dog and noticed a foul smell. When she pulled the dog back she saw a foot and phoned 9-1-1."

I look up at Jilly. "How is that possible? I know I saw him yesterday—alive."

Jilly's frowning. "I'm surprised I didn't twig to the photo after all that time we spent on the composite sketch yesterday. I glanced at the headline, but didn't read further."

She rises from the sofa and walks over to the table by her easel where she sorts through various papers and sketches until she finds yesterday's drawing. We both sit back down on the sofa and compare the sketch against the photo in the paper.

"Same guy," Jilly says, nodding. "I guess I really didn't look at the photo."

"Well, I got a good look at Ethan in the coffee shop yesterday."

Jilly looks at me. "I guess he really did have a case for you."

"Not if he was already dead." I find myself shivering. "God, this is so creepy."

"Maybe the case was to catch whoever killed him."

"Yeah…I don't think so."

But Jilly's not listening to me.

"You know what this means, right?" she says. "We need to take a trip back to the coffee shop."

"And do what?"

"Investigate."

"I think we should just leave it to the police."

"Aren't you curious if anyone else saw him yesterday?"

I hug my chest and look at her. "I didn't see him. I saw a ghost."

"Still."

If only I hadn't looked at that newspaper.

"You've got prints to sign," I say to redirect the conversation.

"This is more important."

"Plus I thought you were going to the soup kitchen this morning."

"We can stop in at the Half Kaffe on the way."

I sigh. "You pretty much have an answer for everything, don't you?"

"So that's a yes?"

The truth is, I might be creeped out, but I am a little curious.

"Sure," I tell her. "Why not?"

Jilly bounces to her feet. "Do you hear that, Bobo? The circumstances are tragic—no question—but we're going to investigate a crime with Nora Constantine."

"Not you, too."

"It's a team up!"

"You know Nora's a fictional character."

Jilly smiles. "So you keep saying. Yet here you are."

"Except I'm not," I tell her. "Nora, I mean."

But Jilly's already on her way out of the room, the little dog trotting at her heels.

~

JASON's behind the counter when we get to the Half Kaffe Café, except this time the name tag is pinned to the chest of a tall, African American woman with her hair in corn rows and the most gorgeous skin you could possibly imagine. She just glows. I've seen her in here before, but I can't remember what her name tag said then.

I expect to be told that Bobo can't come in, but as we stand to one side of the counter waiting for the line to be served, no one says a word. When a lull finally comes Jilly steps up to the counter and turns

her high-wattage smile on the barista. She takes the sketch out of her
pocket and unfolds it before handing it to—I guess we'll have to call
her Jason.

"Do you know him?" Jilly asks.

"Oh, wasn't it just horrible what happened?" Jason says. "Ethan's…
was…a regular here."

"We were wondering when you saw him last."

"Why would you—" her eyes widen. "Hey, you're Jilly
Coppercorn. I love your art. I've always wanted to tell you that."

"Thanks. Sorry about your friend."

"He wasn't a friend, just a familiar face. I only knew his name from
writing it on the cup. Rough, what happened to him though."

She closes her eyes and shakes her head as if clearing her mind,
then looks back at Jilly, her eyes bright once more. "I can't wait for
FaerieFest this weekend," she says. "I've got a different outfit worked
out for each day."

Jilly smiles and prompts her to talk about her costumes, but
another customer shows up so Jason deals with the man's order. When
she's done she calls to the back room to get someone else to come out
and handle the counter. The girl that appears has short spiky hair and a
lot of piercings. Her name tag reads "Tess," which I suppose might or
might not be her name.

"Can you cover me for ten minutes?" Jason asks her.

"Sure."

"Hey!" Tess calls after us as Jason leads the way to a free table.
"You can't have a dog in here."

"He's not a dog," Jilly tells her. "He's an alien abductee who got
trapped in this shape by Venusians. He used to work in a coffee shop
just like this one before it happened, so he's like your brother-in-arms,
if you stop to think about it. You're not going to toss out a fellow
barista just because he's had some bad luck, are you?"

The confused look on Tess's face is priceless.

"It's okay," Jason says. "They're only here for a couple of minutes."

"It's on your head, Amana," Tess tells her.

I adjust to the name change as we sit down.

"Why were you asking about Ethan?" Amana asks.

"Juniper," Jilly says, giving a nod in my direction, "met him in here
yesterday."

"But the news said…"

"Exactly! It's uncanny, don't you think? We were wondering if anybody else saw his ghost or if it was just Juniper he was haunting. Were you working yesterday?"

"I'm still trying to get my head around the idea of an actual ghost being in here," Amana says.

"This city's full of mysteries," Jilly says.

"Yes, but…" Amana turns to me. "And you'd never met him before?"

I shake my head.

"Then why would he be haunting you? Just saying he existed." She looks around the café. "I'm not being pranked, am I?"

"He wanted me to take on a case," I tell her.

"A case? Are you some kind of a detective?" She cocks her head as recognition dawns in her eyes. "Damn it if you're not Nora Constantine! I wondered why you always looked so familiar."

"Except I'm not. I just played her on a TV show. But Ethan was convinced that I was her for real."

"You mean…Ethan the ghost."

"I know how it sounds," I tell her. "But I also know what I saw."

"We thought we should find out more about him," Jilly says. "And if anybody else saw him yesterday."

"Around what time was it?" Amana asks.

"Noonish to one," I tell her.

"Robert and Emma were working that shift. I could ask them."

"That'd be great," Jilly says. "Do you know any of his friends?"

Amana shakes her head. "Like I said, I never really talked with him. But sometimes he was with a guy who works in the used bookstore down the street."

"Burns' Books?"

Amana nods. "But I don't remember his name."

"That's okay," Jilly says, getting up from the table. "We can find out. You've been a big help."

Amana gives a nod, not really hearing her.

"A ghost," she mutters, mostly to herself.

She's still sitting there with a dazed expression when we leave the Half Kaffe.

~

BURNS' Books is across the street and down the next block, tucked in between a little Vietnamese pho restaurant and a card and paper shop. The window's full of old fairy tale books—Andrew Lang, K.M. Briggs, the Brothers Grimm—no doubt to take advantage of the festival this weekend.

"I haven't been here in ages," Jilly says as she checks out the window display.

Bobo puts his paws on the wall and tries to look in, but he's too short.

"Where do you go for used books?" I ask.

"Sometimes I go to Turtle Moon but mostly I go where I always have. I get Christy to drive me out to Holly's shop." She glances at me. "I like to support my friends—plus she's got a hob. I wonder if they have a hob in here."

"I never know if you're kidding me or not."

"Why would I kid you about a hob?"

"Why indeed?"

"You were much better about the Nora Constantine thing with Amana," she says, abruptly changing the subject. "Good for you. We should all embrace our triumphs."

"I wouldn't go so far as to call the show a triumph. It's not like we ever got nominated for an Emmy, and we did get cancelled."

"But after three seasons. That's pretty good for TV, isn't it?"

"I suppose."

Jilly gives me a serious look. "You know, you're a promising artist but you're a great actor, or at least so I've been told."

"What do you mean, so you've been told?"

Jilly smiles. "You know me. I don't watch much TV. I've never seen your show."

I have to shake my head. This is so her.

"So what makes you think I'm any good?"

"Isn't it obvious? Someone came back from the dead just to meet you." She waits a beat. "And Wendy loves the show. I think she's watched all three seasons a half-dozen times."

"She could have bad taste."

Jilly shakes her head. "Oh, no. She has impeccable taste. She's our friend, isn't she?"

With that, she opens the door and steps inside the store. A little bell sounds above the door, summoning a clerk from a closed doorway behind the cash counter. There are books stacked on the counter, books everywhere. The shelves are stuffed, more titles lean in tottering piles wherever there's a spare inch of room. The store smells of old paper—not the kind of musty smell that comes from a book stored in a damp basement or a garage, but a dry, whispery smell that promises everything to a book lover.

I follow Jilly to the counter. The clerk is seriously good-looking but he carries himself as if he has no idea. A girl can tell this kind of thing. Kind of hip, but no hipster. Nerdy glasses like Elvis Costello used to wear, a button-down shirt with the top button undone. Short brown hair, a little messy, but none of that shaved-sides crap that I'm so over.

I'm so busy checking him out that it takes me a moment to realize that he's doing the same. He smiles when our gazes meet. His eyes are a golden, greenish-brown and I don't want to look away.

"I know you," he says.

And just like that, the spell is broken. Here we go again.

Except he says, "You used to work out at Power Fitness—the one on Yoors, down by the mall."

Really? How does he know that?

"You've got a good memory. It's been a couple of years."

He smiles. "What can I say? You made an impression. I used to see you in the weights room while I was working on my cardio."

I'm very aware of Jilly smiling beside me, but I can't help flirting right back at him.

"Stalker," I say.

He laughs. "What made you stop going?"

"All the glass walls and mirrors, and people in their perfect workout gear. I decided to get back to basics."

"So you're still working out?"

"Two or three times a week. I go to O'Shaunessy's now where I can just wear a T-shirt and sweats." I don't see any recognition so I add, "It's an old boxing club on Palm Street, north of Grasso."

"Yeah? That's a rough area."

I shrug. "Besides weights, I've taken up boxing. They've got all the fancy fitness gear out front, but it's like a classic boxing gym in the back. They've even got a ring." I lift my arms and do a couple of air jabs like a boxer warming up. "I love working the heavy bag."

He steps back in mock alarm, which is when I notice Jilly leaning on the counter, grinning even harder at the pair of us. I drop my hands.

"You guys are so cute," she says.

Bobo gives a little shimmy and grins up at us as though in agreement.

I feel a flush rise up my neck.

The clerk clears his throat. "Right," he says.

He looks from me to Jilly, at Bobo, then back to me again. "How can I help you?"

"We were told that someone here is a friend of Ethan Law's," Jilly says.

All his humour drains away.

"Fuck," he says. "It was just brutal waking up to that news this morning."

"You were close?" I ask.

He shrugs. "I didn't see him much outside the store—though we did go for a coffee from time to time—but he came in a lot. He'd help me sort books when a new collection came in, but I think it was mostly to get first crack before things went up on the shelf. He was really fixated on Emma K. Rohlin—do you know her work?"

I nod, wary. "She wrote the Nora Constantine books."

"Yeah, they did a TV show based on them but I've never seen it. I'm pretty sure Ethan would've had the DVDs. He had multiple copies of all the novels."

"We've all got our passions," Jilly says.

"I guess. He was even emailing with her for a while. He'd talk about it all the time until it suddenly got cut off—I'm not sure who ended it. When I asked him what happened he said they had to stop because it was getting too dangerous." A troubled look crosses his face and he pauses.

"Too dangerous how?" I ask when he doesn't elaborate.

"I have no idea. You don't think it has anything to do with him getting killed, do you?"

Jilly and I shake our heads.

"How do you know him?" he asks.

"Funny thing," Jilly says. "Juniper met him in the Half Kaffe yesterday around noon."

It takes him a moment. "I thought he'd been dead for a few days when his body was found."

"That's what they say," Jilly replies.

"So how…"

He studies each of us for a moment.

"You're sure you saw him?" he asks me.

I nod. "And I wasn't too nice to him. He was pretty intense. It was hard to get him to back off."

"Huh. That's weird. I always thought he was into guys. Or girls who identify as guys."

"What do you mean?"

"His partner came in with him a few times. She—I mean, he—is a trans kid."

"Do you know his name?" Jilly asks.

"Edward something. Sorry. I don't think I ever knew his last name."

"Do you know how we can get in touch with him?"

"I've got a number for Ethan, probably his cell. I guess the police would have it if he had it with him when his body was found. But I'll get it for you."

I'm expecting him to look it up on the laptop that's fighting for space with the crowd of books on the countertop, but he reaches down to a shelf and comes up with an old Rolodex. He flips through until he finds what he's looking for and writes a phone number on a scrap of paper.

"So what is it that you're doing, exactly?" he asks as he hands me the number.

"Investigating," Jilly says before I can answer.

The clerk gets a puzzled look.

"We're trying to figure out why his, you know, ghost approached me," I say.

"His ghost."

Some of the colour drains from his face. He looks uncertain for a moment, then sighs and pulls a cell from the pocket of his jeans.

"I thought this was a sick joke," he says. "Or maybe one of those instances when a text goes bouncing around the internet before it finally gets to you. It also makes no sense. But it's from Ethan—and it came this morning."

He hands the phone to me and Jilly leans in close to have a look.

All it says is: Tell Nora that Palmer is back.

"Nora being—" the clerk starts.

"Rohlin's teen detective," Jilly says before he can finish.

He nods. "I don't know who Palmer is."

Jilly turns to me.

"He was the Big Bad in season two," I say. "I can't remember which book he also appeared in, but he died in the season finale."

"So," the clerk says, "this is a message to a fictional character about another fictional character?"

"Apparently," I say. "Why would he send a message for Nora to you?" I hesitate before I add, "Unless you're a big fan, too?"

"All I know about the character is what Ethan told me."

"Maybe it's some kind of code," Jilly says.

We both look at her.

"Well, it makes more sense than what—" She looks at the clerk, waiting for him to fill in his name.

"Nick."

"It makes more sense than what Nick said." Suddenly she gasps and grabs my arm. "Unless it's a message for you."

Nick looks lost.

"When he was bugging me at the Half Kaffe," I say, "he acted like he thought I was Nora. He wanted me to take a case."

Nick shakes his head. "That's crazy. Jesus. You think you know somebody…"

Jilly nudges me with her elbow.

I sigh. "Maybe he just got confused," I say, "because I played Nora on the show."

His eyes open wide. "Really?"

Happily, he doesn't ask for an autograph or if we can take a selfie.

"So do you know what any of this means?" he asks.

"Not a clue," I tell him.

"But we're going to find out," Jilly says. She glances at the clock on the wall behind Nick. "But right now we have to get to the soup kitchen."

"Let me know what you find out," Nick says.

I'm still holding his phone. I go to his contacts and enter my name and cell number.

"Or you can call me," I say. "I mean, us."

Damn it. And now I'm blushing again.

Nick smiles. "I will."

Jilly takes a business card from the holder on the counter.

"Nick Burns" she reads. "Do you own the store?"

He shakes his head. "My uncle does. I just manage it for him."

"Well, it was nice to meet you, Nick," Jilly says, pocketing the card. "Come on, Bobo. You've been a very patient boy."

The pup has collapsed at her feet. Now he jumps up, tail wagging madly, head going back and forth as he looks from Jilly to me.

"Don't, you know, get caught up in anything dangerous," Nick says. "Maybe you should take what you know to the police."

"We will," Jilly assures him. "We're super-conscientious that way."

As if, I think. But I let it ride.

"Bye, Nick," I say and I follow Jilly out the door.

I find myself wishing I could have met him under circumstances where I don't seem quite so crazy, but like most things in the world, we don't get to choose our circumstances. We just have to muddle through as best we can.

I SHOULDN'T HAVE BEEN SURPRISED that room was made for Bobo at the shelter while we joined the other volunteers getting ready to prepare and serve lunch. I am surprised that he lies patiently in a corner on a folded blanket for a couple of hours after Jilly explains to him why he has to chill. She talks to him as though he can understand every word. That's not so strange. I get the sense that most pet owners do that. But I'll bet not many pets actually seem to get what's being said to them the way Bobo does.

It's mid-afternoon before we're walking back to the house on Stanton Street. One of the things I love about this street is the succession of giant oak trees that line either side of the pavement. Bobo loves them too and has to stop and sniff at every one, often leaving little pee messages for other dogs.

"So you don't watch any TV?" I ask Jilly.

She shakes her head. "Not really. I don't watch movies much either —at least not on a computer. I don't use an e-reader." She smiles. "I hardly go online."

"How can you live in this era and hardly go online? Even I do email and lurk around on the socials."

"I don't have to. If I need to use the internet, I just ask Saskia since she pretty much is the internet."

I have no idea what that means.

"After my accident, I couldn't paint for the longest time," Jilly explains. "I could barely get around. The only art I could make was digital, where I pretty much painted a pixel at a time. But I prefer messy art. Charcoal on my fingers. Paint slopping about. And I like my books to be paper, to have pages and not need to be charged just so that I can read them."

"You have a music system in the studio. That's kind of technological."

She nods. "But I only play vinyl on it. I like the fact that the musicians figured out a story and you have to listen to a whole album to get it."

"Most albums don't tell a story."

"Oh, but they do," Jilly says. "Or they used to. There was a reason why one song followed another. Their relation to each other told a story. Or at least they should."

"You'll have to show me."

"I will. But you know, you should get used to Luddites. I'm pretty sure Nick's a bit of one. Did you see that Rolodex?"

"Nick's not interested in me. After the way we carried on, he's got to think we're delusional crazy women—especially me."

Jilly grins. "Right. He remembered you from a gym from two years ago. That hardly seems disinterested."

"Except that was before we went all Looney Tunes on him."

"*He* got the text from a ghost, not you."

"I suppose. But I doubt he'll ever call."

She produces his business card from her pocket and offers it to me, held between two fingers. "You could always call him."

I hesitate for a long moment before I take the card and stow it away in my own pocket. "I'll think about it."

We wait for Bobo to finish whatever's got him so fascinated with yet another tree, then move on. At this rate it'll be dark before we get to Bramleyhaugh.

"Now we need to decide what to do next," Jilly says. "Do we contact Emma Rohlin first, or Ethan's boyfriend Edward?"

"Or," I say, "we could get those prints signed. You know it's only going to take a few hours."

Jilly shakes her head. "If I do that, someone will just find something else that just has to be done before the festival."

I smile. So there's a method to her madness.

"Maybe we should follow Nick's suggestion," I say, "and bring what we have to the police."

"There's no point. They can't deal with ghosts and ghostly texts. And it's not weird and dangerous enough for the Spook Squad."

"The what?"

"The Spook Squad—you know, what everybody calls NPD's Paranormal Investigations Task Force."

"That's a real thing?"

Jilly nods. "The professor used to consult for them. Christy still does."

We follow Bobo to the next tree.

"So what do they investigate?" I ask.

"Supernatural goings on."

"And a ghost wouldn't count?"

"Well, not a benign one. If a phenomenon doesn't present a danger to the public, they leave it alone."

"Um, somebody got murdered."

"This is true," she says. "But we don't know that Ethan's death was supernatural, and that's their bag."

"I can't believe we're having this conversation."

"Why not? Magic's all around if you take the time to pay attention."

"Magic."

She nods.

A hundred little comments over the years suddenly rearrange themselves into a new configuration in my brain.

"So when you talk about hobs and Faerie, and Lyle being a werewolf…"

"I'm being literal."

"Stop," I tell her. "You're making my head explode."

"You're the one who talks to ghosts," she says.

"One ghost. If that's what he was."

"He was."

I give her a dubious look.

"But still," she says.

I look into those sapphire eyes.

"But still," I agree. "He probably was."

~

THERE's music playing when we step inside the house. Jilly lets Bobo take the lead and the pair of them immediately head up the stairs in the direction of its source.

"The prints!" I call after her.

"Yes," she calls back over her shoulder. "Someday your prince will come. Or you could go find him."

I shake my head and follow her up the stairs.

We find the pickup band Geordie's put together for FaerieFest rehearsing in the second floor parlour. I remember there used to be just as many books in here as in every other room, but we hauled them all out to make a rehearsal space for Geordie's various musical endeavours. What was once a crowded library, badly lit and dense with furniture, is now a welcoming open space that's more often than not filled with music.

There's a circle of chairs in the middle of the room where the musicians are sitting. More chairs are set up along a couple of the walls. Instrument cases are everywhere. As are instruments. They're hanging from the walls and leaning up against chairs. Fiddles, mandolins, banjos, guitars, ukuleles and a couple of bodhrans. An old upright piano fills one corner. Beside it is a small table with a big fat pot on it holding dozens of whistles and flutes. Under the table is a doumbek and a couple of other hand drums. In the other corner is an old sideboard, the top of which has been repurposed to hold a stereo and some recording equipment. The body of the sideboard is stuffed with records. The overflow leans against the walls on either side.

Geordie grins at us around the whistle he's playing, his fiddle and bow across his lap. Beside him, his bandmate Amy Scanlon is also playing whistle. She has her pipes on her lap. Next to them are Meran Kelledy and Lesli Batterberry playing Irish wooden flutes. Both have green streaks in their Pre-Raphaelite hair. Jilly claims Meran's are natural, but please. Across from them is Miki Greer on button accordion and my own Tam on guitar. I don't know a lot about Celtic music, but he sounds like he's fitting right in.

The music is joyful. Maybe it's a jig, could be a reel—I can't tell.

Jilly sits happily in one of the empty chairs and coaxes Bobo to dance on his hind legs in front of her. He keeps it up for a few measures, but quickly gets bored and drops to all fours where he shakes himself vigorously from head to tail before settling down under her chair. He may be bored, but I'm not. I have the mad urge to twirl around the room like an unwinding spool. Instead I sit beside Jilly and bounce a little in my seat.

No prints get signed that evening. On the plus side, no one talks about Nora Constantine or ghosts, either.

~

"I THINK I'm spending too much time at Bramleyhaugh," I tell Tam as we're walking home.

He gives me a puzzled look. "Why's that?"

"It's just…you know how they're always joking about faeries in the garden and how the people in the Rookery—" I nod to the tall gabled house we're passing. "—can turn into birds, stuff like that?"

"That's just Jilly," he says. "Hang around her long enough and you'll start believing you can see things, too."

"It's too late for that. I'm seeing things when I'm not even with her."

"What kinds of things?"

"That guy I told you about yesterday—the one in the Half Kaffe who was convinced I was the real Nora Constantine?"

"I remember."

"Turns out he was a ghost."

Tam stops dead. "He was a ghost? And you didn't think that bit was interesting enough to add to our conversation yesterday?"

"I didn't know then. I found out this morning that he died a few days ago."

"Wait," Tam says. "You mean the guy they found in the park last night?"

I nod. "Ethan Law."

"And you're sure you saw him?"

I give Tam another nod. "And it's not just me. I met a guy this morning who got a text from Ethan today—again, long after he died. Not only that. He sort of knew Ethan and said that Ethan had a bit of a Nora fixation."

Tam starts walking again and I fall into step beside him.

"That's just weird," he says.

"I know. And now Jilly's got us playing detective to find out what his story was and why he was killed."

"Tell me you're kidding."

"I'm not."

Tam stops again. "Somebody killed that guy, Joon. You shouldn't be messing around with this. It's too dangerous."

"Tell that to Jilly." I hold up a hand to forestall any more discussion about what's dangerous and what's not. "We're getting off the topic. The point is, if a ghost can be real—and I'm damned convinced it was—then what else might be? Jilly told me the other night that Lyle's a werewolf. What if he really is?"

Tam shakes his head. "Come on, Joon. There's no such thing as werewolves," he says and starts walking again.

"Tell that to the girl who's seen her first ghost. Maybe I should get a birder's book, except it'll be for supernatural creatures. I can check ghosts off my life list straightaway."

Tam doesn't say anything for a half block.

"Hello?" I say. "A little feedback here? What do you think?"

"Well, first off, don't take Jilly so seriously. Her imagination mingles with her art, that's all. And I'd stop playing detective before you end up like Ethan."

"And let whoever killed him get away?"

"Of course not. The police will handle it."

"Except they don't have our intel."

"So go to them and share what you know."

"Right," I say. "Go to them and, when they ask what I know, I can tell them I saw his ghost. That'll go over well."

I put my fingers through my hair as I realize I'm turning into Jilly —arguing for the continuation of what we're doing.

Tam pretty much copies my gesture without thinking about it. "This is messed up."

"Tell me about it."

"You need to be careful."

"We will be," I assure him.

But I'm thinking of Ethan's text to Nick. *Tell Nora that Palmer is back.*

A shiver whispers up my spine.

Bret Palmer. The scumbag who pretty much reduced Nora's life to tatters and then almost killed her.

The *fictional* Bret Palmer, I remind myself.

Tam breaks my train of thought. "So, you think Lyle is a werewolf?" he asks.

I shrug. "Jilly says he is. Like you said, could just be Jilly being Jilly."

"Yeah, but it would explain so much."

"What do you mean?"

"Dogs always freak out around him. I can't tell you how many times I've been walking with him and Mona, and some dog pulls away as far as his leash will stretch to avoid him."

I remember Bobo's reaction last night.

"Seriously," I mutter. "My head is going to explode."

"What?"

"Nothing. Let's pretend today never happened."

Except then I think of Nick. Maybe I should give him a call, like Jilly said.

"On the plus side," I say, "I met a nice guy today. His name's Nick and he runs Burns' Books."

"I've been in there. They've got a great sheet music section. Is he the one with the Buddy Holly glasses?"

"That's him."

"He seems like a good guy. Did you give him your number?"

I nod. "And I took his business card."

"You should totally call him. What's the worst that can happen?"

I don't know if it's because Tam's a musician, good-looking, or maybe both, but he's a bit cavalier about meeting girls because they're forever approaching him. He's not full of himself, just unfazed, and he's always upfront about how much his music means to him—he's basically married to it, if we're going to be honest—but he's still left more than a few disappointed would-be girlfriends in his wake. It's not that he's mean, or that he doesn't have a good heart. It's that he lives in a constant state of distraction for everything except for music and that is not good boyfriend material in anybody's book.

"Joon?" he says.

"No promises," I tell him. "But maybe I will."

3

WEDNESDAY

"You know what the real problem is?" Jilly says over breakfast the next morning.

We're in the Deer Mouse Diner on Lee. For some reason Bobo is allowed to lie on the floor under the table in our booth.

"We're not actually detectives?" I say.

Jilly waves that off. "We're not quippy. All the best detectives are quippy. Were you quippy on your TV show?"

"Is that a real question or do you just like saying the word 'quippy'?"

"A bit of both," she admits.

"All the best detectives are fictional," I tell her. "The writers give them all those snappy lines. I'm just like everybody else. I don't think of the perfect thing to say until the moment's already passed."

"I think we should practice being more quippy."

"And that will help us how?"

Jilly laughs. "We'd be stylin'. Isn't that enough?"

I have to laugh along with her.

"So who do we talk to next?" Jilly asks. "The author or the boyfriend? Or maybe we should have a séance and talk directly to Ethan."

I get a little chill. "You can do that?"

"Sadly, no. I vote you phone the author."

"Me? Why don't you?"

"She's more likely to talk to you," Jilly says.

"Oh, I think she'll talk to a famous faerie painter."

"But you're the one who brought her character so skillfully to life."

"Says the woman who's never seen the show."

"Not true," Jilly says. "Last night I read *Nora Constantine and the Secret of the Red Corvette*, and then Wendy showed me the first two episodes of the show. I think you did a wonderful job. I totally believed you. Though I have to admit I liked the late sixties setting of the books better. Why would they change that for the show?"

"I never thought about it," I say. "They probably didn't have the budget."

"I wonder what Emma G. Rohlin thinks of the change. You should ask her when you're talking to her."

"So that's settled, is it? I'm the one talking to her?"

All Jilly does is give me an expectant look.

"Fine," I tell her. "Though it's not like I have her phone number. It's probably unlisted."

"We'll ask Saskia. She's good at finding out things like that."

Which is how, after breakfast, I find myself with Jilly back at Bramleyhaugh, climbing the stairs to the third floor where Saskia and Christy live. Their rooms are much like the rest of the house, crowded with books and antique furniture, all except for Saskia's study.

We pause at the threshold. Jilly knocks on the doorjamb by the open door, and Saskia looks up from where she's sitting in one of a pair of chairs in the corner. She's tall and gorgeous, blue-eyed with a generous mane of yellow-gold hair. It seems like every woman in this house has gorgeous curls and ringlets except for Mona and me. Mona's is short and blond, while my thick red mop is boringly straight. Boring because it refuses to hold a curl and takes forever to dry.

"Can Bobo come in?" Jilly asks Saskia before stepping inside.

"Of course. Can I get him a pillow or something to lie on?"

"He can tough it out," Jilly says. "We're not going to keep you long."

The contrast between the study and the rest of the house is striking. Outside the room, it's all wooden wainscoting and Persian rugs, paintings and framed photographs hanging in every spare inch that isn't blocked by a bookcase—much like the rest of the house. But the furniture in Saskia's study is spare and modern, the floor polished wood. There's a contemporary bookcase with a tidy array of poetry books and notebooks, and her window overlooks the yard in the back of the house. The two other walls hold only one painting each, abstracts by Isabelle Copley, who doesn't live here in the house, but is among Jilly's family of choice.

And there's no computer.

The expanse of the desk holds just a single notebook with a fountain pen in the gutter to keep the pages open.

Saskia sets a poetry book on the glass table between the chairs and stands. She motions us to sit down and pulls over the chair from the desk when we do. Bobo eyes Jilly's lap and hops up. Saskia reaches over to ruffle the fur on the top of the pup's head and he closes his eyes. If he were a cat he'd be purring.

"How can he not always have lived here?" Saskia says.

Jilly beams. "It's really like that, isn't it?'

"Have you formally adopted him yet?'

"Geordie took care of it yesterday."

"Oh, those Riddell boys," Saskia says. "They treat us well, don't they?"

She glances at me. "You look surprised," she adds.

"Not about Geordie or Christy," I assure her. "I've just never been up here before. It's not like I expected."

"What were you expecting?"

"For it to be like the rest of the house, except more writerly."

She smiles. "You'll have to go to Christy's study for that. I like to have open space so that the words can find me more readily. Christy prefers to let them creep around the baseboards or swing in through the window from the trees outside, but really, how can you even tell where they've been?"

"God help me," Jilly says. "Why does that even begin to make sense?"

I turn to her. "It does?"

But I kind of know what she means because I can just picture Christy waiting on the arrival of a pack of scruffy words, coaxing them onto the page with the whispered promise of being tucked comfortably into his latest story.

"Can I get either of you something to drink?" Saskia asks us. "Maybe some water for Bobo?"

Jilly shakes her head. "But we were hoping you could track down a phone number for us."

"Anything to stay off a computer," Saskia says.

She looks at me. "You're probably just as bad."

"Hey, I do email and stuff," I say.

"The one I want is probably unlisted," Jilly says with just the right amount of being terribly misunderstood in her voice.

Saskia smiles. "Whose number do you want?"

"Emma K. Rohlin's."

"The writer?"

Jilly nods. Saskia closes her eyes for a moment then rattles off a phone number.

"Just a sec," Jilly says. She pulls a little notebook from her pocket and scribbles the number into it. "Thanks, Saskia. You're the best."

"How did you do that?" I ask. "Did you already know the number? No, wait. Why would you even know the number?"

"She talks to the spirits in the wires," Jilly explains, but as is often the case when she tells me something, I have no idea what she means.

Saskia laughs. "More like spirits in the wireless these days."

I look from one to the other. "What am I missing here? Did you guys set this up to amaze me? Because rest assured, I'm amazed."

Saskia seems confused, but Jilly's bouncing happily in her seat, enough to get a protest from Bobo.

"Ask her anything," Jilly says. "Or at least anything you'd ask Google."

"What?

"Go ahead."

"But…"

You know how it is. As soon as someone says something like that your mind goes blank. Or at least mine does.

"I'd show you," Jilly says, "but then you'll just keep thinking that we've had this planned."

Then I remember something Jilly told me yesterday.

If I need to use the internet, I just ask Saskia since she pretty much is the internet.

I just put that down to being one more of all the crazy things she's been telling me over the years. But I'd seen a real, honest-to-god ghost and, despite what Tam said last night, it looks like I'd better start entertaining the idea that maybe she's being factual rather than whimsical.

I take out my phone and open a browser.

"What's the speed of light?" I ask and type the words in the search bar as I speak.

Saskia answers before my browser page loads. "186,000 miles per second."

A few seconds later the same answer comes up on my phone.

"What did I tell you?" Jilly says.

I don't respond. I just look at Saskia for a long moment before I finally say, "You're the internet?"

"What? No." She laughs. "Who told you that? Wait, never mind." She shoots Jilly an admonishing glance. "No, I just have a connection to it that lets me bypass using a device."

"How's that possible?"

She shrugs. "Maybe I was born there."

I close my eyes and try to process that, but it makes no sense. When I open them again, Saskia is looking at me without guile.

"No, seriously," I say. "Where's the science for that? Wait—*were* you born there?"

"It's magic," Jilly says. "Just like faeries in the garden and brownies in the attic, or Christy's shadow, although she hasn't been around for a while."

"Magic," I repeat.

Jilly nods. "Only different."

She puts Bobo on the ground and stands up.

"Come on," she tells me. "You have a phone call to make. I'll be with you and you can put us all on speakerphone if that makes you feel more comfortable."

As I sit there in stunned silence, she tugs me to my feet.

"Thanks, Saskia," Jilly says as she pulls me by my hand out of the room.

"She's really the internet, isn't she?" I murmur as we head down the stairs. "You said that."

"I'm sure I didn't. But if I did, I only meant she's my internet."

"Oh, that's so much more comforting."

"Life isn't meant to be comforting," Jilly tells me. "It's big and it's messy, and there's always another mystery for every one we think we've solved."

On our way to the studio we pass through the kitchen where Wendy's sitting at the table with a mug of tea and a sandwich. She grins when we appear and holds up the book she's flipping through.

"Look," she says. "Hot off the press. Marisa just dropped it off a few minutes ago."

Marisa and her husband run East Side Press. Every year for FaerieFest they do a limited run of signed prints—this year's run being the pile still waiting in the studio for Jilly to sign. A couple of years ago they also published a collection of her paintings in a lovely hardcover edition that did so well they decided to follow it up this year with a reproduction of Jilly's sketchbooks.

The finished book's a little bit of a cheat because they took pages from a whole mess of her sketchbooks and put them all together as though they were simply one, but I saw the galleys a few months ago and it came together beautifully. The finished copy, which we all pore over for a few minutes at the kitchen table, is stunning.

At first Jilly had been less than enthused about the idea. She only warmed to it as we all started going through the various sketchbooks to pick our favourite pages. The finished book is called *Jilly Coppercorn's Faery Sketchbook,* but it contains at least as many taken from her endless rambles through the backstreets and alleys of Newford as there are of actual faerie beings.

"I guess it didn't turn out too badly, did it," she says now.

Wendy and I exchange a knowing look at yet another example of what Sophie calls "the humble Jilly." Don't get me wrong. Jilly's passionate about her art. She just can't seem to understand why anybody else would make a fuss over it.

"No, it's just brilliant," Wendy says.

I nod in agreement.

Jilly smiles. "Well, I pay you to say that. Money well spent."

Wendy fakes a punch at her but Jilly dances back out of reach.

"I'd be happy to exchange fisticuffs with you later," she informs Wendy in a la-dee-da sort of a voice, "but right now Juniper and I have a phone call to make."

She heads off toward the studio with Bobo.

"Did Marisa only leave the one copy?" I ask Wendy.

She shakes her head and points to a box by the door.

"There's plenty for everyone," she says.

I grab a copy for myself before following Jilly to the studio. She's already sitting on the sofa, a phone on the coffee table in front of her. Bobo gives a little groan when he has to shift to make room for me to sit beside them.

"So we're actually doing this," I say.

"Justice waits for no woman," Jilly tells me.

"Right."

She opens her notebook to the page with the number and I punch it in, then press the speaker phone button. Emma Rohlin answers after a couple of rings.

"Hello, Ms. Rohlin," I say. "This is Juniper Wiles. I don't know if you remember me, but—"

"Dear girl, of course I remember you. How lovely to hear your voice."

"I've got you on speaker phone," I say, "and my friend Jilly Coppercorn is with me. Is that okay?"

"Of course. To what do I owe this mysterious pleasure? Somehow I suspect I'll like it."

"And I like you," Jilly says. "Hi Ms. Rohlin."

"Please. 'Emma' will do just fine. Now, are you the same Jilly Coppercorn who does those exquisite paintings of faeries living in alleyways and junkyards?"

"I guess I am."

"You should do another book," Emma says. "My granddaughters and I are coming close to wearing the first one out."

"My publisher just put out a new one, a collection of mostly faerie sketches. I can send you a copy if you'll tell me your address."

Emma does, adding, "Aren't you a dear. I'm hardly surprised that the two of you are friends. Did Juniper tell you how, whenever I visited the set of the show, she went out of her way to take me around and make sure I was always comfortable?"

Jilly gives me a stern look. "She did not tell me that."

"Now, how can I help you girls?"

"It's about Ethan Law," I say.

There's a brief silence before she responds with a clipped, "I see."

I wait for a moment. Before I can go on to say—I'm not sure what. Apologize? Ask her why the name disturbs her—she asks, "Has he been bothering you?"

"Not exactly. He's dead."

"Oh dear. What happened?"

"No one knows, exactly, but it seems he was murdered several days ago. We're looking for the reason why," I say. "We heard you'd had a correspondence with him that you suddenly broke off, and wonder if you'd mind telling us what it was about."

Emma chuckles. "It seems a bit of Nora has rubbed off on you after all those years of playing the character."

I pause and glance at Jilly, who nods encouragingly and motions for me to continue.

I want to say, no, Jilly's put me up to all of this, but I realize it's not entirely true. At least not anymore. Now I need to know what happened as much as Jilly does.

"I guess it has," I finally say. Jilly smiles and pats my knee.

"Just remember the trouble that Nora's curiosity could get her into."

"I will."

"So," Emma says, drawing the word out. "Ethan Law. He seemed like such a disarming young man at first, and to be fair, he was unfailingly polite in all the emails he wrote to me."

"But," Jilly prompts her.

"Turned out he was slightly off his rocker. He had this mad idea that I hadn't created Nora and the rest of the characters from the books. The first few emails were pleasant enough, but as time went on he kept pressing me for details on how I'd come to discover this parallel world in which the actual people lived—the ones I'd based my characters on. I stopped responding to him when he asked me if I was aware that the real people were bleeding into this world, and whether I could give him information about these supposed people."

I take a deep breath. "He really thought I was Nora," I say.

"I'm sorry to hear that, dear," Emma says, "but from what I knew of him I'm not surprised. Oh well. Let's hope he's found his peace."

"At the risk of you hanging up on us," Jilly says, "we should tell you that Juniper only met Ethan on Monday, after he'd been dead for a few days."

There's another silence before Emma says, "I don't believe I heard that correctly."

"And then yesterday morning," Jilly goes on, "Nick—an acquaintance of Ethan's—got a rather cryptic text from him, asking Nick to tell Nora that Palmer is back."

The silence that follows that is longer.

"I'm disappointed in you, Juniper," Emma finally says. "I don't know what you hope to gain by this ridiculous story, but I think we're done here."

"Please, please don't hang up," I say. "Emma, I swear we're not pranking you. I'm as confused about all of this as you are. As strange as it sounds, I know for sure that I met Ethan on Monday in a café. He was very pushy about me being Nora and I shut him down. I only discovered his death yesterday morning when the newspaper reported his body having been found. According to the coroner, he'd been dead for several days."

"The article said he'd been missing for a week," Jilly puts in. "It was all reported in *The Newford Star* Tuesday morning, the same day Nick got that text. All we're trying to do is figure out what happened to him —and what his ghost wants from Juniper."

"I don't believe in ghosts," Emma says, her voice firm.

"I didn't either until this week," I tell her.

The dead air that follows is long enough that I start to think she's hung up. But there's no dial tone.

"There is something else that I didn't mention earlier," Emma says. "When Ethan Law first contacted me his name was very familiar because I once had a character with that name."

"I don't remember that," I say, "and I've read all the books, including the novelizations based on the show."

"Novelizations?" Jilly says. "I thought the show was already based on Emma's books."

"Yes, but it was quite different from my books," Emma tells us. "They updated the setting, dropped some characters, added new ones. The novelizations grew out of the television show."

"So where does Ethan fit in?" I ask.

"There was going to be a subplot with a gay couple in one of my original books," Emma explains, "but this was the late sixties and my agent told me that the juvenile market wasn't ready for that. You have to remember the times. It was still a few years before Judy Blume's groundbreaking work. Come to think of it, there wasn't even a specific young adult market at the time. That wouldn't come for years. In the end, I let her talk me out of it."

"And Ethan Law was the name you gave one of those gay characters," Jilly says.

"Indeed. I thought it was only coincidence that this young man would have the same name. He could have had no access to my unpublished manuscripts. The only people to have ever read them are my daughter and my agent, and they would have no reason to tell anybody about it."

"There's no such thing as coincidence," Jilly says. "There are only connections we haven't figured out yet." She looks at me and adds, "Either the professor or Christy told me that."

"Regardless," Emma says, "it was enough to intrigue me. If I'm going to be honest, I found it amusing to consider that I was corresponding with one of my own characters—at least on the surface. It didn't become disturbing until I realized he knew details about the character that I hadn't even written into a rough draft."

"A good con man," Jilly says, "can be just vague enough for you to fill in the details in such a way that you don't realize you're doing it."

"But what would be the point?" Emma asks. "Our correspondence was only about the books. It was cordial and he was charming—until he began pressing this absurd idea that I'd been somehow reporting on actual events taking place in some other world."

"Did he ever say that he was from this other world?" Jilly asks.

"Don't be ridiculous. That's almost as outlandish as the idea of ghosts."

Bobo suddenly lifts his head from Jilly's lap. I turn to see Sophie come in. Jilly puts a finger to her lips, then points to the phone. Sophie nods and tiptoes across the room to the area where she works.

"I'm not saying the stories aren't yours," Jilly says, getting back to our phone call. "It's just…I've had the experience where an artist creates such, I don't know, let's say true characters in their work that they can manifest in this world."

"Are you listening to yourself?" Emma says.

I see Sophie turn to us, curiosity creasing her brow. I shrug as Jilly goes on.

"Okay, forget that. Can you tell us if there was anything in his correspondence to indicate that he was scared of something?"

"I'm afraid not."

Jilly presses on. "What about this Palmer guy that he was warning Nora about?"

Emma sighs. "Please. This young man was sorely deluded. These are fictional characters."

"Right. Of course. Well, you've been a big help, Emma."

"I hardly see how. But I can certainly see how the art in your faerie book is so evocative. If one didn't know better, one might think you were painting from life."

I hold up a hand, palm out, to stop Jilly from responding.

"It was great to hear your voice again, Emma," I say. "If you're ever in Newford, give me a call and we can go out for some tea. I promise there won't be any talk of ghosts and such."

"Yes, well…" She pauses to clear her throat. "You've certainly given me some food for thought. Will you let me know how the case proceeds?"

I laugh. "It's hardly a case."

Jilly gives me a little huff, and Emma inadvertently backs her up.

"A young man is murdered and you're trying to discover his killer," she says. "What else would you call it?"

"I guess when you put it like that…"

"Be careful, Juniper," Emma says. "I'm sorry, but I have to go now."

"Thanks, Emma, we'll be careful."

We hear the click as she hangs up.

"What," Sophie says as I cradle the phone, "was that all about?"

"The short version," Jilly says, "is that we're trying to figure out why a ghost wanted to hire Nora Constantine to take a case."

"But Nora's—"

Jilly nods. "Fictional."

Sophie crosses over and sits down on the coffee table, facing us.

"You think he was a numena?" she says.

"Or something like. If he was a numena, somebody wouldn't have had to physically kill him, would they?"

Sophie nods. "How would you kill a numena born from writing?"

I raise my arms and wave my hands in the air.

"Um, guys?" I say. "What are you talking about? What's a numena?"

"It's like I was telling Emma—who, by the way, you didn't tell me was your bestie."

"It was only on set and it was a long time ago. She always looked a little lost, and nobody else paid much attention to her. Don't change the subject."

"Numena," Sophie says, "or at least the ones we know, are created when a certain kind of artist makes a painting that somehow brings the subject to real life."

"You're kidding me," I say. But I don't even have to look at their faces to know they're serious—not after the past few days. "You're not kidding me. Do you know any?"

"Well, Isabelle—" Sophie begins.

"—She's a num…ah…what you said?"

"Numena. And no. She's that rare artist that can bring them to life."

"You know that crowd from the island that comes with her to FaerieFest?" Jilly says. "They're all her numena and none of them are wearing costumes."

Isabelle Copley used to be part of Jilly's inner circle of friends before she moved back to Wren Island. The people Jilly's referring to… well, I always thought they were amazing cosplayers.

"Wow," I say.

"Plus the kids who live up in the attic with the brownies," Sophie says. "Izzy and Kathy."

"And you've met John Sweetwater," Jilly adds.

"Ethan wouldn't be a numena," Sophie says, "but what about an Eadar?"

Jilly thinks about it

I look from one to the other. "Should I ask?"

"They're another kind of being," Jilly says. "They're created out of imagination and exist only so long as someone believes in them—a lot of someones, normally, so that wouldn't fit here because no one else is supposed to know about the Ethan Law who didn't make it into Rohlin's books or the TV show, except for Emma herself, her daughter and her agent."

"According to Emma," Sophie says.

Jilly nods. "This is true."

"Oh boy." I fall back against the sofa cushions and stare up at the ceiling.

"She's only just figured out that the others of the otherworld are real," Jilly tells Sophie.

Sophie puts a comforting hand on my knee. "It starts to feel normal way more quickly than you think it will."

I tilt my head. "Yeah, I'm starting to get that. But is everything magic?"

"Jilly would say yes," Sophie tells me, "but that's only because she's as amazed by a flock of birds all flying in perfect unison as she is by a faerie made of sticks."

"The world is a magical place," Jilly says. "Even without faeries and such."

She stands up and hauls me to my feet again before giving my back a motherly pat. "Come on. Let's go walk some dogs at the shelter before we interview Ethan's boyfriend. Are you coming, Sophie?"

"Not today. I've got a workshop at the Arts Court this afternoon."

"Have fun with that," Jilly calls over her shoulder as she hustles me out of the studio. Bobo runs circles around us all the way down the hall. It makes for a weird dance, but somehow, both of us manage to avoid stepping on a paw.

ANOTHER VOLUNTEER HAS JAMES TODAY, so I get a bull terrier named Sonora while Jilly clips her leash to Charlie, a husky/shepherd cross with one blue eye and one brown. It makes him look very dashing. Bobo doesn't wear a leash anymore—he hasn't since Jilly brought him home. He trots right at Jilly's feet as we head outside. I don't think I've seen him farther than ten feet away from her since they first met at the shelter.

Unlike James, Sonora is skittish and I find her hard to handle. The more my anxiety goes up, the worse she gets. She's not big, maybe forty pounds, and I'm stronger than a lot of people realize from looking at me, but I still feel like she's about to pull my arm right out of its socket.

"Hold up," Jilly says.

She squats down until she's pretty much nose-to-nose with Sonora.

"Now listen, girl," she says. "I know it's horrible having to live in a jail when you never even did anything wrong, but we're trying to break up your day here and give you some exercise and a little love. That's not going to work if you can't stop being pissy."

Sonora's ears and tail droop and she looks at the ground.

"So are you going to be a good girl instead and not freak Juniper out with all that pulling?"

Sonora looks up at Jilly, then tilts her head in my direction. After a moment she steps closer and licks my hand.

When we start walking again she's as well behaved as Bobo.

"How do you do that?" I ask.

Jilly shrugs. "It's just this gift I have."

We take the dogs across the canal to Butler Common and let them romp around, all of us running in circles and chasing each other until we have to drop to the grass to catch our breath. Jilly pulls a collapsible dog bowl and a water bottle from the little army surplus shoulder bag that serves as her purse. She fills the bowl with water for the dogs then shares the rest with me.

There's time for another crazy game of chase, but all too soon it's time to take the dogs back. I feel a little pang in my heart when I say goodbye and find myself thinking about Sonora all the way to Ethan's apartment.

THE PERSON who answers the door is pretty with short black hair, no makeup, and wearing a boy's shirt and jeans. Yellow high tops poke out from under the rolled up cuffs. Their eyes are red from crying, but they brighten up a little when they see me standing in the hall outside her apartment with Jilly and Bobo.

"Oh my god," they say. "You're Nora Constantine."

I don't even bother to correct them.

"Are you…Edward?" I ask and he nods.

'I can't believe it's you," he says. "I tried to believe that it was true —Ethan was so persuasive—but it didn't seem possible that you could actually step out of a book and just be walking around."

"You're aware they made a TV show based on the books?" I say. "You know—with actors and everything?"

He nods, but I don't see him make the connection between the show and me. I shoot Jilly an exasperated look and she shrugs.

I clear my throat. "So," I say. "Um, Ethan wanted me to look into a case for him, but unfortunately I wasn't able to meet up with him until it was…too late."

His eyes well up with tears.

"We're so sorry for your loss," Jilly says.

He nods, but says nothing.

"Do you mind if we come in?" I ask. "We wanted to talk to you a

little bit about Ethan to see if we can figure out what happened to
him."

"Do you really think you can?" he says, dabbing at his eyes with
his shirt sleeve. "The police have already been by and…you know.
They asked a lot of questions that I couldn't really answer because I
didn't know how."

Jilly steps past me and steers Edward back into his apartment.
"We're certainly going to do our best," she says.

I roll my eyes, but I'm still standing in the hallway and there's no
one to see. Even Bobo's gone inside.

Ethan and Edward's apartment is furnished thrift shop style. It's a
study in mismatches. Like how the floral pattern on the armchair
clashes with the floral pattern on the sofa, both of which clash with the
drapes and the worn Persian rug. There are lots of bookcases filled with
DVDs and books, many of which have catalogue stickers on the
spines, which shows that they came from library sales. A modestly
sized flat screen TV stands on a beautiful antique walnut sideboard.

Jilly and Edward sit on the sofa. Bobo is the perfect gentleman
dog, lying by Jilly's feet.

"So when did you first realize something was wrong?" Jilly asks.

"He didn't come home last Tuesday. I went around to all the usual
places he'd go, then started calling friends. I went to the police on
Wednesday, but at that point they weren't concerned."

Jilly nods. "A lot of people take off for a couple of days and then
just show up again. Sometimes it's drugs, sometimes it's alcohol.
Sometimes they're having an affair."

"Not Ethan," Edward says. "He doesn't do drugs or drink, and he'd
never have an affair. He just disappeared until…until…"

Jilly pats him on the knee. "I know. It's so hard, isn't it?"

Edward gives her a grateful look, his eyes glassy once more.

"Can you think of any reason why someone would want to hurt
Ethan?" Jilly asks.

I browse the bookshelves while Edward shakes his head.

"So he wasn't having problems with anyone?"

"No one would want to hurt him," Edward says.

"Then why do you think he wanted Nora's help?"

Edward sits a little straighter. "He wouldn't tell me. He told me
everything, but he wouldn't say why he needed to see Nora—just that
he did."

Jilly nods thoughtfully.

"Can I use your bathroom?" I ask.

Edward nods and points down the hall. As I go by, I take a quick peek into their bedroom. There are bookshelves in there. Jilly's still talking, so I slip in, do a fast scan of the titles, then tiptoe back out of the room. I close the bathroom door quietly, wait a few moments before flushing, then run some water in the sink.

"If you can think of anything that could help," Jilly's saying as I come back to the living room, "will you give us a call?"

She writes her number on a page in her notebook, tears it out and sets it on Edward's knee.

"How did Ethan come to know about me?" I ask.

Jilly was starting to get up, but she gives me a curious glance, drops back onto the sofa, and looks at Edward.

"I don't know exactly," he says. "But he probably discovered the show back when he was in Santa Feliz."

"At the community college," I say.

Edward nods.

"Do you know what happened to his cell phone? Do the police have it?"

"He would have had it with him, so I suppose they must."

"Of course," I say. "Well, thanks so much for your time."

I walk to the door. It's not until we're walking down the stairs , Bobo in the lead, that Jilly asks me, "What was all that about?"

"They don't have any of the Nora books or DVDs in the apartment. Maybe they only have digital copies, but seeing the rest of their stuff, it doesn't seem likely. Don't you think that's odd for someone who was so into her?"

Jilly nods. "And didn't Nick say he bought whatever Nora stuff came into the bookstore?"

"He did. So where is it all?"

"Good question. Maybe at his office?"

"What office?"

"Edward told me Ethan had an office while you were off having your wee."

"My 'wee'? Who says that anymore?"

Jilly smiles.

"And I wasn't having a wee. I was snooping."

"For clues."

I sigh. "Yes, for clues. Did Edward tell you where the office is?"

"He gave me the address and the keys so that we can go have a look. Apparently Ethan's Nora Constantine obsession got to be a bit too much to keep all the stuff in their apartment so he rented this place to store it."

She hands me a pair of keys and waves me off when I try to hand them back. "You might as well hang on to them," she says. "You know me and how things can get lost."

"Did Edward say what he did in this office?" I ask.

"He did a lot of buying and selling of Nora memorabilia so I guess that's where he did it. He said he didn't tell the police about it."

"Did he say why?"

She shakes her head. "Why were you asking about his phone?"

"Anyone could have sent Nick that text. All they'd need is Ethan's cell."

Jilly gives me a broad grin. "And here you thought you weren't a proper detective."

I aim an elbow in her direction but she dodges it easily.

"Where to now?" she asks as we step out onto the street.

"You're probably going home to sign prints," I say. "Or not," I add at her look of mock horror.

"And you?" she asks.

"I'm going to work out at O'Shaunessy's."

I DO SOME CARDIO, some weights, then wrap my hands and work the heavy bag, punching and kicking until my T-shirt is soaked and my muscles ache.

"I wouldn't want to be whoever pissed you off," a voice says behind me.

I turn to find Pearse O'Shaunessy sitting on a bench behind me, a big smile on his lips. I guess he's well into his sixties by now. He's stocky with a thick neck and a full head of white hair. But old or not, he could probably still whup half the kids who work out here, including me.

I come over to where he's sitting and do my cool-down stretches by the bench, first one leg, then the other. Shoulders, neck, arms.

"I'm not mad at anybody," I tell him when I finally sit down. "I just needed to blow off some steam."

He hands me a towel, which I drape around my neck.

"Coulda fooled me," he says.

"I'm just confused about a bunch of things."

He laughs. "Welcome to the world."

"Yeah, well…"

I wipe my face with the towel, then let it fall back around my neck. I turn to look at him.

"Do you believe in magic?" I ask.

"In my world, not so much. But are you still hanging with Jilly Coppercorn and her crew?"

I nod.

"In her world, I think maybe, yeah. Do you know Sam Cray? He's with the NPD."

I shake my head.

"He runs this task force that looks into—oh, crap, I don't know. Weird shit."

"The Spook Squad," I say.

"So you have heard of him."

"Not really. The name of the squad just came up in a recent conversation."

Pearse nods. "He and some of his team work out here—usually at night when there's no one else around. I stay late for them, get caught up on my paperwork, but I hear them talking to each other about the things they deal with."

He looks across the room for a long moment, lost in thought.

"Magic?" I try.

"Kind of. More like monsters. The things you don't want to believe exist."

"Huh."

He stretches out his legs, leans back against the wall. "So I guess maybe I do." He turns to look at me. "Have you seen something?"

"I had a ghost ask me to take a case."

"What? Like you're some kind of PI like the one you played on TV?"

"Something like that."

"A ghost."

I nod. "That young guy whose body was found in the park? It was his ghost."

He studies me for a long moment. "So what's bugging you the most? The idea of meeting a ghost, or the fact that he wants you to play the part for real?"

"A little of both. Not to mention how I can see him when other people can't. He came up to me in a café but nobody else saw him."

Pearse nods. "I don't know about why you can see a ghost nobody else can, but the world's a big place with room for all kinds of things in it—those that make sense and those that don't. But I do know that the past can hold you back or it can push you forward. I like to embrace the past—the good and the bad—and use it to build something better."

"Except I was never an investigator. I just played a part. A team of writers figured out the clues for me." I smile. "When it comes right down to it, they're the ones who got my character into trouble in the first place."

"But...?"

"It's weird, but now I can't stop thinking of...the case."

I use the term reluctantly.

"Well," Pearse says, "I know this much. If you get in a little deep, you know how to take care of yourself."

"Even if there are ghosts and monsters?"

"Everybody on the Spook Squad is human."

"I'm kind of surprised you're taking all of this at face value."

"Like I said," Pearse tells me, "the world's a hell of a lot bigger and stranger than the little corner I live in. My dad used to leave milk out for the brownies."

"Have you ever seen a ghost or one of those monsters?"

"Hell no. I'd probably crap my pants if I did."

I STOP in at the Half Kaffe after I leave O'Shaunessy's. I'm not feeling as sore after some more stretches and a hot shower at the club. The hipster Jason is behind the counter and he chats away to me while he draws me a cup of coffee. I have no idea what he's saying because I'm not really listening. I just nod in what seem like the appropriate places.

I'm thinking about a bunch of things. Sonora, back at the shelter. The weirdness that Ethan has brought into my life. And yeah, Nick.

When I finally get my coffee and claim a table I take Nick's business card from my pocket and lay it down beside my takeout cup. I dig my phone out but only to check the time. Quarter to six. He'll be closing up soon. Tam's playing at Your Second Home with one of his bands. Maybe Nick would want to come along.

I could call him, but I decide to go by the bookstore before it closes. At five to six I step inside to the sound of the store bell and see a stranger behind the cash counter. She's a cute college-age girl with blond hair and black horn rims, which makes me wonder if eyeglasses are to Burns' Books what the Jason name tag is to the Half Kaffe Café.

At the sound of the bell, her head lifts from the book she's reading and she smiles.

"Can I help you find something?" she asks.

"No, I—is Nick in?"

She shakes her head. "I'm afraid not. He usually leaves around five. Did you want to leave a message?"

"No, it's okay. It wasn't important."

I leave and wander aimlessly for a while, eventually finding myself standing in front of the animal shelter. Which is closed at this time of day. I wonder how Sonora's doing. If Jilly were here, I bet I could convince her to help me break Sonora out and she'd know just how to do it. But I don't have Jilly's fearlessness. I don't think many people do.

As I put my hands in my pockets and start for home I feel the keys to Ethan's office.

It's a long walk down Stanton Street to Flood. I take Flood Street north for a couple more blocks before I arrive at my destination. Ethan's office is in the old Sovereign Building, a tall brick structure that has seen better times. I remember my parents' lawyer had an office in it before he moved closer to the waterfront. The neighbourhood surrounding it has been decaying for years, though I suppose that makes for cheaper rents.

The day is slipping into dusk when I step inside the foyer. There's a bank of names to my left with buzzers and I look through them for

Ethan's, but come up blank. It doesn't matter. He's not keeping office hours anymore and I don't need to be buzzed in.

The first key doesn't work, but the second lets me in. I take the elevator up to the third floor. It's a smoother ride than I was expecting from how the doors stuttered and wheezed like an old man as they were closing. When they open with the same difficulty I promise myself to use the stairs when I leave.

It takes me a moment to get my bearings and follow the office numbers down a long hall until I get to Ethan's. It's not breaking in, I tell myself as I unlock the door and step inside. I've got a key and Edward's permission. But I can't help feeling like a burglar.

I hit the light switch on the wall inside the door and stop. I immediately see the books and DVDs I was expecting back at Ethan's apartment. There's a bookcase full of them against one wall, with multiple copies of both. There are even foreign translations. The bottom shelves hold action figures still in their packaging, packs of collector's cards, the Nora Constantine board game, and a set of coffee mugs featuring the main characters from the show. Me, naturally. My two boyfriends, James Hearne and Toby Cannon. Carmen Hale, the frenemy who could never decide if she wanted to help or hinder me. Roland Anders, the teacher's assistant I meet in the pilot, who keeps getting sucked into my investigations. And of course Gabi Ramos, who was played by Allison Bennet, the only member of the cast that I'm still in touch with.

Gabi was the typical computer hacker that every mystery show seems to have—sort of punky, sort of Goth, with the spiky black hair, piercings and tattoos we've all come to expect. I blame *The Girl With the Dragon Tattoo* for that. The ironic thing is, off-screen Allison has nice wavy blond hair and neither tats nor piercings. Plus she dresses like the Valley girl she is.

A desk with a closed notebook computer on top faces the door. The other furnishings are an old beat up sofa and a three-drawer metal filing cabinet with a coffee maker and hot plate on top. My face looks back at me from a poster above the sofa. The other walls are papered with more posters from the show, mostly me, often in action with another character.

I quietly close the door behind me in case someone comes along, and let out a gasp when a life-size cutout of me behind the door catches me off guard. It takes me a minute to recover my equilibrium, but I'm left with a nervous chill.

I don't have any of this crap—the mugs, action figures, posters. I left it all behind in L.A. I did bring along a set of the books and DVDs, but they're still packed away in a box in my closet.

It's creepy, standing here surrounded by all this memorabilia with my face looking out at me. I cross over to the desk and sit down to try to tame my wobbly knees.

I check the drawers, which are mostly empty, but have a few of the usual things you'd expect in an office: an unopened two-pack of memory sticks, notepaper, a couple of pens, the power cord for the notebook. The top of the desk's not much more interesting, just the computer and a copy of *Nora Constantine and the Secret of the Yellow Steamer Trunk*.

I open the computer, expecting to need a password, but Ethan's background image fills the screen. Naturally, it's the publicity shot of the cast from the third season.

So much for finding incriminating evidence. If you've got nothing to hide, you're not going to bother with security.

There aren't any programs open to see what he's been working on most recently, so I click on the Documents folder. I find a whole bunch of files named TNCS with a number following the acronym. I open the first and groan as its title appears at the top of the page: The Nora Constantine Sexcapades 1.

I don't need to read the text below the title. Allison told me about this blog last year, and now I know who it belongs to. Beyond his fixation on the show, it seems Ethan writes fanfiction, specifically raunchy fanfic.

I think about this for a moment. Ethan's obsessed with the show. He buys and sells show memorabilia. He's got a trans boyfriend whom he seems to really love, yet he writes raunchy porn fanfic that he publishes in an online blog. Does this make sense? Why does he do this?

Allison thinks this stuff's hilarious. Me, not so much. But Allison gets a kick out of putting on her Gabi wig and gear and making appearances at conventions.

I take a look at his browser search history but it's wiped clean. His emails are all about various transactions—things he's sold, things he's bought—and notices of when someone's posted a comment on the blogs he follows. There's spam. What there doesn't seem to be—at least from a cursory look—is a reason why someone would want to kill him. Or why he'd want to hire me. I mean, Nora.

I shut down the word processor program and close the lid on the notebook.

I still don't have a clue why he was killed or what that cryptic text he sent to Nick is supposed to mean.

Palmer was a truly despicable character, but he was also just that. A character. A character who got killed and buried on screen—there was a pretty moving scene of Nora and a couple of the girls she'd rescued from him standing at his grave in the last episode of season two. And off-screen, Adam Hendrix, who played Palmer, is one of the sweetest guys you could ever meet, so this has nothing to do with him.

I sit there for a while, staring at the cutout and posters of myself across the room, but I don't find a single bit of insight, the way Nora would have by now.

Finally I cross the room, lock up behind me and head for home.

~

I HAVE a weird dream when I finally go to bed. I'm in an unfamiliar room, locked in a big cage like the kind they have for the animals at the Crowsea Animal Shelter. The lights are off and it's hard to see. I have the sense that there are other cages with other people in them all around me.

I'm lying on a ratty old blanket and don't seem to have much strength but I manage to get my fingers in the mesh sides of the cage and pull myself up into a sitting position.

That's when a door opens across the room and this vague Nosferatu shape of a man glides into the room and comes up to my cage. It's hard to make out anything except for his pale face, which seems to float in the darkness, but I instinctively know he's some kind of vampire, and if I meet his gaze he'll trap my soul as well as my body. My pulse drums as he stands there looking down at me, radiating menace.

I can't bear the tension. I feel that I've lived this moment many times before. I know that I'll eventually look up and then he will feed on me.

I wake up when he reaches for the lock on the cage.

4

THURSDAY

"You never showed last night," Tam says when I come shuffling into the kitchen the next morning in my pajamas. "And when I got home your light was off. Is everything okay?"

I look around, trying to blink the sleep from my eyes. "I just didn't feel like seeing people, so I decided to stay in and finish off my outfit for tomorrow. Then I realized I was beat and just went to bed."

Tam pushes a mug of coffee across the table to me and I take it gratefully.

"Thanks," I mumble. I take a swig and wait for the caffeine to do its job. It doesn't take long. Sometimes I feel just the idea of caffeine is enough to wake me up.

"Do I really have to get dressed up?" he asks, scrunching up his nose.

"What did Geordie say?"

"Pirate shirt or anything with poufy sleeves. Jeans are okay. Maybe add a scarf for colour."

I shake my head. Boys.

"Come on," I tell him. "It's not like he's asking you to go full Renaissance Faire which, do I need to remind you, you've done in the past. What's the big deal, anyway?"

"Poufy sleeves." He sticks out his tongue.

I laugh. "Oh, grow a pair. It'll be fun. I've got wings and pointy ears to go with my dress."

"The sleeves will get in the way of my strumming hand."

"So roll them up."

This coffee is so good. I have another big sip then loll back in my chair, content.

"I'm thinking of getting a dog," I say.

He rolls his eyes. "If Jilly jumps off the bridge are you going to jump off, too?"

Now I stick out my tongue at him. "Oh, please. It's nothing like that. I just really felt connected to Sonora—that's her name—and I hate the idea of her being stuck in a cage at the shelter when she could be living with me."

"I'm kidding," Tam says with a smile, then adds with more seriousness, "It's a big commitment."

"I know. Will you come and meet her with me?"

"Absolutely. Will you help me find a shirt with poufy sleeves?"

"Only if I get to make you try on dozens of them before we settle on one."

"Why can't it be simple?"

I straighten up and give him a haughty look. "Fashion is never simple."

He holds up his hands in surrender and I settle back in my chair.

"How's your case going?" he asks.

"Don't ask."

"That bad?"

I shrug. "I'm not a real detective, so it's no big surprise that I suck at it."

"You're good at lots of other things."

"I know. Like picking out poufy shirts!" I stand up and grab my mug. "I'm going to put on some clothes and then I'll be ready to go."

WE'RE PLANNING to go to the thrift shop up on the corner of Lee and Kelly before heading down to the animal shelter, but take a short detour over to the house on Stanton Street to drop off Tam's guitar. They have another band rehearsal this afternoon.

Bobo comes tearing down the hall when I open the front door, his high-pitched barking followed by Geordie shouting, "Inside voice!" from the kitchen. Bobo's barking drops to a lower woof, but he continues to dance around our feet as we make our way to the kitchen.

We find Jilly, Geordie and Wendy sitting around the table. Bobo hops up onto Geordie's lap and immediately looks as if he's been there for hours.

"Don't buy a shirt just for this gig," Geordie says when we explain our errands. "I've got a bunch and I can lend you one." He absently strokes Bobo as he talks.

"Can I come to the shelter with you?" Jilly asks. "I want to see Sonora's face when she realizes she's got a forever home."

In the end we all go traipsing down the street, Bobo leading the way, head and tail held high. As we walk, I tell them what I found in Ethan's office.

"What's fanfic?" Jilly wants to know.

"It's when readers," Wendy explains, "get so invested in the world of an author that they write their own stories set in that world. They might make up their own characters, but they usually use the ones from canon—meaning the original books and movies and shows—and either continue those characters' stories, or make up new relationships for them. Like Captain Kirk and Spock being a gay couple."

"Really?"

Wendy nods. "There've probably been more pages of Harry Potter fanfic written than there are in the original books. Fanfic's huge. The people writing it focus on anything that's popular. *Star Trek. Star Wars. Twilight.*" She looks at me. "*Nora Constantine.*"

"Aren't there copyright laws to stop that kind of thing?" Geordie asks.

"Well, sure. But it's hard to go after somebody when they're not trying to make money from your intellectual property. In the old days, the people writing it would trade mimeographed and photocopied versions. Now it's all up on the 'net."

"And Ethan Law was one of them?" Jilly asks.

"Looks like," I tell her. "He put them up on a blog called *The Nora Constantine Sexcapades.*"

She grimaces in sympathy.

"And what do they get out of writing this stuff—besides titillation?" Tam asks, also shooting me a sad face.

Wendy shrugs. "It's not all titillation. Their stories get read. You have to remember that they do this out of love for the original material. They just want more, or they think they know better how the stories should go and who should end up together. Apparently there's a lot of steamy romance."

"I am so innocent," Jilly says.

"Well," I say, "from all I've heard, the Nora of fanfic fame sure isn't."

We've reached the shelter now. Wendy and Geordie wait outside with Bobo while the rest of us go inside. Everybody knows Jilly, of course, because she's in here so much, and after a couple of visits I'm starting to know some of the staff as well. The girl behind the counter is Judy, twenty-something, brown hair pulled back in a ponytail, a ready smile that jumps to her eyes when she finds out why we're here.

Judy has us wait in a side room while she goes to get Sonora. I feel like I'm going to vibrate right off my chair from anticipation. Sonora's just as beautiful as I remember, with the pink of her ears and her muzzle, and the black fur around one eye so she looks like she's wearing a patch. But I can tell there's something wrong. In temperament, she seems completely different from the cheerful Sonora I walked and played with yesterday. She still holds her head high, but she won't quite look at any of us. Her tail isn't between her legs, but it's droopy.

"Baby," I say as I kneel on the floor and hold out a hand to her. "What's the matter?"

She sniffs my hand and lets me pet her, but it's pretty obvious that she's uncomfortable and it makes my heart break. I so wanted this to work out, but she doesn't seem to like me anymore.

"I don't get it," Judy says. "She's never been like this before."

"She's scared," Jilly says. "And I'll bet I know why."

Tam and I exchange puzzled looks.

"Scared of what?" I ask. "What are any of us doing that's scary?"

"It's not you," Jilly says. "It's more a defense mechanism. I don't think she trusts that any of this is real." She looks up to Judy. "She got like this when you told her why we're here right?"

"I guess," Judy says slowly. "But she's a dog. It's not like she can actually—"

Jilly interrupts her. "Oh, they understand way more than people give them credit for."

Judy gives her a doubtful look.

"I don't blame you," Jilly says. "I know you love the animals that come in here. Sonora's just got issues." She holds out a hand. "Can I have the leash?"

Judy hands it to her and Jilly promptly lets it fall on the floor. She sits down cross-legged in front of Sonora. Putting her hands on either side of the dog's narrow face, she looks deep into Sonora's eyes.

"Hey, girl," Jilly says. "Remember me? Remember Juniper and the fun we all had yesterday?"

The tail lifts a little and gives a small wag.

"Well, Juniper brought her brother Tam to meet you," Jilly goes on, "because she fell head over heels for you. And you know why? It's because you're such a good girl."

Sonora looks past Jilly's shoulder, her grave gaze settling on me for a moment, then on Tam.

"And you know what she told me?" Jilly says.

The gaze returns to Jilly's face.

"That she can't live without you. That she thought about you all night long and first thing this morning she just had to come down here to break you out so that you never have to come back here again. She's offering you a forever home, sweetie. What do you think of that?"

Sonora looks at me again. Her tail wags once, twice, before she returns her attention to Jilly.

"I promise you it's true," Jilly says. She takes her hands from where they rest on either side of Sonora's head and puts her right palm on her chest. "You know me. Ask anybody. I don't lie."

Sonora bumps Jilly with her head then steps around her to where I'm still kneeling in front of my chair. I don't know why I thought she had a serious gaze. Her eyes are bright like a good-natured clown. She puts her forepaws on my knees and gives me a big lick on the cheek. I put my arms around her and she burrows in under my hair, licking my neck.

I could burst with happiness.

"She's been in and out a couple of times," Jilly says as she stands up. She's looking at Judy.

"How did you know that?" Judy asks.

Jilly shrugged. "I didn't. But it had to be something like that. Why did the people who took her bring her back?"

"She can be a little willful."

Jilly laughs. "Who isn't?"

But now Tam's got the doubtful look. "I don't know, Joon. If she's got a moody temperament…"

Jilly stands up, a thoughtful look on her face.

"When's she being sent away?" she asks.

Judy won't meet her gaze. "Monday. After the weekend. We have an anonymous benefactor who apparently has a big farm out in the country. He takes in all the old animals and the ones…you know, with attitude problems. We never want to do it. You know we're a non-kill shelter and we want the animals to get to bond with a person like you and Bobo have. But she's already been returned twice and I swear she'll be fine there."

And now I know why Jilly really wanted to come inside with us. Somehow she knew there'd be a problem she'd need to smooth over for me.

"There's no way I'm leaving here without her," I say.

"But if she's developed behavioural problems," Judy begins.

"I'll sign a waiver," I tell her.

"Joon," Tam tries.

"What if nobody believed in you?" I ask him.

He knows me well enough. I'm pretty easygoing, but once I make my mind up about something, you'd have more luck pulling the moon out of its orbit with a lasso than get me to change it.

The corner of his mouth lifts in the ghost of a smile. He goes down on one knee beside me and reaches out a hand for Sonora to sniff.

"Welcome to the family," he says.

～

IT TAKES another half hour to get through the paperwork and pay. The guys leave in the meantime for their rehearsal. When Jilly, Wendy and I leave, we take three other dogs along with our own to the park for a walk and a romp.

I've got James again and I feel a little bit guilty because in my head I imagine he knows I picked Sonora over him and it's making him sad. But that's the movie running in my head. In reality he just seems happy to be out of the shelter and part of a pack. Wendy has Rubie, who's part black lab, while Jilly has a shepherd/setter mix named Ginger.

We were warned that Ginger's a runner, but when we get to the park Jilly lets him off his lead anyway. He starts to bolt, but stops dead when Jilly calls his name. There's something in her voice that makes all the dogs go still and turn to look at her.

"Where do you think you're going?" Jilly asks Ginger.

She doesn't raise her voice or look angry, but Ginger ducks his head, tail lowering.

"You stay close and play nice with everybody," Jilly goes on. "Can you do that for me? Can you be a good boy?"

Damned if that dog doesn't come right back. He's still a little diffident, but he perks right up when Jilly fusses with him, then he runs off to play with the others.

"How do you do that?" I have to ask her.

"It's just this gift she has," Wendy says.

Jilly shrugs.

"Well, I hope you can teach me," I say.

"Oh, don't worry," Jilly tells me. "You'll get the hang of it in no time."

I doubt that, but I'm sure going to give it my best try.

We spend another hour in the park before we bring the dogs back to the shelter. Then it's off to the pet store to pick up stuff Sonora and I will need before we return to the house on Stanton Street. Wendy has lunch with us then heads down the hall to the library to work on her blog for *In the City*.

Jilly and I go into the studio, dogs at our heels. Sonora jumps up onto the sofa and curls up against one fat arm. Bobo waits a moment before he jumps up beside her. When he cuddles up against Sonora I have to get my phone out to take a picture. I have the feeling I'll be doing this a lot in the future.

"Come see," Jilly says.

She's standing by her hedge faerie painting. There's something different about it, but I can't tell what from where I'm standing. Tucking my phone in my back pocket, I join her by the easel.

"What do you think?" she asks.

It takes me a moment to figure out what she's done. At first it doesn't look any different, but on closer inspection I realize that now my gaze is travelling through the painting as if it's on a planned journey. Which it is. Using only light and shadow, she's turned the whole busy unfocused scene into an absorbing narrative.

"It's brilliant," I say. "How did you think of that?"

Jilly shrugs. "I sat and stared at it for most of the night. Then I went and sat on the sofa and dozed off. When I woke up the dawn light was coming through the windows and as soon as I saw the play of that light moving across the studio it came to me."

I have so much to learn. I could never have fixed it. I step closer to see just how she made the haphazard scene it was the last time I saw it into something that now makes sense.

Allison was really surprised when I mentioned I was painting in Jilly's company. She said, "You don't have any interest in painting fairies, so why are you studying with her?" But the thing is, the subject isn't important. Hanging around with her and Sophie, I absorb insane amounts of technique just by watching them work. It's such a gift. Then I apply what I learn to the subjects that I'm passionate about, which is mostly cityscapes or the details of buildings.

"I should sign some prints," Jilly says. "Keep me company?"

I nod and go over to the long table where the prints are stacked. We sit down beside each other. She signs one from the undone stack, then I take it and start a new stack.

"Okay," she says as she finishes signing one and reaches for the next. "Let's list what we do know about Ethan Law."

"Well, he's dead," I say.

Jilly nods. "And before that he was fixated on the fictional you, collecting all kinds of memorabilia."

"And let's not forget documenting made-up versions of my sex life."

Jilly pulls a face. "He either really thought he came from another world where the Nora Constantine books are real, or he wanted Emma Rohlin to think he had."

"His ghost is still hanging around—or at least it was a few days ago. And he wants me to think that a dead villain is walking around in the real world."

"It's not much to go on," Jilly says.

She lets me take the print she's just signed and pulls another in front of herself.

"And we're no closer to finding out the big answers," she says. "Who killed him and why. And how does Nora Constantine fit in."

"With great discomfort," I say.

Jilly smiles. "I got Christy to talk to Sam Cray at the NPD."

"The Spook Squad guy?"

"The very one. Apparently the M.E. hasn't got a cause of death. The consensus at the moment seems to be that he simply stopped living."

I look at her. "What's that supposed to mean?"

"That it's not a homicide. They've ruled that he died of natural causes even though they can't determine the actual cause. But Sam told Christy that this got him curious, so he ran a background check on Ethan. Want to guess what he found?"

I shake my head.

"There's no record of him until a couple of years ago. When Sam dug deeper, he came up with nothing. No record of birth, no school records, no work history. Zip, zilch and nada. He told Christy that he's heard of people going off the grid, but that this is the first time he's run into a case of someone coming on the grid. Even criminals, apparently, make some effort to sketch out a life for themselves when they get a new identity."

"Are you…are you saying he really did come from some other world?"

"Your guess is as good as mine. But he had to have come from somewhere."

"So what do we do now?" I ask.

"I don't know. Maybe we should hold that séance? Did you ever do that on the show?"

"Yeah, but it was just part of some elaborate con."

Jilly pauses with her pen above the paper to look at me.

"Maybe that's what this is," she says.

"It seems really complicated and bizarre to me. Why would anybody go to so much trouble?"

I take the print after she signs it.

"We need to know the end game," she says, "before we can figure that out."

"Good luck with that."

"We could start with his computer," Jilly says. "We'll get Wendy to go through it and see what she can find."

"I thought Saskia was the computer whiz."

Jilly shakes her head. "Saskia's the internet, Wendy's the whiz."

"I've still got the keys," I tell her. "I can go by and pick it up. Though we should probably run it by Edward first."

"Giving us the keys already implies that he won't mind."

"Okay."

"And if we hit another wall, maybe we really should try a séance. Christy must know a half-dozen spiritualists."

I open my mouth to say something like, it'll just be a waste of time, except these days I'm still trying to navigate through a whole world of things that I never would have thought possible. For all I know, Ethan's ghost will show up as soon as we join hands and call his name.

I THINK about that episode with the séance later as I'm walking over to Ethan's office on Flood Street with Sonora. I remember how Dean —Dean Farris who played my boyfriend James—got upset while we were shooting that particular episode because he took the idea of spirits and ghosts very seriously, but everybody else thought it was a laugh and teased him mercilessly.

Maybe I should call him and see what advice he can give me. I could ask him if anything weird's come into his life. Or for that matter, I could reach out to all the cast.

Hey guys, I met the ghost of a guy who has the same name as a character in an unpublished Emma Rohlin novel, except he was real and walking around but now he's dead. Hence the ghost part. What's new with you?

No doubt Dean would think I was pranking him. Everybody would think I was pranking them.

I hope Wendy can find something to help us on Ethan's computer because I don't love the idea of a séance. But suddenly the need for one becomes irrelevant.

Sonora and I have just passed a bus stop. Sitting on the bench is a guy staring down at his shoes. I'm a few steps past him before I realize who it is. I return to stand in front of him but he doesn't look up. Sonora shifts her weight a few times and I try to stay patient.

"So, Ethan," I say finally. "What was this case you wanted me to take on for you?"

He lifts his gaze. He seems defeated. Worn out.

"I don't have a million dollars," he says.

I sit down beside him. "Yeah, sorry about that. You caught me at a bad moment and I was just being pissy. I shouldn't have come down on you the way I did. On the other hand, you have a sex blog featuring me front and center, my face pasted on some porn star's body, so maybe I was prescient and have every right to be pissy."

Instead of responding, he goes back to looking at his shoes.

It's weird, what can come to you at a moment like this. I never really thought about meeting a ghost, but if I ever had, I wouldn't have thought it would go like this. I'm even finding myself feeling a little sorry for him, which he so doesn't deserve, but I can't help myself.

"It's funny," I say when he continues to give me the silent treatment. "I thought you dead guys just hung around because you had unfinished business, but here I am offering to help you finish yours and you won't even talk to me."

He looks up again. "Wait. I'm dead? How did I die?"

He goes from a moment of surprise to immediate resignation. I watch it happen in his eyes.

"Nobody knows." I tell him. "The medical examiner says you just stopped living."

"I don't feel dead."

"I can't help you there. I don't know what it's supposed to feel like."

He holds his hands in front of himself, turning them palm to back, back to palm. "I don't think it's supposed to feel like this—you know, exactly the same as being alive."

His gaze goes to where Sonora lies with her chin resting on top of my foot. Her rear legs are splayed out behind so she looks a bit like a frog.

"Is that your dog?" he asks.

I nod.

"You're not supposed to have a dog. You never have a dog."

"Focus," I tell him. "You had a case for me. What was it?"

He looks away from Sonora. "I'm trying to find this guy who sold me a book."

"Let me guess. A Nora Constantine book."

"But not just any Nora book," he says.

"The one that has you in it."

"But not the one you're thinking of. I thought it was that one, too —*Nora Constantine and the Secret of the Blue Diary*, the unpublished book from when the series was set in the sixties. The one the guy sold me was also unpublished, but it carried on from the last season of the TV show."

"So you got ripped off. What were you planning to do if I had found him for you?"

"You don't understand," Ethan says. "He sold me a manuscript with Rohlin's byline on it—not just the title page, but on every page."

"That's easy enough to fake. And dumb, too. Everybody knows she stopped writing Nora books in the sixties."

"I don't think she did. I've studied her style and if she didn't write this manuscript, then the person who did could mimic her perfectly. And here's the thing. I'm in it. It's like she rebooted *Blue Diary* to fit into the modern version of the series. I think she wrote all the novelizations."

"That doesn't make any sense. Why wouldn't she publish them under her own name?"

"I don't know. I was hoping the guy who sold it to me could tell me. What I do know is that it looks like she was toying with the idea of shifting the series so that it would fit the current paranormal/post-apocalyptic craze."

"That really doesn't make any sense. I used to talk to her on set. She could see the shift that was coming after the Harry Potter books took off and hated that kind of story. She said they wouldn't have any longevity—not like a book set in the real world."

"Tell that to a million Tolkien fans."

I give a slow nod. I don't know about longevity, but the bookstores are filled with clones of *Twilight* and *The Hunger Games* and there doesn't seem to be any sign of the trend coming to an end.

He's studying his hands again, squeezing the fingers of one in the palm of the other. I've never seen anybody actually wring their hands before. It's a little mesmerizing.

"I can't believe this is happening," he says.

"What part can't you believe?"

"That Palmer's gotten this close."

"Yeah, I saw the text you sent Nick—that was you, right?"

He nods.

"Why'd you do it?"

"To warn you about Palmer. I knew if you started to investigate you'd end up at Nick's store. I couldn't think of any other way to get in touch with you."

I hesitate for a moment, then decide to play it as if the books are real. "Palmer died. I saw his grave."

Ethan shakes his head. "Nothing's permanent over there. Palmer died and then he came back as this monster called Charlie Midnight. That's why I wanted to escape. I stole this life for myself, but now he's stealing it from me."

"What do you mean you stole this life? Was there another guy named Ethan Law?"

He shakes his head. "No, but there was the potential for him to exist so I stole the space where his life would have fit in if he did exist."

"That makes no sense."

He doesn't bother explaining. Instead he taps a finger against his temple. "But I can feel Palmer in here, like he's watching me. Or looking for me. I thought I'd be able to get away from him, but even if I did, what if he comes after Edward? What if when he's done with me he starts in on everybody else I know in this world?"

My head's hurting like it did when Jilly was explaining that magic is real.

"So…what are you saying? That Palmer—or this Charlie Midnight—is trying to cross over to this world and somehow he got to you?"

"Why else would I be dead?"

I think of hobs and faeries and werewolves. Of how the city has a special task force devoted to dealing with the supernatural.

"No," I tell him. "This isn't right. It's too much. Nora Constantine is a fictional character. So are her friends, and Crescent Beach, and everything to do with the books."

"Here, sure," he says. "But over there—"

"Over there, over there. There is no over there. Emma Rohlin made all of this up."

He nods. "Except it's based on things that are real, only they happened somewhere else. Or maybe she makes them happen by writing about them. All I know is that in *Nora Constantine 10: The Rising Dark* she brings Palmer back, except now he's some kind of a vampire creature named Charlie Midnight and he's trying to end the world. The book's either unfinished or it ends on a cliffhanger, but you can plainly see where it's all heading."

He pauses a moment before he adds, "And that's exactly what happened over there. Crescent Beach was on its way to becoming a disaster zone that would be the jump off point for the whole world to fall apart."

"No. There is no Crescent Beach. It was just a set, with parts of Long Beach and Santa Feliz filling in for the establishing shots. Those sets are all long gone now."

"You have to stop saying that. In the book, Charlie Midnight feeds on us—the people in Nora's life—and he's going to do the same to those of us who have escaped here. According to you, he's already gotten to me. But *you're* still in danger, Nora."

I sigh, exasperated. "I'm. Not. Nora," I tell him. "I'm just an actress who played her on a TV show."

He shakes his head.

"So if I'm Nora, why would I look exactly the way Nora looks on the show? Why wouldn't I look like the girl on the covers of the original books, or even completely different? This is ridiculous."

"Read the new book," he says. "Figure him out so that you can find a way to stop him before he gets to you."

"Forget it," I say. "I'm not going to read some stupid book." I reach out to poke him in the shoulder with a stiff finger, except there's nothing there. My finger goes right into his shoulder and he just dissolves away.

My hand drops to my lap and I stare for a long moment at where he was sitting, then I lean over and bury my face in my hands. Sonora whines but I can't comfort her. I feel like I'm going insane.

I might have stayed like that forever except my cell pings, telling me I've got a text. I sit up slowly and dig in my pocket for my phone, reaching down to pat Sonora with my other hand.

"It's okay," I tell her. I'm surprised at how steady my voice is. "I'm just having a mental breakdown, but someone will take care of you. Tam. Or Jilly."

She pushes her head against my leg.

I finally get my phone out. The text says: *Read the book. Edward can tell you where I keep my Nora stuff.*

What? Now a ghost has my cell number?

I slide off the bench and sit on the pavement beside Sonora, hugging her to me. I'm dimly aware of traffic on the street. There's not a lot, just a few cars until a bus pulls up in front of me with a hiss of its brakes. The door opens and the driver looks down at me.

"Are you all right, miss?" she asks.

I give her a slow nod. "Just dandy. Thanks."

"You can't come on with that dog."

"I know." I didn't, but right now I don't know much of anything.

"Do you want me to call someone?" the driver asks.

That gets me to my feet. "No, I'm fine. Really. I was just resting."

The driver gives me a dubious look. She must think I'm stoned or drunk. But finally she closes the door and the bus pulls away. I watch its taillights as it continues down the street.

Read the new book, the ghost wrote.

Which I assume is at his office since that's where Edward told us Ethan keeps his Nora Constantine memorabilia.

"Okay," I tell Sonora. "I can deal with this. We can deal with it. Sorry about the meltdown."

A man's been coming down the street as I talk to her and gives us a wide berth, stepping off the sidewalk to keep some distance between us. I don't blame him. If I look the way I feel, I must be wild-eyed with crazy.

I concentrate on steadying my breathing. Once I feel my heart rate drop, I bend down to give Sonora another reassuring pat and set off again for Ethan's office.

∽

WHEN I OPEN the door and switch on the lights, nothing has changed. It's still creepy in here. My own face still looks at me from too many places. Sonora heaves a sigh and stretches out on the floor.

"I know," I say. "We won't be here long."

This time I decide to give the bookcase a closer look, noting the books, DVDs, and merchandise. The manuscript's not hard to find. It's in a shallow box on the bottom shelf under the Nora Constantine board game and a couple of unopened cartons of collector's card packs.

I pull the manuscript box out and lift the lid. The title page reads *Nora Constantine 10: The Rising Dark* by Emma K. Rohlin.

I sit back on my heels.

I start thinking about the authors of the novelizations. When I look for Ethan's copies, I find them a couple of shelves up. Emmett Rowland wrote three of the books, one for each season of the show. The other two authors were Erica Roberts and Evelyn Roome.

They all have the same initials. Emmett Rowland could almost be Emma Rohlin.

How come I never noticed that before?

I have a feeling I'll be making another phone call to Emma in the very near future.

I spend another half hour poking around the office, not really sure what I'm looking for. Nothing jumps out at me. Finally I take the manuscript box and Ethan's notebook computer and slide them into my backpack. I start to zip it closed when I remember the power cord. I add that and heft the backpack. It's not light, but I've carried heavier loads.

While I'm sitting at the desk I have another look at the text message I got at the bus stop. There's no return number, which just adds to the list of impossible things I've run across this week. There's always a name or a number under the title bar.

I try responding with a message of my own. But when I hit send the app won't deliver.

I swing the backpack onto my shoulders and adjust the straps.

"You're a good, patient girl," I tell Sonora.

I grab the end of her leash and step into the hall, locking up behind me.

The trek back to Bramleyhaugh on Stanton Street takes less time than going to Ethan's office did, but that's only because there's no pause for a conversation with a dead boy. When I get there, Wendy tells me that Jilly and Sophie have gone over to the Memorial Court to give the kids day passes to FaerieFest. Tam's gone too, having taken Sonora's food and sundries with him. I hand over the laptop to Wendy and readjust my pack. With only the manuscript in it, I have a lighter load. After dinner I'm going to start the book.

"Are you hungry?" I ask Sonora as we leave the house. "I know I am."

She wags her tail and gives me a goofy grin.

I laugh and give her a pat on the head. "I'll take that as a yes."

Tam has dinner waiting for me when we get home, some kind of Thai soup, rich with vegetables and chicken, seasoned to perfection, flavourful and spicy hot. I feel sorry for Sonora with her kibbles, so I save a few pieces of chicken, which I give to her after I've rinsed them off.

"And so the spoiling begins," Tam says with a smile.

"I waited till we were finished."

"That's true. I was expecting you to feed her from the table."

"But look at those kibbles. Can you imagine what it would be like if that was all you could eat? I'm going to look up some recipes and make her food myself."

I take the dishes to the sink.

"Do you want to watch a movie?" Tam asks.

"No, I've got some reading to do."

I don't tell him about meeting Ethan again. I didn't tell Wendy either, and I don't know why. I think I'm still trying to process everything.

I was going to read the manuscript in bed, but the loose pages make it awkward, so I sit at the dining room table, Sonora collapsed on the floor by my feet. I guess she isn't used to all the walking we did today.

The book's pretty much the way Ethan described it. I can't tell if he's right about Emma Rohlin really having written it or not. I haven't read any of the other Nora books in forever, so I can't compare the styles.

I don't like the story. The addition of the supernatural elements takes away the charm the original books had. I always liked the interaction of the characters and their relationships, and that seems to take a back seat to Charlie Midnight and his monster allies. It's all action with no mystery.

I set it aside after I'm about halfway through and get my laptop. I know I shouldn't be doing this because it's just going to irritate me, but morbid curiosity has me going to Ethan's fanfic blog, where I skim through the last few entries.

I'm not a prude. I believe people should be allowed to do whatever they want in the privacy of their own homes so long as they're consenting adults. And I know I'm not Nora. But the sex romps he writes piss me off.

From talking to Allison, I expected the gay pair ups of James and Toby, and Gabi and Nora. Even the pair up of Nora with her frenemy Carmen, though I didn't see the heavy S&M and bondage coming. What pisses me off is that my face, and those of the other actors from the series, have been seamlessly Photoshopped onto the bodies of porn stars, creating explicit illustrations to go with his stories.

Allison thinks they're hilarious but I never went looking online to see how bad they were. I don't find them funny at all. The thing is, I knew that people reading this trash would be picturing us in these roles. The photos just add a further level of debauchery to the whole tawdry mess.

If Ethan were here right now, I'd punch him in the face. Except he'd probably dissolve away before he could feel it.

"Whoa," Tam says from behind me. "Sorry. I didn't realize you were—"

"Oh stop it," I tell him. "I'm just doing some research. These pictures are on the blog the dead guy had. Can you believe it?"

He comes over to the table, making sure to not step on Sonora, and takes a seat. Reaching over, he closes the lid of my laptop.

"These are obviously pissing you off," he says, "so why put yourself through it?"

"I told you. Research." I sigh. "And morbid curiosity."

"We should see about having that blog taken down. Get Greta to deal with it. She must know a million lawyers."

"Monday," I tell him. "Right now I'm going to bed. We've got a long day tomorrow, you know, what with the poufy sleeves and all."

"Lay off, little sister. I'm bigger than you. I could whup you."

"In your dreams."

I stick out my tongue at him and head off to bed, Sonora following at my heels.

I have bad dreams all night, fuelled by the unpublished Nora novel and Ethan's stupid blog, and maybe the cages from the animal shelter. I don't remember much when I wake, only flashes of S&M gear, a lot of running, hiding, whips and chains. At one point I'm hanging on a wall beside Nora's boyfriend Toby, both of us decked out in sleazy leather bondage gear. Carmen is cheerfully flailing away at us with a whip, hitting the wall, thankfully, more than us. At one point I'm also back in the cage.

It's awful, but the worst is, I keep catching glimpses of the monstrous Charlie Midnight who, just like last night, looks way more like the classic Nosferatu than Adam Hendrix who played Bret Palmer on the show.

I know that no matter how disturbing the kinky sex elements of these dreams have been, I really don't want Midnight to lock his gaze on me. Even if it's just in a dream.

I stare up at the ceiling, willing myself not to drop off again.

Sonora was sleeping at the foot of the bed at the beginning of the night. Now she's cuddled up against me, her head on the spare pillow. I turn on my side and throw an arm over her. She sighs but otherwise doesn't stir.

I can see the digital numbers of my clock from here. It's almost six-thirty. The alarm's set for seven but I get up anyway. Sonora stretches, one eye peering at me as I go about packing the stuff we'll need for the day.

She watches me dress in my workout clothes and follows me downstairs. I take her out to do her business in the backyard, then give her some breakfast while I put on the coffee. Tam walks into the kitchen just as the coffee's ready.

"You're up early," he says.

He helps himself to a mug then fills one for me when he sees I haven't taken any yet.

"Yeah, I need to go punch something."

His eyebrow goes up.

"Bad dreams," I explain, "courtesy of Ethan Law and his pervy blog."

"Not cool," Tam says. "If he wasn't already dead I'd have a go at him myself."

He eyes my workout clothes and nods approvingly. "Throw a few slugs for me. Want me to bring Sonora to the park?"

I shake my head. "No. I want to introduce her to Pearse."

~

WHEN SONORA and I reach O'Shaunessy's I open the side entrance and we wait just inside until I can catch Pearse's attention.

"Can my dog come in?" I ask when he approaches us.

Pearse looks down at her. "Is it housetrained?"

"It's a she. Her name's Sonora and she's as housetrained as you."

"Then I don't have a problem. But that might change if I get any complaints."

"Don't worry. I won't bring her out front where she might scare the yuppies."

Pearse smiles. "Play nice, Juniper."

"Always."

Sonora's good. She lies quietly and watches me go through my routine like we've been doing this together forever. By the time I get to the heavy bag, I've worked up a good sweat. After twenty minutes on the bag I'm drenched and I've punched away the last of my dreams. Pearse has been sitting and watching me for the past five of those twenty, absently rubbing Sonora under the ear.

He tosses me a towel.

"Maybe you could help me with something," he says.

Pearse never asks me for anything, so I'm curious.

"Sure," I say. "What's up?"

"Be good if you could work a few sessions with this kid I've taken on. She's showing a lot of promise, but I think she'll really blossom with another woman as a sparring partner."

"That could be fun," I tell him. "But I'm busy this weekend. How does Monday morning sound?"

"Perfect. I'll let Gabrielle know."

"Pretty name for a boxer."

"Don't worry. She's got steel in her."

I sit down beside him and we watch a couple of guys sparring in the ring until I realize I need to clean up and get over to the park.

"I'll watch Sonora for you," Pearse says.

I bump fists with him and head for the shower.

~

THE RENTAL TRUCKS are already at the park when Sonora and I get there. Alan Grant and his wife Marisa, the owners of East Side Press, go all out for FaerieFest. It makes sense since this is their big moneymaker of the year.

I tie Sonora up where she can hang out with Bobo, and help unload the last of the boxes from the trucks. We've all been doing this for so many years that we've got it down to a fine art. Before you know it we've got the giant tent and the smaller tent up, the displays and stage assembled and the merchandise all laid out. Books, posters, cards, CDs, figurines, T-shirts. A few original paintings are on easels and the big banners are in place. The smaller one says "East Side Books." Above it hangs a much larger one that reads, "Jilly Coppercorn Faerie Art," which embarrasses Jilly every year.

As soon as the banners are hung, the air fills with the sound of wings. Dozens and dozens of crows drop to perch on the tent top and the nearby trees. It happens every year, regular as clockwork. They come as soon as we're done setting up and stay through the weekend until Sunday evening when we take everything down.

"Isn't that weird?" I said the first time I was helping out a few years ago.

"What? The crows?" Geordie said.

I nodded.

"They're security," he told me.

I didn't understand until that evening when we were all about to head over to the final concert. All the merchandise, even original paintings, were still on display.

"Um, guys," I said. "Anybody can just walk in and help themselves."

At that point, Jilly's friend Joe stepped out from the shadows inside the tent. Joe's a tall Native man with a loose, lanky stride and intense eyes. He's always been nice to me, but to this day I still think he's a little scary. It's those eyes. And it doesn't help that people also call him "Crazy Dog" and "Bones." Only scary people have names like that.

"Don't worry, Juniper," he told me. "We've got this."

Jilly put her arm around my shoulders. "Joe and the birds are keeping watch."

Through all these years we've never lost a single piece of merchandise. Even during the day, the occasional thief attempting a five-finger discount gets dive-bombed by crows until they drop whatever they grabbed.

"Who trained those birds?" I asked the first time I saw it happen.

Everybody just laughed.

Behind the storefront of the main tent is a second adjoining tent for hanging out. At the moment, we're using it to change into our outfits.

Jilly's sticking to a simple pair of leggings and a painter's smock, so she's already outside with the guys and the dogs. Meanwhile, the rest of us are transforming ourselves from boho city girls to woodland faeries, some with a touch of steampunk. I've even made Sonora a collar with bits of extra fabric from my outfit. All sorts of dangly bits of ribbon and cloth hang from it as Sonora patiently lets me put it around her neck.

I stand back to admire her and she grins up at me.

"Too much?" I ask Sophie, who's standing closest to me.

She smiles. "I think it's darling."

Marisa has posted the schedule for who's working when. Everybody checks it out before heading off to see how the set up is going at the other booths, wandering away in groups of two and three.

I stay with Jilly, waiting for Alan and Marisa to get back from bringing the trucks to their house where they'll be parked until Sunday evening teardown.

"Wendy didn't get to Ethan's computer yet," Jilly says as we make ourselves comfortable behind the counter.

Geordie found an outdoor chaise cushion somewhere and the dogs are drowsing on it behind our chairs. They're so cute. Bedazzled Sonora's lying on her side, while Bobo's cuddled up against her.

"She wanted to get all her work done so she'd have the weekend free," Jilly goes on.

I want to say no rush, because I'd just as soon take a break from our "investigation" for the weekend, but what comes out is, "I saw Ethan again yesterday."

I go on to tell her about our conversation, the unpublished book, what I found on his blog. I study her as I'm talking and two things strike me as weird. She's not interrupting as much as she usually does and—

"You don't seem surprised," I say. "Have you actually run into this kind of thing before—fictional characters that can walk around in the real world?"

But then I remember a conversation I had with her and Sophie the other day. About people stepping out of paintings and characters in books becoming so well-loved that they take on a life of their own.

"Sort of," she says. "But it was different. It was kind of in my head and real at the same time."

My eyebrows go up.

"It was when I was recovering from the accident, so who knows? But with everything I know, it's certainly plausible."

"Plausible."

She shrugs. "I've seen it with characters from old books. It's never occurred to me that the same could be true for TV and movies."

"So fictional versions of the Nora Constantine show characters could actually be running around."

She nods. "They're called Eadar."

I remember she used that term when we were talking to Sophie.

"They don't like the term fictionals," she goes on, "and they usually don't like it when you refer to here as the real world. They like to think that their worlds are real, too."

"Are you serious?"

"Well, consider it from their point of view."

"I mean, *how* is it plausible?"

"We told you about Isabelle's friends, didn't we? How is a book that different from a painting?"

"My head's threatening to explode again," I tell her. "I was only just getting used to the idea of faeries and ghosts."

She gives me a sympathetic look.

"Let's forget about it for now," she says. "I'm terrible at explaining the finer workings of the otherworld. Joe'll be around later. After the concerts are over we can come back here and he'll make sense of all of this for you."

I don't even see how that's possible, but I nod all the same. I doubt I'll be able to just shake it off, but Jilly has no problem. She starts chatting away about what vendors she hopes will be at the fair, the bands that are playing, the latest installment of Mona's "Life As a Bird" comic strip, how she feels like she's always had a dog even though Bobo's only lived with her for a couple of days. Before I know it I'm not thinking of anything else either.

When Alan and Marisa return I promise to have Jilly back at the booth for when the fair opens, then she and I take the dogs to go exploring.

One of the benefits of being a vendor is that you get to check out what everybody else is selling before the crowds show up and it's all been picked over. Neither of us are planning to actually buy anything today, but it's fun going around and looking at everything. There's beautiful tooled leather, paintings, dolls and figurines, steampunk gear, musical instruments, books and CDs and movies, every kind of good food you can imagine, and of course clothes.

Oh God, the clothes. Whether you're human or faerie, I suppose, you still want to look good. If I bought everything I wanted at FaerieFest I'd have to take some of those comic con gigs Greta keeps offering me, just to pay for it all.

Jilly's very good about not bringing even a whiff of magical things into our conversation as we wander around, but I can't help eyeing everybody differently than I have any other year. Before, I'd be admiring the costumes and outfits. This year, I'm trying to figure out if any of the people we see and chat with are actual faeries.

Eventually, we make our way to the main stage where Geordie and his friends are setting up for the show later in the evening. Many of them, along with some other invited locals, will also be playing short sets on the smallest stage by the East Side Press tent when there isn't music happening on the other festival stages.

We sit in the grass with Sophie and Mona and listen to the band do their sound check before we all head off to check out the side stage at the far end of the park. I always like this one best because every year they transform it into something different. Last year, it was decorated like an enchanted woodland where the musicians were playing in a forest. The year before, the whole stage was a pirate ship.

We grin at one another in anticipation as we approach the site of the small stage, then gasp in delight as it comes into view. This year it holds all the trappings of a desert nomad camp. The stage is painted in an array of rich desert hues, contrasted by a soft midnight-blue backdrop painted with iridescent stars. Artisans have made realistic slabs of "rock" upon which the musicians will play. Above it all hang several exotic brass filigreed and stained glass lamps. Imagining this scene later on, lamps aglow, music wafting, fills me with warmth.

We all stand there soaking it in until I realize it's time for Jilly and me to get back to the East Side Press tent. The festival's opening in fifteen minutes.

Sophie and Mona come back with us and help me keep Jilly on track. Left to her own devices she'd be hanging out at every booth having long conversations with whoever she happens to meet. Marisa is obviously relieved as she sees us approach. She sets Jilly up at a long table where she'll be able to talk to her fans and sign things for them. While Jilly settles in the rest of us see to last minute preparations. There's really not much for us to do yet. I get the dogs back on the cushion, then sit at the end of Jilly's table and start to flip through her new faerie sketchbook, which I haven't had a chance to check out until now. Just as I'm beginning to feast my eyes, a fanfare of trumpets signals the opening of the fair, and because we're the first of the Faerie Market booths inside the gates, we're immediately swamped.

I love watching the people approach Jilly. They're of all ages and temperaments, ranging from nervous girls clutching battered but well-loved copies of her first art book, to middle-aged women and men with excitement twinkling in their eyes, making them look years younger. It's all the more delightful because everybody is in some sort of a faerie costume.

Jilly spends the next three hours signing books and posters, complimenting people on their costumes, accepting gifts of art, candy and various trinkets with a smile. She gives everybody their moment of undivided attention. A couple of girls have brought portfolios and she asks them to come back later in the weekend when it's not as busy so she can sit with them to look through their art.

I give the dogs a couple of opportunities to stretch their legs and do their business, dutifully picking up after them and putting their waste in trash cans, which are already starting to fill up with the usual festival debris.

Christy comes by to do a round of signing. Wendy and Saskia also take their turns in the booth. But finally, the Faerie Market closes for the evening.

As we talk about getting something to eat before the music starts, Joe arrives with his wife Cassie. He smiles a greeting when I look his way, the crazy in his eyes toned down a little, the way it always is when Cassie is with him.

Cassie will have a table by the East Side Press tent tomorrow and Sunday where she'll be reading fortunes. I'd think the rainbow flood of colours she's wearing is for the festival, except she always dresses like this, her hair in cornrows, her dark skin seeming to shimmer with an inner light.

Joe kneels on the ground and both dogs immediately rise and approach him.

"Handsome and Beauty," Joe says, each hand busily scratching a dog behind the ear.

"It's actually Bobo and Sonora," Wendy says.

Joe smiles. "Good names." His gaze finds me, then Jilly. "You should let them visit with me while the bands are playing, save them from getting stepped on."

Jilly walks up to him and kisses the top of his head.

"You're the best," she says.

~

GEORDIE and his friends play a killer set. I'm so proud of Tam. It's not really his usual style of music, but you'd never have known from his relaxed performance. After them, a German band called Faun plays traditional music from the Continent on an array of acoustic and electric instruments that's pure magic. Local steampunk darlings The Clockwork Noise Smiths close off the night with a rousing set that still has us all buzzing and pumped when they leave the stage.

We all return to the East Side Press tent to collect our stuff. Most of the others leave, laughing and chatting, until it's just Joe and Cassie, Jilly and Geordie, and me. We take the festival chairs from the back room and set them out in front of the tent along with a couple of small pails containing beeswax candles. It seems so quiet now that almost everybody has left the grounds.

Cassie lights the candles, then produces an enormous thermos and passes around cups of steaming hot tea. For a while we just sit and enjoy the quiet and each other's company, sipping our tea.

"So Jilly says you've been seeing ghosts," Joe finally says to me.

And we're back to crazy times.

Sonora senses my discomfort and gets up so that she can lie down pressed against me. Once she settles, I lay a hand on her back. I feel the calmness emanating from her flow into me.

"That's the tip of the iceberg," I say. "How much did Jilly tell you?"

"Just enough to make me curious," he says. "Maybe you should start at the beginning."

"I don't want to bore everybody…"

"I only know the little that Jilly's told me," Geordie says, "so I probably know less than Joe."

"I'll help," Jilly says. "You were in the Half Kaffe when you first met Ethan—though you didn't know his name yet—and he thought you were Nora Constantine."

"That's a character from a TV show I was in," I explain to Joe and Cassie.

"I know," Joe says. "I've seen it."

"You have?"

"What? You think we don't have TVs on the rez?"

I feel my face redden and am grateful it's dark out.

"Um…I didn't know you lived on the rez."

"Oh, sure. Our teepee's got cable, WiFi—"

"Joe," Cassie says, a warning tone in her voice. "Don't play the clown." She turns to me. "He only lived on the rez when he was a pup. These days we live in an apartment here in the city, and I always liked the show. Wendy got me started on it and Joe's only seen a couple of episodes, which is quite amazing since it's hard to get him to sit still long enough to watch anything."

Even in the relative dark, I can see the twinkle in Joe's eyes.

"Anyway," Jilly says, reaching over and giving my wrist a little squeeze.

I nod and pick up from where we left off.

It takes a while, even with Jilly and me taking turns and trying to keep it short. I'm glad I can't really see Joe watching me, but I feel his undivided attention. When Jilly and I finally get the other three up to date I wait for Joe to speak. I'm afraid he's going to echo what Jilly said —that a Crescent Beach with Emma Rohlin's characters is actually plausible—but I'm hoping for the opposite.

Except when he does speak, it's only to ask, "Is there any of that tea left?"

Cassie passes him the thermos. He pours himself a refill then offers it around. Jilly and I take him up on it since we've been talking so much.

Joe leans back in his chair, sipping his tea and staring up at the sky.

"Well?" Jilly says.

He looks over to her. "I'm trying to find a way to frame this so that it makes sense to…you know…"

"An unbeliever?" I say.

He shrugs.

"I've talked to the ghost," I tell him. "Twice. I don't think there's anything you can say that can really freak me out after that."

Liar, I think, but one way or another I have to know.

"What do you know about the otherworld?" he asks.

"Just what Jilly's told me. It's like a parallel world or something that kind of exists a step sideways from this one, right?"

"Yes and no. There is an otherworld just out of sight of this one, but it's only one of…" He waves a hand to the night sky above us. "As many as there are stars above us. And the one closest to us is more like a between place that you have to move through to get to the deeper otherworlds."

I swallow, uneasy with the idea.

"Some people," he goes on, "call the otherworld the dreamlands because it's where sleeping spirits go when they dream. The truth is, there are as many otherworlds as can possibly be imagined, and then times that to infinity. Out there, the past, present and future all exist at the same time.

"Some of those otherworlds are as complex as this world we're living in, others are simpler, almost like pocket worlds. The size of a country, a city, an acre of land, even just a house—like the place Christy's sister Christiana has made for herself."

He gives me a questioning look. "You with me?"

I shrug. "I don't know her that well," I say. "We've only met a couple of times at Bramleyhaugh."

Joe nods. "Okay, but I was talking about the concept. Where it gets really interesting is the origin of many of them. Dream about a place often enough, and it comes into being. Share the idea of a place, and the same thing happens. The size and permanency of the world depend on how many people share the idea of it and how strongly they believe in it. Some become permanent. Others fade away after a time, or leave just a ghostly echo behind."

He pauses again, to make sure I understand, I suppose.

"Like the Eadar I met over there," Jilly says.

Joe nods.

"So people are just flitting back and forth between here and worlds they've made up?" I ask.

"Again, yes and no. You know how, in your European mythologies, they talk about the gods disappearing because people didn't believe in them anymore? Or how faeries exist only so long as people believe in them?"

I nod. I can see where this is going.

"You're saying there could be a Crescent Beach somewhere out there in the otherworld if enough people believe it exists."

"I am."

"And all the people who love the show and the books, and all the people writing fan fiction—they're making it more real."

"And the people that live there," Joe says, "are becoming more independent beings in their own right, the longer that world exists."

I think of the debauched crap that Ethan wrote and pray he didn't have much of an audience. I can't repress a shudder. Sonora stirs and looks up at me. Thankful for the distraction, I switch to another train of thought.

"Okay," I say. "So if there is a Crescent City out there, why did Ethan tell me it's under attack? Instead of the usual stories of Nora and her friends solving mysteries and having their relationships with each other, now there are monsters running around tearing everything down. But that situation couldn't be based on a lot of people believing in it. That story is in a single unpublished book that hardly anyone has read."

"I suppose it depends on the potency of the creator."

I think about Emma Rohlin, and shake my head.

"I don't see Emma making actual worlds," I say. "Or should that be otherworlds? She kind of freaked when we just talked to her about ghosts."

Joe shrugs. "Maybe it's not her. But somebody is."

"So how can we stop what's happening there?" I ask. "How do we get rid of Charlie Midnight?"

"How does the book end?" Joe asks.

"I don't know. I haven't finished it yet. But Ethan gave me the sense that the book doesn't have a tidy ending."

"Maybe Emma Rohlin needs to write another book," Cassie says. "To fix the mess she's made."

"Let me check into this place first," Joe says.

"How would you even find it?" I ask.

"I'm good at finding my way around on the other side. It'd be easier if I had something that belonged to Ethan."

Jilly looks at me. "We could go back to his apartment and ask Edward for something."

I dig in my pocket. "Would these work?" I ask, holding up the keys to Ethan's office.

Joe reaches over and takes them from me. He closes his fingers around them for a long moment, then hands them back.

"That's it?" I say.

"I got what I need from them."

I stare at him.

Again, Jilly reaches over and gives my hand a squeeze. "How's your head?"

"Exploding."

She smiles. "Yeah, I thought that was going to happen."

I turn back to Joe. "So the faeries that Jilly says come to the festival —they're here because people believe in them?"

"Some. But faerie have always existed on some world or other, regardless of anybody's belief in them. Among my people, we call them the little mysteries."

"The Kickaha?"

"Sure," he says. "Let's go with that."

I want to ask what he means, but then I think about being a kid scared of the monster in my closet. So many kids are afraid of these bedroom monsters.

"How about the boogieman?" I ask. "Is he real?"

"Somewhere out there, anything you can imagine is real." Joe waits a beat, then adds, "We're all going to be busy this weekend. I'll get to this on Monday."

I nod. "We can wait that long?"

"I think so. It's not like there's an army poised on the other side just waiting to invade us."

I think of Charlie Midnight and shiver. I so didn't want him to actually exist. And I really don't want him coming over here to wreak havoc.

"Do we know that for sure?" I ask.

He shrugs. "I haven't seen any signs of one and I keep an eye out for that kind of thing. But to be on the safe side, you should stop dreaming about the place. That's like offering an invitation."

"I don't know how to do that."

"Cassie," he says. "Do you still have those mints?"

She rummages around in her big colourful purse and pulls out a little tin that rattles when she hands it to me.

"Mints?" I say dubiously.

"We got them the last time we were in Mabon," Joe says. "They let you sleep without dreaming."

"I was wondering why I bought those," Cassie murmurs.

"Mabon?" I ask.

"You know," Jilly says. "Sophie's always dreaming about going there."

"That's a real place?" I catch myself. "Of course it's a real place."

I give the tin a little shake, then tilt it toward the ambient light coming from the candles. There's a picture of a girl sleeping peacefully under the calligraphed words, "Esmerine Undream Mints."

"So what makes them work?" I ask.

"Medicine," Joe says.

"Magic," Cassie says at the same time. "Don't worry," she adds. "We got them from a trustworthy source."

"Right. Magical mints."

I tuck them in my pocket.

"What about Edward?" Geordie asks. "Could he be in danger?"

Joe nods. "Good point. Jack's mooching about in the middleworld. I'll get him to watch out for the kid."

"Middleworld?" I ask.

"The part of the otherworld that you first step into from here," Jilly says. "It's the between place Joe was talking about earlier. You have to pass through it before you can get into the crazy quilt that makes up the rest of the dreamlands."

"And it's not as dangerous," Joe puts in. He lifts his head. "Hey, cousins!" he calls up into the sky. "One of you want to carry a message to Jack for me?"

There's a stirring in the trees and on the canvas of the tent. One black-winged bird sails down to land on the arm of Joe's chair.

"Make sure Jack knows that Edward is transgender," Jilly says. "Otherwise he might pass him over thinking he's a girl and not the person he's looking for."

Joe gives her a look.

"Right," Jilly says. "Of course Jack's going to see deeper than the skin someone's wearing."

"Just make sure he looks out for him," Joe tells the crow.

The bird dips its head before launching itself back into the air. I watch its flight, but a couple of yards above Joe's head it disappears as though it was never there.

I sigh. I want to be quiet, but it's hard to hide my discomfort. The way that crow vanished makes everything too real.

Cassie's sitting on the other side of me. She reaches over and touches my arm. "What is it?" she asks.

"Oh, I don't know," I say, trying to keep the anxiety out of my voice. "But I've got a ghost talking to me. Charlie Midnight can maybe drag me into the otherworld version of Crescent Beach unless I don't dream. And, oh yeah, the boogieman in my closet was real."

"It's not all dreary and dark," Jilly says. "I promise you."

I try to give her a smile.

She turns to Joe. "We have to show her. Can you take her home?"

I try to hide my alarm. Joe's been nice all evening, if a bit of a tease, but he still makes me nervous. Being alone with him is not going to make me feel less anxious.

Joe nods in response to Jilly. "Sure."

I guess even in the dim light Jilly sees something in my face.

"We'll all go," she says.

She's brimming with the excitement she always gets when something special is about to happen.

"I'll keep the crows company till you get back," Cassie says to Joe.

Jilly puts Bobo down on the ground. When I stand up I can tell Sonora's picking up on my anxiety because she stays pressed against my leg and keeps looking up at my face.

Geordie steps into the tent and reappears in a few moments carrying his fiddle, my backpack and Jilly's bag.

"Take my hand," Jilly says, "and hold onto the end of Sonora's leash."

I put my knapsack on as Geordie scoops up Bobo, then I grab the leash.

Jilly takes my free hand and puts a hand on Joe's arm. Geordie does the same on the other side of Joe.

"Anytime," Jilly tells Joe, then adds, "See you tomorrow, Cassie."

Anytime what? I wonder.

But then Joe's moving forward, the rest of us fall into step, and the world goes away.

It's a disconcerting sensation. For a moment, the ground feels spongy underfoot and I get a touch of vertigo quickly followed by a wave of nausea. Jilly lets go of my hand and steps up to steady me, putting her arm around my waist.

The weird feeling goes away almost immediately and I look around myself. The four of us and the dogs are standing in a moonlit meadow. There's forest all around us. The air smells clean, the way it only can on top of a mountain or when it's snowing. The sound of crickets is loud. From a little farther away I can hear a frogs' chorus.

"Welcome to the otherworld," Jilly says, stepping away when she sees I have my balance. "Well, the middleworld, if we're going to be specific, but I find it easier to just think of it all as Faerieland."

Any lingering doubts I might have had about magic and faeries and otherworlds wash away as I turn in a slow circle, trying to take it all in.

"You can let Sonora off her lead," Joe says. "She'll stick with us."

I look down to see her trembling, but it's with excitement. I unclip her lead as Geordie puts Bobo down and the pair of them go running in gleeful circles around us.

Joe laughs. "I love seeing this. Every time."

I'm smiling too, watching the dogs romp, but I ask, "See what?" Because I feel he means more than a couple of dogs playing.

"Cousins experiencing the world the way it's supposed to be," he says. "No pavement. No constant drone of electricity. No cars. No satellites watching us from the skies. Just a pure world, the way the thunders created it for all us living things."

"What do you think?" Jilly asks.

"It's beautiful," I tell her. "It feels…deep."

I don't really know how to describe the rush of feelings inside me, but she seems to get exactly what I mean.

"C'mon," Joe says. "I'll take you all home."

I DON'T KNOW how long we follow a deer trail through lush fields and stands of tall trees. We probably walk for no more than a half hour, but it seems so much longer, as though we're moving through a stretched-out moment stolen from time. It lasts forever, yet it also goes by all too quickly.

When Joe steps me back out, Sonora by my side, we're right at my front door.

"Thanks, Joe," I say.

He gives me a nod and a small smile before he vanishes. I hear Jilly calling, "See you tomorrow!"

I stare for a long time at the place where Joe disappeared before I finally shake my head and turn to the house. Sonora has a quick pee then bounds up the steps to wait for me on the porch.

Tam's asleep when we go inside, but he left the hall light on for us. I lead the way upstairs. Sonora jumps on the bed while I change into my pajamas and brush my teeth. I come back and sit on the edge of the bed, my little tin of Esmerine's Undream Mints in my hand. Sonora watches me, her chin resting on her folded forepaws.

I feel a sense of elation, like I just woke up from the best dream ever. It seems ridiculous to not try to recapture it tonight when I'm sleeping—but only until I remember my dreams last night and the horror show of Charlie Midnight's face. I pop open the tin and put one of the mints on my tongue. It doesn't taste at all like I expected. There's a hint of peppermint, but mostly it tastes like a spring day, fresh and expectant.

I slip into bed, one hand behind my head, the other resting on Sonora, and I'm not aware of anything again until the next morning.

6

THE WEEKEND

There's a girl I don't know at the stove the next morning making an elaborate omelet with peppers and tomato and who knows what all. She's pretty, twenty-something, slender with jet-black hair cut in a sleek bob that really suits her. She's wearing one of Tam's Bill Frisell T-shirts and looks startled to see me.

I give her a nod and take Sonora out into the backyard. By the time we return, Tam's in the kitchen and he introduces the girl as Lydia, telling me how they first met a couple of years ago at a gig in Tyson and hadn't seen each other again until they hooked up at the festival yesterday.

"You look familiar," Lydia says.

Please don't, I think. At least not before I've had a coffee.

"I've been at the festival every year for the past few years," I tell her. "In the East Street Press tent. You've probably seen me there."

"I guess…"

I can tell she knows me from Nora Constantine. She just hasn't connected the dots yet.

I put some kibble in Sonora's bowl. As soon as this weekend's over I'm going to learn how to make better meals for her. Then I grab a coffee and head up to my room to get ready for the day.

I'm not trying to be unfriendly to Lydia. I've just learned not to bond with Tam's girlfriends because they're never around for long.

Whenever I made the mistake of getting close, it felt like losing a friend when they went away. And eventually they all go away. I wonder sometimes if Tam even notices. Though maybe I'm being unfair. He treats them all really well when the music isn't distracting him.

Upstairs, I lay out the two outfits I have left for the weekend, trying to decide which I'll wear today. I can't tell if Sonora's amused by my fussing or if it's just the natural smile she has when her mouth is in repose. I finally make up my mind and hang Sunday's outfit back in the closet.

Sonora lifts her head just before there's a knock on the door. I respond and Tam pokes his head inside.

"She figured it out," he says.

Meaning Lydia.

"Of course she did."

He comes in and sits on the edge of my bed. "I asked her not to talk about it."

"Thanks."

"But," he says, "I can't figure out why you keep running from having been in the show. You were great—it was like it was written for you. So why does it embarrass you?"

"It doesn't. I'm proud of the show."

"Then what is it?"

"I'm not Nora, but so many people still see me as her even though I haven't played that role in years. That's what makes me uncomfortable." I sigh and sit down beside him. "And it doesn't help that I made a whole bunch of poor film choices outside of the show and after."

"Do you miss acting?"

"A little. But I like painting more. I'd probably be calmer about everything that's been going on this week if I could've had my paints out even once. But you know what it's like the week before FaerieFest."

"I didn't really," Tam says, "but I do know now. Are you working the tent again today?"

I nod.

"Bring your sketchbook. You can sit and draw people from the crowd while Jilly's doing her thing—at least for part of the time."

I lean forward and kiss his cheek.

"You're a genius," I tell him.

"I wouldn't go that far," he says, then grins. "Oh, who am I kidding? I'm the best, right?"

I give him a push. "Get out of here. I've got to finish getting ready."

He leaves, laughing.

~

A LITTLE LATER, I go to meet Jilly at Bramleyhaugh before we head off to the festival. We decide to walk to the park this morning to make sure the dogs get some exercise in.

"So," she says as we set off, "can we talk some more about the case, or do you want a Nora moratorium for the weekend?"

"We don't have a case."

"But we don't know how Ethan died or who killed him."

"If anybody even did."

She gives me a look.

"Okay," I tell her. "There's something hinky going on, but let's go with the moratorium—the temporary moratorium," I add as she opens her mouth to speak.

She pouts. "You don't even know what I was going to say."

"What were you going to say that has nothing to do with Nora?"

"I was going to ask if you liked your first trip into the otherworld."

I remember the glorious walk under the moonlight, the pure air and the joy that seemed to run through my veins instead of blood.

"Are you kidding me?" I say. "I loved it. I could live there forever."

"You could move into the house with us," Jilly says.

I give her a considering look. "What are you saying?"

"The Professor's house kind of straddles the otherworld."

"What?"

"Actually a lot of Stanton Street does. There's a kind of a nexus because of the Rookery, the Kelledys' house, and our place."

"I know you told me about the crow people who live in the Rookery," I say, "but how does Meran's house fit in?"

"Are you kidding me? You know how you were asking me about who's magic the other day?"

I nod.

"Well, the Kelledys," she says, "are some kind of faerie royalty."

"Say what?"

I'll admit their music is pure magic, but they seem like two of the most down-to-earth people you could ever meet. Kind of whole-earth vibe meets old hippie.

"Watch how the faerie at the festival treat them," Jilly says. "Some of the hobs pretty much faint when they catch sight of either one of them."

"I've never seen a hob," I tell her.

"I'll point one out to you."

Oddly enough, my head doesn't feel the least bit explody. I guess once you've been to the otherworld everything else just slips into some kind of twisty logic that actually makes sense.

"Bobo, no," Jilly says suddenly. "What did we say about eating bird poop?"

Bobo quickly steps away from the questionable snack. He gives her such a sad and guilty look that we both end up leaning against each other and laughing as we continue on our way.

~

THE GIRLS who wanted Jilly to look at their art are waiting at the booth when we arrive. Anybody else would have them wait a little longer while we set up for the morning signing, but not Jilly.

"Come on into the back," she says.

The girls look like they're going to burst with excitement as they follow her into the back room of the tent.

Their names are Maddie and Carla. Maddie has red hair like mine, except hers has a ton of waves and curls. Carla has short dreads that hang to her shoulders, and she's the taller of the two. They're dressed like woodland faeries in raggedy greens, browns and yellows, their tunics and leggings sporting all sorts of dangly bits as though they're draped in vines. They don't have elf ears like I'm wearing, but they do have wings, which I don't today.

Jilly sits cross-legged on a pillow with a girl on either side as she pores over their portfolios. There's tea and coffee and muffins on a side table, and we've all helped ourselves. With her mouth half full of a bite of banana muffin, Jilly asks the girls if they want some honest criticism. When they nod, she starts to talk about perspective, line work and shading, how to use colour and light to tell a story, the rule of thirds, and all the little things that help make the common extraordinary. The girls hang on to her every word, beaming when Jilly exclaims over the things she likes in their art.

Marisa pops her head into the back room.

"We should get started," she says. "There's already a bit of a line."

Jilly sighs and closes the portfolio on her lap.

"You guys should come by the studio sometime," she says to the girls. "You know, after the festival's over."

The girls share a disbelieving glance with one another.

"Really?" Carla says.

Jilly smiles. "Sure. It'll be fun."

She pulls out the little sketchbook she's always got stuck in one pocket or another, and hands it to Carla.

"Write out your contact info for me," she says, "and I'll give you a call next week."

If those girls were beaming before, now they're positively glowing.

This is one of the reasons I love Jilly so much. If she thinks someone is genuinely serious about their art, she's super generous with her time. Here, over at the Memorial Court, pretty much anywhere. She loves people anyway, but she really loves to nurture young artists. In the couple of weeks after every festival there's always a handful of visitors to the studio, earnest young artists, greedy to learn. They come barely able to speak or contain their excitement. Jilly immediately puts them at ease, drawing out the best of what they carry inside, and they all leave with a better understanding of what they're trying to accomplish.

I know, because once upon a time I was one of them.

Jilly has the last bite of her muffin and stands up.

"Finish your drinks," Jilly tells the girls. "And for God's sake have something to eat or Alan will try to feed us stale muffins tomorrow morning. Joking," she adds, patting Alan on the head as she walks by him.

He's poring over figures on the screen of his tablet, but looks up long enough to give her a mock frown before returning to whatever he's doing.

We bring our coffees outside to where a line is forming in front of Jilly's table. The dogs follow us and settle on their cushion. Mona and I sit on either side of Jilly, chatting to the people as they wait for their turn, opening books to their title page for Jilly to sign.

After a while things get a little less busy and Jilly starts to entertain

herself by pointing out faeries to me—the real faeries, she says. I take
her at face value now.

"Those two boys?" Jilly says, nodding with her chin toward two
boys looking at the leather headpieces, bracelets and belts in the booth
across the way. "They're both hobs. Those three girls? The middle one's
a faerie."

"Really?" I say, "because the costumes her friends are wearing seem
more magical to me."

"Mmm. Oh and look—a derrydown. That's a kind of finding
sprite and it's rare to see them—hardly ever outside of Mabon. They're
related to derrynimbles which are the original finding spirits and the
tiniest of things so they can't ever pass as human."

I see what looks to be an eight- or nine-year-old child dressed
much too sexy goth for her age, except when she looks in my
direction, her eyes show a depth of knowledge beyond that of any little
girl I've ever met. The smile she sends my way is almost feral.

Another customer approaches the table. As Jilly begins to chat with
him, Mona leans back in her chair and talks to me behind Jilly's back.

"I know it can seem a bit much at first," Mona tells me, "but it all
starts to come together much more quickly than you'd think."

I lean back in my own chair. "It does feel a little overwhelming.
I'm trying to be cool about it but…" I give her a bit of a helpless look.
"I'm kind of out of my depth."

Mona laughs. "Don't worry. You're being very cool."

"I think the most embarrassing part of it all is that this has been
going on under my nose for years and I've never noticed."

"Don't be," she says. "If you don't have some magical being
standing right in front of you it can be easy to think it's all just stories
and talk."

"Excuse me," someone says from the other side of the table. "Are
the original paintings for sale?"

The girl asking the question is a teenager in a gorgeous costume
that's all shimmers and silk. I don't make the assumption that the
paintings are out of her price range. Last year the biggest sale was to a
boy about her age.

"Sure," I tell her. "Do you want to come around the table to have a
closer look?"

She nods eagerly and maneuvers her tall faerie wings around a
couple of people to come into the tent. Marisa comes over to talk to

her, so I return my attention to what's happening out front. I spot a couple of people I know: Izzy and Kathy, the two girls that live up in the attic of the house on Stanton Street. As I wave to them, I remember what Jilly said about people born from books and art. These girls seem so, well, real, as they wave back at me before disappearing into the crowd with a gaggle of their friends.

There's been another pause in customers and I find Jilly looking at me.

"There's no difference," she says, "not once they're here in our world."

"Now you read minds?" I say.

She smiles and shakes her head. "But I can read faces, and I knew just what you were thinking. I know their origins are different from ours, but they were as much born as we were. And once they're here, you have to treat them as real because…" She shrugs. "Well, because they are."

"What did you call them before? Eadar?"

"No, Eadar are the beings that require someone to believe in their existence. Izzy and Kathy… Isabelle calls them numena—or maybe it was Christy who first used the term. I can't remember. I just know that it doesn't matter if you believe in them or not, they still exist."

"I'm not sure I can keep all of this straight in my head."

"Don't worry," Jilly says. "There's not going to be a test."

"But how do you know which are magical beings and which are people like you and me?"

"They have a bit of a glow to them—or maybe it's a feeling that we get and we just perceive it as a glow. I haven't thought about it for a while, so I'm not sure which comes first. But you'll figure it out."

A new wave of customers starts to form a line in front of the table and we get too busy to talk. As the time gets closer to noon, Sophie and Saskia arrive to relieve us. Mona and I take the dogs for a stroll through the festival. I see Lydia and return her wave, but I don't stop at the clothing booth where she's working. We find Tam with Geordie and the other musicians in the middle of an impromptu jam behind the main stage. They're taking over the side stage later in the afternoon for a series of mini showcases, each taking their turn in the spotlight with the others backing them up as needed.

On the way back to the East Side Press tent, the dogs suddenly start pulling on their leashes and we see Mona's boyfriend Lyle making his way through the crowd. I try not to stare at him too much because all I'm thinking is: werewolf. He fusses over the dogs. I offer to take both dogs back by myself so that he and Mona can have some time to themselves.

When I get back I let the dogs return to their cushion, then go watch the singer on the small stage that's set up between the tent and the table where Cassie is doing her fortune telling. I spend a happy twenty minutes or so sketching the performer and various people listening before I return to help out in the tent.

~

IT'S A CRAZY DAY, but Saturday is always the busiest one of the festival weekend. I don't know how many copies of the new book have sold, but as the hours go by we're kept busy restocking it and all the other merchandise. When Jilly takes a break I sit with Christy while he does his signing, but without a new book out he's not nearly as busy as Jilly has been. Lots of people stop to talk to him though. I let their conversations wash over me and do more sketching.

The day finally winds down and I'm really looking forward to the music tonight. The Goblin Kings are the headliners and they always put on a great show. They can get the whole crowd dancing from their opening bars, and I think we all need to blow off some steam, though you wouldn't know it to look at us now. We're sprawled out in chairs in front of our tent waiting for Alan and Saskia to get back with our supper.

"I'm not sure I can walk all the way to the stage," Mona says. "Will somebody carry me over later?"

"And then me?" Sophie adds.

"They should have little rickshaws to ferry people around the grounds," I say.

Sonora's ears twitch at the sound of my voice. She's lying with her head on my lap and her butt on the seat of the chair by my thigh. I give her a scratch between the ears and she lets out a long contented sigh.

Mona grins. "That is a most excellent idea."

Each and every one of us is exhausted from talking all day, except for Jilly, of course. I don't know where she gets her energy. She's been interacting with people since we got here this morning—and she's still talking to a couple of fans by the side of the tent—yet all it seems to do is give her a boost.

"Hey," a man's voice says from beside me.

I look up to see Nick standing there.

"Annie said you came by the store the other day," he adds.

"Annie?"

"My part-timer."

"Oh, right. Cute girl with glasses like yours."

"It's a prerequisite to get the job," he says.

"Really?"

He laughs and tilts his head as if to say, seriously?

I feel a telltale blush rising. God. Why did I say that?

"So how are you doing with your investigation?" he asks.

"It's not really an investigation—"

"Oh, but it is," Jilly says, coming up behind us and cutting me off. "But we've had to take a break to regroup and do more research."

He gives her a curious look. "What kind of research?"

"Well, for starters did you know about his blog?" Jilly asks. "That's one of the things we're looking into."

"What kind of a blog?" When Jilly cocks her head he adds, "You want me to guess. Okay. It had to have something to do with that TV show."

"So you haven't been on his blog?"

I know exactly what Jilly's up to but I don't say anything because I'm curious myself. Because if he was into it how creepy would that be?

Happily, he shakes his head. He gives me an apologetic look. "No offence, but I'm not really into network TV. I had no idea he had a blog. Is it helping your investigation?"

"Not really. But we're following all kinds of leads."

He looks from her to me. "You guys are really serious about this, aren't you?"

"It's a tough job," Jilly starts, "but—"

I cut her off with a wave of my hand. "Pay no attention to her."

He gives us a smile. "I get it. You can't really talk about the case because it's ongoing. That's cool. Ethan and I weren't exactly close but I liked him. It's good to know that someone's looking into it."

He has a sweet smile, totally natural. I want to say that the police are looking into it but instead I ask, "How'd you know to find us here?"

"Just good luck. I came to see The Goblin Kings and noticed you sitting here. I've been hoping to run into you again."

Jilly leans on the back of my chair and rests her head on top of mine. We must look like a very short totem pole. I wonder what my face is doing.

"Have you eaten?" Jilly asks. Her chin pokes into the top of my head as she talks.

He shakes his head. "I was going to grab something from one of the food booths."

Jilly straightens back up. "Perfect! Come eat with us. Hey, everybody. This is Nick from Burns' Books. Nick, this is everybody."

Tired hands rise to wave a greeting as Jilly rattles through the names of the people he doesn't know. She pulls an empty chair over beside mine.

"Have a seat," she tells Nick.

"I don't want to intrude."

"Oh, please," Jilly says before wandering off to the other side of the tent.

Nick sits down. He reaches out a hand to let Sonora sniff his fingers before giving her a pat.

"Is this your dog?" he asks.

I nod. "Her name's Sonora. She's a rescue that I just got this week."

"She's beautiful. I love her eye patch."

"Me too. She is gorgeous, isn't she?"

"So…" He glances over to where Jilly is sitting on the ground playing with Bobo. "I was serious about what I said. You guys are obviously tired and already had plans. I didn't mean to push my way in."

I smile. "You couldn't leave now if you tried."

"Because…?"

"You'd run up against the immovable force that is Jilly Coppercorn."

He looks in Jilly's direction again then back at me.

"So is she…?"

"Matchmaking?" I finish for him. "Definitely."

I duck my head so that my hair falls in front of my face.

"Well, she's got good sense—and taste."

I look up to see he's smiling.

"Aren't we full of ourselves," I say, returning his smile so that he'll know I'm only teasing.

"But I was talking about you."

I laugh. "Smooth."

He just keeps smiling.

"So what got you into The Goblin Kings?" I ask.

"I saw them when they played the festival a couple of years back. One of the best shows I've ever seen."

"Huh. I didn't take you for a FaerieFest type."

"What did you take me for?"

I smile. "A bit of a hipster?"

"Ouch."

"Okay, I take it back. I guess there's a lot we don't know about each other."

"But we have things in common," he says, numbering them on his fingers. "We're both here. We both like to work out. There's at least one band we both like. And we definitely both like your dog."

"Food's on!" somebody calls out.

I turn to see Alan and Saskia approaching, hands full of takeout bags from The Light of India, one of my favourite restaurants ever.

"So you'll stay to eat with us?" I ask Nick.

He grins. "Are you kidding? I love that restaurant."

"And now we have five things in common," I tell him.

Sonora jumps down from her chair. Nick offers me a hand up before I can get out of my own.

"What happens with Sonora while you're watching the show later?" Nick asks.

"Oh, we've got—"

I don't get to finish. Both Sonora and Bobo give happy barks and race to where, as if on cue, Joe appears at the side of the tent with a crow perched on his shoulder. It looks like he's saying something to the bird. It bobs its head in response, then lifts from his shoulder to join the rest of the crows already in the trees. Nick follows its flight before looking at me again, eyebrows raised.

"That's Joe," I explain. "He and the crows are kind of like our booth security. He doesn't mind looking after the dogs and they love him to pieces."

We watch Joe fuss over Sonora and Bobo, then go over to accept our plates of food from Cassie. Her clothes are such a swirling kaleidoscope of primary colours that if a spotlight were to hit her, we'd probably all be blinded.

"You've got some interesting friends," he says.

"You don't know the half of it," I tell him.

~

DINNER IS NICE. The food is terrific and Nick fits right in with our crowd. It helps that he already knows a few of them who frequent his store, but it's more than that. He seems to have just the right easygoing vibe that lets anybody be comfortable around him.

I like that. I like how he makes me laugh. I like pretty much everything about him. So when we all head off for the main stage, I get a little butterfly as he takes my hand.

He dances with me when The Goblin Kings start playing, making up in enthusiasm for what he lacks in dance floor skills, but I don't mind. He gets points for making the effort. He gets points for being present and attentive throughout the night, and if I didn't have to be back the next day I might well have taken him home and it would have been Tam's turn to find a stranger in the kitchen making breakfast.

"Do you make breakfast?" I ask him.

"I can certainly do the basics. Why?"

"No reason. I'm just taking a poll."

Later on Nick walks Sonora and me home. I don't invite him in but I get a most excellent kiss before he goes off on his way.

~

SUNDAY MORNING, it's back to business again. We're all a little bleary-eyed and moving slowly except for Jilly, but luckily the main crowds haven't arrived yet. Sundays don't usually pick up until noon and by then the rest of us will have caught a second wind, or at least have stolen a little nap in the back room.

The girls all want to talk about Nick. They know he walked me home after the main stage closed.

Mona puts her hands on my shoulders, a conspiratorial smile on her face. "I just want to know," she says. "Is there love in the air?"

I let my eyes go wide. "I think you're mistaking me for my brother."

"Ouch," Wendy says.

"Except it is true," Jilly offers. "Tam's not exactly the settling down type."

I didn't even think she was paying attention. She's been fussing at the food table with her coffee, her back to us.

But Mona won't let it go. "Come on. A little detail, please."

"He was a perfect gentleman on a first date, which, technically, this wasn't even, and I really don't sleep with someone that I've only just met."

"Except," Mona says, "if you're going to get all technical, you first met him earlier in the week."

Marisa pokes her head in from the front part of the tent.

"What if I told you that Nick's standing right out here beside me?" she says.

Mona puts a hand over her mouth.

"Except he's not," Marisa says. "But we do have customers."

Jilly lays the back of her wrist against her forehead. "Slave driver."

Marisa has no sympathy. "I'll set you free at six o'clock."

She lets the tent flap fall back in place. Jilly and I leave for the signing table to a general chorus of laughter.

～

"TELL me The Goblin Kings aren't really goblins," I say later when there's a bit of a break.

Jilly smiles at me, an impish look in her eyes. "I can do that."

"But will it be true?"

"In this case, yes."

"I'm glad to hear that. I don't want everything good to be rooted in magic."

Jilly lays her hand on my arm, her gaze as serious as I've ever seen it.

"Don't ever think it could be otherwise," she says. "Faeries, fabulous creatures, the otherworld—it's all beguiling and wonderful. They make the world seem bigger, the stars shine brighter, the dark woods appear darker and more mysterious. I'll be the first to tell you that, and the first to add that the world would be a sorrier place without their wonder in it."

She pauses, her gaze thoughtful as she looks away to the hustle and bustle of the festival.

"But," I prompt.

She turns back to me. "But this world we live in has just as much charm and magic all on its own. The problem is, most of the time we don't pay attention to it. We're distracted by what sparkles so bright, like a crow girl convinced a pop can tab is an ancient and secret ring of power and magic, and so we miss the little everyday mysteries and enchantments that are going on all around us, all the time.

"I can find just as much wonder sitting quietly in some corner of a park or a hidden acre of wood. In a vacant lot, a busy street corner, or a cobbled alley in Lower Crowsea. The trick is, you have to actually pay attention. And understand what you're looking for.

"It might be a flowering weed growing up through a crack in the pavement. Some hipster bringing a homeless guy a coffee and a sandwich. The light in the eyes of a couple in love. These things are all their own kind of magic. The difference is, it belongs to us—the human us—and anyone can partake of it without the casting of spells or receiving a boon from a faerie godmother."

"Is that something you really believe?"

She presses her forearms across her chest. "With all my heart. And remember, I've been to the otherworld for longer periods of time than that little midnight jaunt we had the other night. I rub elbows with magical people all the time. But when I witness some small act of kindness, or take the time to appreciate the pure wonder that nature holds, I'm just as overcome with the beauty of it as I am with faerie."

"That's good to know," I tell her.

She nods. "And worth remembering. The faerie world can be addictive, and not always to our benefit. There's a reason so many stories are filled with dire warnings about interacting with them."

"But you haven't had any trouble?"

Jilly smiles. "Let's just say that I can recognize addiction when it comes sniffing around me and have learned when to cut myself off from falling back into that black hole."

Everybody knows the story of her teen years when she scrabbled to get by on the streets.

"But that was a long time ago," I say.

"It was," she agrees. "But addiction is the demon that never goes away. It's always sitting just behind your shoulder, ready for the right temptation to come along so that it can give you a push."

∽

LATER IN THE afternoon a girl asks if there's ever going to be a collection of Jilly's non-faerie paintings.

I'd love to see that as well.

One of the things I find so fascinating with her work is how all the figures are rendered with an intricate, almost photographic, detail, which should be at odds with the loose, painterly quality of the settings and backgrounds. It makes no sense. It shouldn't work. The two styles should be fighting with each other, but instead the figures blend perfectly with their surroundings.

That said, her cityscapes absolutely mesmerize me. The loose strokes only hint at detail, but I recognize each setting because she presents it in a way that's familiar but makes you look at it with a whole new eye.

Alan has published a run of cityscape cards, as well as a couple of posters, but they don't sell nearly as well as the faerie paintings, so I doubt he'll ever do a book of them.

Jilly tells the girl as much and she walks away with the same disappointment I feel.

∽

WE'RE tired by the end of the day, but there's a feeling of sadness, too, as we box up the unsold merchandise and take down the infrastructure for another year. Both Nick and Joe show up to help and the "many hands make light work" truism proves itself once more as we get the rental trucks loaded up in what seems like no time.

When we're done I watch the crows fly away before I join the others for our last FaerieFest meal. This one's catered by a vegetarian booth at the festival and everybody's here, including all the musicians and their various partners. By the time we're done, we can hear the announcer at the main stage. We bag up our garbage, put away the chairs, and head in that direction en masse.

We leave the trucks where they're parked. Nobody stays behind to keep watch because even Joe wants to see the Kelledys, who are closing the festival as they do every year. It's one of the few official gigs they do in town and nobody wants to miss it.

I glance back at the trucks as we're leaving and note a pair of crows perched on the roof of one of them. Then I see a shimmer in the air between the two trucks and there's suddenly a small crowd of a half-dozen kids coming my way. The foremost one is wild-haired Cosette, and I realize it's the gang from Wren Island. That's confirmed when I spy Isabelle and her friend Rosalind bringing up the rear.

Nick stopped with me, but didn't turn around in time to see how they all just stepped out of the air. The kids go bounding past us while we wait for the two women to join us.

I let go of Nick's hand to give Isabelle a hug. "I didn't think we were going to see you this weekend," I say.

Isabelle smiles. "And miss tonight's music? Not a chance."

I make introductions. Isabelle shakes Nick's hand then crouches down to fuss over Sonora. Once Rosalind's done the same we follow in the wake of the kids and make our way through the grounds to the area in front of the stage that Jilly and the others have claimed with a bunch of spread out blankets.

It's almost dark by the time we're all settled in. The quiet murmur of the big crowd that fills the space in front of the main stage dies away as a recording of harp music begins a stately march. Lights come on to illuminate a line of kids dressed in their best FaerieFest gear as they come on the stage and begin an intricate dance. I recognize some of them from the group that came from Wren Island, others from having seen them around the festival over the weekend.

Like everybody in the crowd, I'm entranced by the music and the hypnotic movement of the dancers. The lights seem to make the dancers glow with their own inner light until I remember something Jilly said to me.

I turn to where she's sitting beside me and bring my mouth close to her ear.

"So those kids…" I begin.

"Are faerie," she whispers back. "And numena from Wren Island."

"And the harping?"

"Isn't a recording."

"How is it not a recording? I don't see anyone playing it."

"Magic," Jilly says and returns her attention to the stage.

Damn.

Nick gives me a quizzical look. I don't know what to say. My heart is so full of the wonder of the moment and it's not like I can tell him what we're talking about. So I squeeze his hand and smile.

The dancers leave the stage, or maybe the lighting just makes it seem that way since it all goes dark. A moment later a small spotlight captures Miki Greer sitting on a stool on the right side of the stage as she begins playing long notes on her accordion to accompany the harp, which is still playing. A second beam lights up the harp and Cerin, his fingers moving deftly on the strings.

"Once upon a time," he says, "or perhaps it was yesterday, there was an old man who wanted nothing so much as to learn the music of faerie."

He's got the kind of voice that draws you in. It carries easily, but you still lean a little closer.

"And what music it is, a music seldom heard in this world or even the next."

Another beam slowly brightens to reveal Meran, drawing long harmony notes from her wooden flute. Now spots focus on Geordie, Amy and Lesli as they begin to play a sprightly tune on fiddle, whistle and flute. More stage lights follow a pair of dancers moving lightly from one side to the other as they mime playing instruments. Another finds a figure bent like an old man walking slowly to the front of the stage, one hand cupping an ear as he listens to the music.

I elbow Jilly lightly when I realize it's Tam. Jilly gives me a grin and we return our attention to the stage. How can he not have told me about this?

Cerin keeps telling the story. Sometimes he plays his harp, sometimes the other instruments take the lead. Meran's flute. Amy switching to her pipes. Lesli on a low D whistle. Miki playing a melody on her accordion. Eventually, through guile and trickery, the character Tam embodies takes up his guitar and plays fluid versions of the faerie tunes on his own instrument.

Like the rest of the audience, I'm utterly mesmerized.

This is so different. Every other time I've seen the Kelledys perform, it's been just the two of them sitting center stage, playing music on harp and flute and telling stories. Occasionally, they'd bring in guest musicians for one or two pieces. But this is a full-blown performance, theatrical, yet intimate, as though Cerin is telling the story to each of us individually, and some people just happen to be doing interpretive dance as the tale unfolds.

The story ends with the faerie queen played by Meran giving Tam his comeuppance. The whole stage goes dark except for the spotlight on Tam. He's on his knees, his forehead on the ground. The music swells, then the instruments fade out, one by one, until it's just the harp. When it finally fades as well, there's a long silence before we all rise to our feet and give them a thunderous ovation.

Lights come on, highlighting the musicians and dancers, who stand in a long row. They wave at us before they leave the stage until finally it's just Meran in a single spotlight.

"Thank you so much," she says. "We're going to have a little break, but we'll be back with more music so don't go away."

As if anybody's leaving after that performance.

Everybody's talking during the intermission, except the conversation is only a murmur of soft voices.

"That was amazing," Nick says.

I nod in agreement. "I can't believe Tam kept it a secret from me. And I can't believe how good an actor he is."

"It must run in the family," Jilly says.

I wave off her compliment.

"Did you know they were doing this?" I ask her.

She shakes her head. "Geordie didn't breathe a word."

I'm dying to ask her about faeries and magical harps and a hundred other things that came into my head during the performance, but Nick's standing with us and I'm not sure what the protocol is for talking about magical things around people who aren't aware of any of this. I know Jilly does it all the time, but people just think, that's Jilly, and don't take her seriously. I know I didn't. But I've already noticed that the others don't mention it unless they're among a particular circle of friends.

So I let it go for some later time when I'll be alone with her.

"So you liked it," I say to Nick.

"I'll tell you," he says, "if you'd asked me before this evening if I liked performance art, or this raw traditional Celtic music we just heard, I would have said that I could take it or leave it. But honestly, that just left me speechless. I feel full of—I don't know what, exactly." He laughs. "Starlight and moonshine, maybe."

Jilly gives an approving nod.

"We should give the dogs a chance to stretch their legs before the second half," she says.

So we wander off around the park. Isabelle comes with us, and she and Jilly chat quietly with each other. They're not excluding us, but I don't mind not being a part of their conversation. I'd just as soon walk without talking anyway, Sonora trotting on one side of me, my hand tucked into the crook of Nick's arm.

~

THE SECOND HALF of the show opens with the musicians spread out in a line across the stage, some standing, some sitting. Cerin and Meran are front and center, and lead the band in sets of tunes, occasionally broken with a vocal performance by Meran and Amy singing in gorgeous harmony. Cerin tells a couple of shorter stories. Finally they all run through a lively set of tunes that lasts about twenty minutes. Each musician gets a chance to play a solo, but mostly it's a full band delivering a rousing performance.

At this point everybody's dancing. Nick and I have moved off to the side with the dogs so that they won't get stepped on. Partway into that last long set, Joe appears beside us.

"Go on," he says, taking the leashes.

"You don't mind?"

He smiles and tilts his head. "Do I look like I dance?"

Actually, I'm sure he does. He couldn't live with someone as full of life as Cassie and not hit the dance floor from time to time. But I don't argue. I grab Nick's hand and soon we're in the thick of it all, jigging about in a way that would probably horrify real traditional dancers, but nobody cares. We're all just having fun.

The music seems to end far too soon, but it's almost eleven and FaerieFest organizers are good neighbours and never push the patience of the city's bylaw officers because they want to be able to come back every year. The lights come on around the field and on the stage so that people can collect their stuff and leave without tripping over each other.

The crowd disperses until it's mostly just our gang still hanging around waiting for the musicians to finish packing up their gear and join us. I hear talk of a session at Bramleyhaugh, but while it's tempting, I decide to go home. It's been a long weekend and I have to get up early to be at O'Shaunessy's in the morning.

Nick offers to walk me home again, which is sweet. I start making the rounds to say my goodbyes.

"Are we still on for tomorrow?" Joe asks when I come to where he and Cassie are talking with Marisa.

I nod. "But it'll have to be in the afternoon. I promised my friend at the boxing club that I'd spar with this new girl he's training."

He lifts an eyebrow.

"Girls box," I tell him.

"I know that. I just didn't know that you do."

I give him a smile. "Well, it looks like you're not the only one with mysteries."

Cassie laughs.

"I'll see you tomorrow," I say, and let Nick lead me toward the entrance of the park, Sonora walking beside him since he's holding her leash.

"What was that about?" Nick asks.

I glance back, then shrug.

"Joe's just helping us out with our—" I have to force the word out. "Investigation."

NICK WALKS us right to our door, but I don't invite him in for the same reasons I didn't go to Stanton Street with the others. And sure, we've got a little bud of romance happening, but it's far too soon to get intimate.

"Can I call you?" he asks.

"That would be nice."

I give him a light kiss on the cheek, then Sonora and I stand on the porch and watch him go down the street until he turns the corner.

"Do you need to pee?" I ask Sonora.

She obligingly goes down the steps, does her business, and rejoins me at the door. We go inside and I get ready for bed, but I don't think I can sleep. I remember what Nick said about feeling like he was full of starlight and moonshine. I knew exactly what he meant then and I still feel that now, as though the music and Cerin's stories are still vibrating inside me, along with the sweetness of being attracted to someone.

So I decide to finish *Nora Constantine 10: The Rising Dark.*

When I reach the end, I square the last loose page with the rest of the manuscript and put it all back in its box. I'm not sure how I feel. Disturbed, that's for sure. I don't know why the book wasn't called *Nora Constantine Disappears and the Whole World Goes to Hell.* It's certainly a more appropriate title because, instead of a fun mystery novel, it's set in a bleak dystopia with monsters and the prophecy that only Nora can prevail against them.

But two thirds of the way through the book, Nora leaves to go investigate a lead in the mystery she's trying to solve. The story then switches to third-person perspective, and she's never heard from again. The damn thing ends with the monsters having taken over and destroyed most of Crescent Beach. It's awful. I mean, the story's awful. It might be better if the writing were bad because then I could think of it as fanfic, just a little weirder than most. But it's been written with a skill that draws you in and makes the story feel all too real.

I sit there holding the box and really doubt I'm going to sleep now. Not with all of this darkness and angst floating around in my head. I give Sonora an envious look. She's been conked out for ages, sprawled beside me on the bed.

I reach down and stroke her back. I have to try to sleep, but I really don't want to dream about Charlie Midnight, so I take a mint from the Esmerine's Undream Mints tin on my bedside table.

I lay my head on the pillow and let the mint dissolve in my mouth.

It's the last thing I remember before I wake up the next morning.

7

MONDAY

I wake up to find myself half lying on the manuscript box of the Nora Constantine book. Sonora is pressed up against me. She creaks open an eye to look at me, then closes it again. I turn my attention to the bedside clock.

Crap.

I jump out of bed and have a quick shower then hurry downstairs to put the kettle on while I take Sonora outside. Back in the kitchen, I feed her and make my coffee. I sit at the table long enough to gulp it down and leave a note for Tam.

I don't know if Lydia stayed over again. I don't even know if Tam ever came home. But just in case he did, I want to tell him how proud I am of his performance last night.

Sonora and I leave the house with just enough time to make it to O'Shaunessy's to help Pearse with his new boxer. I'm hoping she's not huge, but she probably isn't. If she is, Pearse would have her sparring with one of the men at the boxing club. Actually, I'm not quite sure why this girl needs another girl for a sparring partner. Whenever I spar I do it with one of the guys.

There's no one around when we get there, so I settle Sonora on a towel beside my backpack and change into sweats and a tee. I'm sitting on a bench wrapping my hands when Pearse comes in from the front of the gym. There's a small woman trailing behind him. I don't get a good look at her until they're halfway across the gym, at which point I draw a quick breath. As they get closer I stand up and glare at the pair of them.

"What the hell is this?" I say.

Pearse gives me a puzzled look.

I focus my attention on the woman.

"Seriously," I say. "What the hell, Allison? What are you doing here? And why do you look like that?"

Allison, who should be in L.A., is standing in front of me decked out like she's playing her character Gabi Ramos from the TV show.

I'm staring at her. She's got the spiky black hair and piercings. Her tank top and spandex shorts show off Gabi's tats in all their glory. Except Allison looks just as confused as I'm feeling.

"Nora?" she says.

And then I get it.

"You two know each other?" Pearse asks.

I sit down heavily on the bench. Gabi sits beside me and takes my hand. I don't want to look at her, but I do. It's so disconcerting and really doesn't make sense. Unless there is an otherworldly Crescent Beach that was born from the imaginations of readers and viewers…

I let the thought die.

Of course she would look just like this. It's why she and Ethan think I'm Nora, because I played the role on the show. These are the images that most people carry.

Except the Gabi looking at me has pain in her eyes.

"What happened to you?" she asks. "How did you get here? We've been lost without you."

A mix of sadness and frustration fills me. I gently lift her hand and place it back in her lap.

"I'm not your Nora," I tell her. "I'm the actress who played her on a TV show in this world. My name is Juniper Wiles."

"Does anybody want to fill me in on what the hell's going on?" Pearse says.

I look up at him. "We need a moment here. I'll explain everything to you later."

He holds my gaze as though trying to read my mind, then gives a brusque nod and walks away to his office. I watch him go, collecting my thoughts before I turn back to Gabi.

"Do you understand what I'm saying?" I ask.

There's still a deep sadness in her eyes.

"Of course I do," she says. "I'm not stupid. I was just hoping—I thought for a moment that I'd finally found you. Her, I mean."

"How did you get here?"

"It was after you… Nora… It was after she disappeared. I was following one of those strays she's always taking in."

"Ethan Law?"

She nods. "You know him?"

"In a way," I tell her. "Why would she befriend him? The guy's a creep."

I feel bad talking ill of the dead and all that, but come on. That blog of his.

"What makes you say that?" Gabi asks.

I wave the question off because it's obvious she doesn't know about his fetish porn. If she did, being Gabi, she'd have punched him in the face.

"Never mind," I tell her. "You were saying?"

"He was acting suspicious, and Nora had been gone for a while by then so I tailed him, thinking he might lead me to her. Instead he crossed over to this world. I watched him step up to an intersection and then he just disappeared. It was the weirdest thing. But when I got up to where he'd vanished I found myself stumbling through a hole in the world and ended up here in yours with no way back."

"And then you…just dealt with it? Being in another world, cut off from everything you know?"

"What else was I supposed to do? Curl up in a ball and start crying? I'm not that girl."

"No," I say. "You never were."

She stares at me. "God, you're just like her. Everything about you, from the way you look and talk, your whole vibe."

"We had a lot of similarities," I tell her. "The character and me, I mean. At least on the show."

"I guess."

"It must have been hard for you, ending up here all alone with no one to turn to. How long have you been here?"

"A couple of years."

"The same as Ethan."

"So you do know him."

I shake my head. "Not really. You know he's dead?"

"Yeah, I saw it on a newsfeed. I didn't really know him either, but he was my only connection to the other Crescent Beach. So I feel bad —I just don't know if it's for him or for me. A bit of both, I guess. Is that shallow of me?"

"No, I get it."

"You—Nora—always did."

"How have you gotten by for two years? What did you do for money or ID?"

She just gives me a look. "I'm a hacker. What do you think I'd do?"

"Did you fix Ethan up with an identity as well?"

"No. Like I said, I didn't really interact with him. You know, when you feel like there's something off about a person?"

I nod, but don't mention his predilections.

"But I kept tabs on him," she adds. "In case he found a way back."

"When the police were looking for him," I say, "they couldn't find any trace of him before two years ago. Nothing. No record of anything."

Gabi smiles. "Well, you can tell I didn't build an ID for him. The cops look me up and they'll get a history that goes back to when I was born."

"Because you're that good."

"I am that good. But not good enough to find Nora."

"What makes you think she's here?" I ask.

"She's not in Crescent Beach, and since Ethan and I ended up here I thought she might have fallen through, too. I've been trying to track her down ever since I got here and there's nothing but the books, some fanfic and the show. I've tried all the pseudonyms that she's ever used. No leads."

She pauses, cocking her head. "There's not much about you online either," she says. "A handful of movies and TV guest spots after the show ended, but that's about it. No social media presence, no driver's license. I had to hack into Internal Revenue to get an address."

"I don't use the internet much. Just for the odd email and lurking on socials. And to Google things from time to time."

"Yeah, I can tell. I couldn't even get an email addy for you."

"It's tams_sister@gmail.com."

She smiles. "Well, no wonder. It doesn't bother you to be known only as somebody's sister?"

"I like Tam. And it's better than having people track me down because they want to talk to me about the show."

She nods. "I get that. People recognize me from time to time, but I just pretend to be a super-fan and they get over me."

"If you hacked my home address, why did you never come around? Especially once you got to Newford."

"I only just got here. But what would I say? I honestly don't get how you're so accepting about all of this. It's like a serious mind-fuck. I thought if we ever met you'd just freak out and not believe a word I said."

"Except you're Gabi. Why would you lie to me?"

"Only you're not Nora."

"Right. But it looks like I'm as close as you're going to get. I—you know, it's weird. Even though I only know you because of a fictional relationship, I still really feel like I know you."

She gives a slow nod. "I get it. Even though you're not my Nora, I kind of feel the same way. Except I don't know anything about you, apart from the bios online. And now I know that you box."

"I only train and spar. I don't have any real interest in getting in a ring."

She smiles. "Me neither. It's like the martial arts classes we took. I just want to make sure I can handle myself."

We each took classes, but it was the other Nora who took classes together. I don't bother to correct her.

"How come you didn't cash in at cons," she asks, "like some of the other actors on the show?"

"It's just not me," I say. "I like things to be quiet. I'm real serious about art—painting and drawing. And now I have a dog."

Gabi smiles at Sonora who's been gazing up at us, head moving from one face to the other, depending on who's talking.

"She looks pretty special," Gabi says.

"She is." I wait a beat then ask, "Do you want to go back to the otherworld?"

"Are you kidding me? It's a horror show over there. Charlie Midnight is like every monster rolled into one and then cranked up to a thousand. He can't be stopped." She gives me a pained look. "Except by Nora."

"Because of the prophecy."

"How do you know about that?"

"It's in the book," I tell her.

"What book?"

"There's an unpublished Nora Constantine novel. The tone's completely different. It's like the writer was playing with the idea of turning the franchise into what's popular now: a dystopia with vampires and monsters."

"That's exactly what it's like."

"I figured as much," I tell her.

"Because of the book."

I nod.

"Does that mean the prophecy's real, too?"

"I have no idea," I tell her.

"So are you still taking in strays?" she asks.

I point to Sonora. "Looks like. But she's the first in years. I just found her and couldn't let her go."

Gabi gets an almost wistful look. "That's how it was with us, too." She catches herself. "I mean, it's how I met Nora."

"I'm not Nora," I tell her, "but I remember that. I remember all we did together in the show and books. If you feel more comfortable, you can think of me as Nora. All the things she felt for you, I feel them too."

She gives me a slow nod.

"You know what scares me most?" she says after a moment. "Charlie Midnight figuring out how to get over here. I have nightmares about it. I feel like he's looking for me."

"I've been having them too."

"Yeah? So I guess we have to figure out what happened to Nora if we want to make sure those dreams don't come true."

"Maybe not. Some friends of mine and I have been looking into all of this since Ethan was killed and we've got some ideas."

She smiles. "So you've put together a new team."

"It's not like that. I don't go around investigating things and solving problems the way Nora does." I pause. "Or I didn't. But I'm doing it now. I think we have to. Not just because of what might happen here, but to help all those people in that other Crescent Beach."

She gives me an admiring look. "Damn. You sound just like Nora."

I duck my head for a moment, embarrassed. "Don't make too much of it. Nora's a lot braver and smarter than I am."

"You only think that because a team of writers put her character together for the show. But you were the one who brought Nora to life."

"I suppose."

"Well, I'm in," she says.

"In?"

"Whatever you've got going—I'm in."

Of course she is.

"Where are you staying?" I ask.

"I've got a room at a hotel on Palm Street."

I frown. "That's not the best part of town."

"It is if you want to stay off the grid."

"Will you come stay with me?"

Her eyes open wide and then she grins. "You know what? I'd like that."

I look down at my hands. One's already wrapped with protective elastic bandages, the other's half done, a long loose strip hanging from it.

"You still want to spar before you meet my friends?" I ask.

"Sure. How much of this are we going to tell Pearse?"

"As little as possible. Hey, how'd you ever end up in his club anyway?"

"Last place I lived was Chicago. I asked the guy running the boxing club where I worked out what the best place here would be and he directed me to Pearse. Even gave him a call to introduce me before I got here."

I smile. "That's the same way I found this place, only my recommendation came from a club in L.A."

She starts wrapping her own hands.

"Enough talking," she says. "Time to start sweating. The good thing about hitting things is that it stops you from thinking."

"Amen to that."

∾

TURNS out we're pretty evenly matched, which makes it a fun practice. After we hit the showers and get dressed, we go talk to Pearse. I don't want to lie to him, so I keep it simple. I tell him there's a bunch of stuff going on and that I can't talk about it now, but I'll fill him in on everything later.

He looks from Gabi to me, studying us for a long moment.

"Does this have anything to do with that ghost you were telling me about?" he finally asks.

"It's related."

"You need any extra muscle?"

I smile. "Not now. But if it comes up, I'll give you a call."

"Don't get in so deep you can't make the call."

"I won't."

"And you," he says to Gabi. "Stop leading with your left. You have to mix it up so that it's not so easy for your opponent to get a read on you."

"I like him," Gabi says when we leave the club.

"You and me both."

WE TALK non-stop all the way to the house on Stanton Street, Sonora trotting happily in between us. I tell Gabi about how I had to leave L.A. after too many poor movie choices, and how becoming friends with Jilly turned everything around for me. She talks about her search for Nora, moving from town to town, staying off the grid, keeping tabs on Ethan and always looking over her shoulder for Charlie Midnight or one of his monsters.

"So you knew about his blog?" I ask.

She pulls a face. "Knowing what you know, why are you helping him?"

"I'm not sure. It's partly because I said I would, partly because I like his partner Edward and he's really broken up about it. And I guess I kind of feel sorry for him. And in the end, isn't Rohlin really to blame since she's the one who originated his character, and he's just doing what she decided was in his nature?"

"Or he's just a creep."

I nod. "That, too."

When we reach the house I unclip Sonora from her lead and she goes racing to the door. She barks once and is answered by a flurry of Bobo's yips.

Gabi hangs back a little as we approach.

"Don't worry," I tell her. "Everybody here is cool."

"But do they know what I am?"

"What are you?"

"A figment of somebody's imagination."

"Nobody's going to think that for a moment. Trust me. These people have seen much weirder things than how you came to be."

She gives me a skeptical look.

"Trust me," I repeat.

"Okay." She cocks her head for a moment. "What did you say your name was again? Because all I can keep in my head is Nora."

I smile. "The alias I'm using for this mission is Juniper Wiles."

She smiles back. "Right. Now I remember. It's an unusual name."

"But better than my brother's. His is Tamarack."

"You're kidding."

"What can I say? We grew up in a commune with hippie parents."

I open the front door and step aside so that Sonora can dash in and run in circles in the hall with Bobo before the pair of them go tearing off to the greenhouse. The music from a solo fiddle comes drifting down from upstairs. Someone's been baking bread today because it smells like heaven.

"Come on," I say, leading the way.

Gabi pauses in the doorway of the greenhouse as three faces turn in our direction. Jilly and Joe look a little puzzled that I've brought a stranger. Wendy beams from ear to ear.

"Holy crap!" she says.

"Hey, everybody," I say. "This is my friend—"

Jilly breaks in, holding up a hand. "Wait, wait. Don't tell me. Let me guess. From Wendy's reaction I'm going to say Joan Jett. Or maybe Joan Jett's little sister." She looks at Wendy. "Does Joan Jett have a little sister?"

"It's Gabi Ramos," Wendy says. "From the other Crescent Beach?"

Gabi gives her an uncertain smile, but lifts a hand in greeting.

"Watch out for Wendy," I warn her. "She's going to nerd out on you if you let her." I point to the others. "This is Jilly and Joe."

Joe's got his crazy eyes thing turned up a few notches, but the warmth of his smile lessens the impact.

"Hey," he says.

Jilly bounces up from her seat and crosses over to give Gabi a hug. I watch Gabi's back stiffen at first, then she seems to relax into the hug and I smile. Jilly does that to people. She takes Gabi by the hand and leads her to the sofa.

"You guys want something to drink?" she asks. "We've got tea and beer. I don't recommend you mix them, but hey, to each their own."

"I think I need a beer," Gabi says.

I nod in agreement and settle on the sofa beside her. I can tell Wendy's dying to ask a million questions, but she manages to keep her curiosity in check. Jilly comes back from the kitchen carrying five bottles of beer. I'm impressed that her small hands can manage the task so easily. Once they've been passed around, she settles in her own chair and twists the cap off her bottle.

"So," she says. "With Gabi here, I'm guessing everybody has some news." She tips the top of her bottle toward Gabi. "Do you want to go first?"

I let Gabi decide how much she wants to tell since it's her story, not mine. She gives them a shortened version of what she told me, but the others see right through what she isn't saying. Jilly leans forward, sympathy in her eyes but no pity.

"Don't think for a moment," she says, "that you are any less your own person than any one of us."

Joe nods. "None of us get to decide how we come into the world. Sure, some people get created and come with a history rooted in whatever story's being told about them, but once they're here in the world, nobody owns them. Nobody can tell them who they're supposed to be. Their own story starts and they get to make their own decisions, fulfill their own potential. And they don't owe anything to whoever created them."

"Like Christiana," Jilly says. "Christy's shadow."

Joe gives another nod.

"Christy's what?" I ask.

"Long story. You know Christiana Tree."

"Not well."

"Well, we call her Christy's sister, but she actually started her life as his shadow—all the parts of Christy that he thought he didn't want. But she became her own person. She took things that Christy thought were negatives and made them into positives."

Wendy laughs and starts ticking things off on her fingers. "She's social where he's not. She's emotionally open where he closes up. She calls people on their crap where he prefers to avoid conflict. I could go on."

I can't believe how clueless I've been to the secret lives of these people I thought I knew.

Gabi has a slight squint in her eyes, her gaze moving from one to the other of them. I know what that look means.

"You're not being pranked," I tell her. "You think what happened to you is strange? Well let me tell you, the whole world's bigger and stranger than either of us could ever have imagined. For instance, did you know that faeries are real?"

Joe raises his palm. "We're losing focus here. Let's stay on track."

Wendy nods. "I went through Ethan's laptop, even dug up the stuff he thought he'd deleted."

"You're a hacker, too?" Gabi says.

"Not in your league," Wendy tells her. "But I can get by. There's a whole lot of Nora Constantine crap on his machine, but nothing particularly revealing. I did find a correspondence between him and the guy who set up his ID, and let's just say an overabundance of fanfic porn." She gives me a sympathetic glance. "I also found the correspondence between him and whoever sold him that unpublished novel. I tried to backtrack to get an IP address, but the seller was using way too many proxies to get a solid lead."

"Maybe I can help you with that later," Gabi says.

I take the manuscript out of my backpack and lay it on the table. "I brought the book for you to read," I tell Wendy, "but to save time let me give you a brief synopsis."

I lay out the main plot points for them.

"That jibes with what I found over there," Joe says.

Gabi's gaze locks on him. "You mean, you can go to the other Crescent Beach?"

Her question spawns a repeat of the explanation Joe and Jilly gave me about how the otherworld works.

"Bad things are happening there right now," Joe goes on. "Looks like the local authorities have given up on the place and the bloods have the town locked up tight—nobody in or out. Inside, it looks like a war zone."

"So we've got three objectives," I say. "We need to find out how Ethan was killed so it doesn't happen to anyone else." I don't look at Gabi or mention her by name, but we all know who I'm talking about.

Gabi shifts uncomfortably in her seat. I take a breath and continue. "We also need to make sure Charlie Midnight doesn't make his way to this world. And we have to do what we can to help those left behind in the other Crescent Beach."

"About that," Joe says. "I agree with you on all counts, but you need to understand that there's no turning back what's happened in Crescent Beach. We can try to stop it, but even if we succeed, the town will have to move on from there. There's no reset."

He looks at Gabi. "It's the same for you. You're who you've come to be. Doesn't matter what anybody writes or believes, your life is your own and only you can make decisions for yourself."

She nods. "Good to know."

I can tell she's way more relieved than she's letting on.

"I don't know where to start with figuring out how Ethan died," I say. "Maybe we can get Edward to talk with the coroner. As for keeping Charlie Midnight out of our world, on the plus side, in the book, he isn't smart. He's cunning, but he doesn't exactly formulate complex plans. So we've got time to come up with something to stop him and I have an idea about how we can do just that."

"The prophecy," Gabi says.

"What prophecy?" Jilly wants to know.

I tap the manuscript box on the coffee table. "It's here in the book. Nora tracks down this vampire hunter who says it was foretold that when the monsters returned a red-haired warrior would rise up to put an end to their master."

I shake my head and continue. "I have to admit that while the novel's well written, it's such a mishmash of everything that's popular in fiction these days, it's kind of embarrassing at the same time."

"But the prophecy applies to Nora," Gabi says, "and we don't know where she is."

I nod. "I know. My plan isn't about the prophecy or finding Nora. I think we need to have another talk with Emma Rohlin."

"Who's that now?" Joe asks.

"She wrote the Nora Constantine books," Wendy says.

"And I think she wrote the novelizations as well," I put in. "Under a pen name. And it's pretty clear she wrote this new book."

"You think there's that much mojo in her writing?" Joe asks.

"There has to be. From what you've said, you've seen firsthand what's happening in Crescent Beach. None of that's in the original books or from the TV show. It's only described in this one, unpublished book."

"She didn't seem too open to the idea of another Crescent Beach the last time we talked to her," Jilly says.

I give a glum nod. "I know. It'd be better to have a face-to-face. I want her to meet Gabi and see her try to say none of this is happening. But she lives in Phoenix."

"Do you have a street address?" Joe asks.

I shake my head.

"I have it on my laptop," Gabi says. "What?" she adds when I give her a surprised look. "I'm thorough when I do my research."

"Good," Joe says. "I've got a jump point near Phoenix, so I can get us there through the otherworld. But after that, we'll have to walk or cadge a ride from someone."

I'm not sure what he means, exactly, but having been to the otherworld once, I know it's not impossible.

"When can we go?" I ask.

Joe stands up. "No better time than the present."

"This is for real?" Gabi asks, standing up as well.

"As real as it gets," Joe says. "So who's coming?"

"All of us," Jilly says.

Joe nods. "Except the dogs should stay here. We can't have them distracting us from the business at hand."

"I'll get Geordie," Jilly says.

"Don't do that," Wendy says. "I'll stay with the dogs. It'll give me a chance to catch up with the book. Maybe I'll see something in it that Joon missed."

Gabi gets her laptop out and kneels at the coffee table. After a few moments she closes it up again and returns it to her backpack. While she's doing that I grab a copy of Jilly's new book and stick it in my own backpack.

"Okay, I've got the address," she says.

"Good," Joe says. "Everybody stay close."

Jilly grabs his hand, I grab hers and hold out my free hand to Gabi.

"Dive right in," she says as she takes my hand.

It's what she always said on the show when we were about to do something crazy.

And then the greenhouse is gone.

～

THE LAST TIME I crossed over to the otherworld, my new
surroundings weren't much different from Fitzhenry Park, just wilder,
with no city around it. This time Joe steps us out onto the top of a
mesa in the high desert. I have that flash of vertigo again as we cross,
but recover almost immediately. It doesn't seem to affect anybody else.
The air here is crisp and dry, and for as far as the eye can see there are
only more mountains and desert. The sky's so blue it almost hurts,
with neither cloud nor jet trail, and the sun washes the rock
surrounding us to the tone of old red bricks.

At the far side of the mesa a tall bluff lifts like a finger pointing up
into the sky. A small campfire burns at its base, logs set around it as
makeshift seats. As we approach, a man holding a tin mug in one hand
rises from one of the logs. He's tall and handsome, with a smirk in his
eyes that says he knows it. He wears cowboy boots, jeans and a
checkered shirt, his jawline sharp, his eyes hidden under the shadow of
a flat-brimmed black hat.

"Hey, Joe," he says with a grin. "Does Cassie know you're running
around with a little pack of pretty women?"

"This is Cody," Joe tells us. "You can ignore most of what he says
because he's got no filters and his social skills are pretty much
nonexistent."

Cody puts a hand on his chest. "Man, that hurts."

Joe ignores that. "I wasn't expecting to find you here," he says, "but
I'm glad we did."

"So everybody says," Cody goes on. "Life of the party and all that."
He cocks his head, not quite leering at us, but definitely checking us
out. "I've got to say, you've really traded up from those mangy canids
you're usually running around with."

I notice that Gabi isn't paying attention to either Cody's attention
or the conversation. She's turning in a slow circle, eyes wide as she
takes in our surroundings. I understand. I'm trying to stay focused
myself, but it's hard to do when my mind feels like it's blown a few
circuits as it tries to catch up with the drastic change in our location.

"I need a favour," Joe says.

Cody's gaze leaves us and returns to Joe's face.

"I'm trying not to meddle anymore," he says.

Joe sighs. "It's not meddling when someone comes and asks for your help. It's only meddling when you think you know what they need better than they do, then go ahead and give it to them without their permission."

"You make that sound like a bad thing," Cody says.

Jilly starts to laugh. "God," she says, "you're worse than ever."

"Darling," Cody says. "Who's been telling tales out of school?"

"Anybody who's ever met you?" Jilly replies.

Cody grins. "That sounds about right." He turns to Joe and, just like that, he's all business. "What do you need?"

"A quick trip to Phoenix. I don't have any jump points there."

"Phoenix in general," Cody asks, "or do you have a particular address?"

And that's how we find ourselves standing outside the door to Emma Rohlin's condo about ten minutes later. Cody tips a finger against his brow and he steps away—back to his mesa, I assume.

～

"LET ME DO THE TALKING," I say as I put my finger on the bell. "At least to start things off."

"It's your show," Joe says. He cocks his head, nose twitching the way Sonora's does when she's catching a scent. "Someone's come to the door," he adds, "and she's watching us through the peephole."

A moment later the door opens and Emma Rohlin is standing there giving us a once over. She looks exactly the same as she did a decade ago on the set in L.A. Tall and slender, short blond hair, a peaches and cream complexion that hardly shows a wrinkle except for the few laugh lines around her eyes. I hope I can still look that good when I'm in my sixties. With my genes, the chances are decent.

"Juniper?" she says. "What are you doing in Phoenix?"

I hold out Jilly's book, which I pulled from my backpack before we left the mesa.

"Delivering a personalized copy of Jilly's new book to you. Emma, meet Jilly Coppercorn. Jilly, this is Emma Rohlin."

Emma nods an automatic greeting, but I can see she's confused. I don't blame her. I would be too, in her shoes. Her gaze goes to Joe, then to Gabi, and I watch her eyes widen.

"Can we come in?" I ask.

"Allison?" she says, still looking at Gabi.

But just as greeting Jilly was an automatic politeness, she moves aside to let us all into her condo. The main room is an open concept combination of kitchen, dining area and living room with a large adobe fireplace. A glass wall with sliding doors opens onto a patio that looks out over a part of her gated community with desert and mountains in the distance. The furnishings are Southwestern— Mission furniture, Navajo rugs, original paintings of desert landscapes on the walls, woven grass baskets and pottery. On the coffee table is an open notebook with a glass of iced tea on a coaster beside it.

"Why are you dressed up as Gabi, Allison?" Emma asks.

She's followed us into the condo. Joe goes and closes the front door and stays there, his arms folded across his chest. Oddly, he seems to blend into his surroundings rather than look intimidating.

I put the book on the dining table and take Emma's hand.

"There's something impossible we need to talk about," I tell her, "but the easiest way to explain it is to show you something else first." I look over my shoulder. "Joe?"

Joe pushes away from the door and comes to lay his hand on my shoulder. A moment later the three of us are standing on the mesa top where we met Cody. Emma sways and Joe quickly comes around me to steady her. There's a panicked look in her eyes as she takes in her surroundings.

"What...where...?"

Words fail her. Joe steps away from her, but I keep hold of her hand.

"It's okay," I tell her, keeping my tone low and soothing. "You're not dreaming and you're not in danger."

"This is impossible..."

"And yet, here we are."

She takes another look around. Scuffs her slipper on the rough rock under our feet.

"This is the otherworld," I tell her. "You can take as long as you like to verify that you're no longer in your condo or Phoenix. You're not in the world you know anymore. But as soon as you're ready, we'll take you back."

She searches my face. "What do you want? Why are you doing this to me?"

"It's like I said. I have things to tell you that you're going to find impossible to believe, so I wanted to give you some proof before we talk."

There's still a flustered look in her eyes, but she seems to be calming a little.

"Why is Allison dressed up as Gabi?" she asks again.

"We'll get to that. Have you seen enough here? Do you want to go back to Phoenix?"

"We're really somewhere else?"

I nod. "Here. Come see."

I lead her near the lip of the mesa where she can experience the full scope and height of our vantage point.

"Those—they look like the mountains outside of Tucson," she says. "But there's…"

"No sign that people have ever been here."

She nods. "Except for that fire."

Cody's campfire is still burning but he's not there. Something stirs deep in the shadows of the rock spire and I see a dog, head on its forepaws, watching us.

"I'd like to go home now," she says.

I start to lead her over to where we arrived, but Joe comes up and steps us back into the living room of her condo.

"Jesus!" Gabi says, startled by our appearance.

She's standing by the glass doors that lead out to the patio. Jilly's sitting in a chair with a magazine open on her lap.

Emma's unsteady on her feet from the crossing, so Joe and I walk her over to the sofa. She sits down and runs a hand across the fabric of the cushions, then reaches down and touches the red dirt dusting her sandals. I didn't have any vertigo at all this time. Joe picks up her iced tea and hands it to her. She nods her thanks and takes a sip. Then another.

"So I'm not hallucinating," she says as she puts the glass back down on the coffee table.

She looks around at us, one by one, as though waiting for someone to admit that this has all been an elaborate joke. Finally she gets to Jilly, who throws her hands in the air as though she's tossing confetti.

"No!" she says. "Magic is real. Isn't it wonderful?"

"I would have said disconcerting," Emma says. "And it doesn't explain why Allison here is dressed like her character from the show."

"That's because she isn't Allison," I say. "She's Gabi."

Emma shakes her head. "No. No. That is impossible."

"You can say that after you've just been taken to the otherworld?"

"The otherworld. My god, what's happening? Did someone drug me?" She puts her hands over her face and leans over.

I hesitate and pat her awkwardly on her back, but it's Jilly who takes charge. She leaves her chair and sits on the edge of the coffee table, then takes both of Emma's hands in her own. Her sapphire eyes hold Emma's gaze.

"You're not drugged or dreaming," she says. "You're not crazy. There is an otherworld and this really is Gabi. You know it's true."

Emma stares at Gabi. "But how…?"

So we tell her everything that's gone on since Ethan Law first approached me in the Half Kaffe. She starts off shaking her head, not wanting to accept anything we're saying. By the time we're finished, she sits there, silent, staring at the polished hardwood floor at her feet.

"I did write those other books," she says finally, "or at least I co-wrote them with my daughter Shannon. When the show was over she kept wanting us to write something else—something that would appeal to today's readers. Vampires and shapechangers and dystopian landscapes. But I had no interest and she didn't trust her own skills enough to do it herself."

"So who wrote the manuscript that Ethan had—and how did he even get a copy?"

"I have the only copy," Emma says. "It's on my hard drive, but I printed off a single copy."

Emma gets up and goes into another room but she returns empty-handed.

She sighs as she sits down again. "The manuscript's gone. I had a break-in a few months ago, but the security guards were quick to respond and scared them off. They took a few things. My tablet. Some jewellery. I never thought to check my file cabinet."

"You said you had no interest in books like *The Rising Dark*," I say. "So why did you write it?"

Emma's eyes close for a moment and she takes a deep breath. "Shannon got cancer. It was terminal. We worked on the manuscript in the time she had left, as a way to be closer. She would come up with ideas, I'd put them into the story and then read it back to her. At that point, I didn't care how outrageous her ideas were. I incorporated them as best I could into the story. I couldn't deny her wish to express her creativity, or myself the opportunity to distract her from what was happening. The book was never going to be published anyway."

She shakes her head. "I still can't believe any of it is real."

"I'm very sorry your daughter had such a short time with you," Joe says, and the rest of us echo his condolences.

"As for what's real," he continues, "I could bring you to the other Crescent Beach and show you, but I couldn't guarantee your safety. It's pretty grim."

"This is awful," Emma says, her eyes glassy with tears. "I'm an awful person."

"You had no idea," I tell her. "None of us did. Well, except for Gabi."

Emma can't look at her.

For a long moment nobody speaks.

"Emma, where is Nora?" I ask finally.

"Nora?"

"Partway through the book she heads out to interview someone, then you switch to a third person point of view, and we never hear from her again. You end the book with the monsters winning."

"That's not the end of the book. I just didn't finish it. I stopped when Shannon…when she died. I haven't looked at it since. I couldn't."

"Of course not," I say. "But you must have planned for Nora to go somewhere—to do something. What would that have been?"

"I don't know. There was no plan. I don't write with an outline or know what's going to happen next until I write it. And as I told you, Shannon and I were working on it together. It's not a story that I would have chosen to write."

"Then you have to finish the book," I tell her.

"I don't think I can."

"If you don't," Jilly says, "that other Crescent Beach will be completely overrun and the monsters will spread to other towns and cities. A lot of people are going to die and get hurt."

"People?" Emma says. "They're not real people. They're characters in a book. It's not like you're talking about actual flesh and blood."

Gabi stiffens. "So what does that make me?"

Emma shakes her head. "You're asking me questions I can't answer."

"Then maybe you should start to try," I say.

"I can't."

"Before you wrote that last book," Gabi says, "my Crescent Beach was a good place to live. Sure, bad things happened, but they were human bad things. We could deal with them. We could prevail. But we can't deal with Charlie Midnight and his monsters. You made this happen and now people are dying."

Gabi's eyes are filled with tears, but Emma keeps closing her own and shaking her head.

I can't help feeling that, even given the circumstances, Emma needs to take responsibility for what she created. I know what I read, and it was gruesome.

I look at Joe. "Maybe you should take her there so that she can see what's happening firsthand."

"I don't think it'll help," he says. "And even if she could finish the book and put a positive spin on how it all turns out, I don't think it's going to make any difference. Just looking at her, I can tell she doesn't have the juice for that kind of mojo anymore."

"Not enough mojo? She made this happen all on her own with an unpublished manuscript."

Joe nods. "Yeah, but it wasn't all on her own, and it was fuelled by the power of a mother's love. By the bond she and her daughter had. There's no medicine in this world or the next that can duplicate that."

"So the other Crescent Beach goes down, and once the monsters have finished with that world, we could have Charlie Midnight clawing his way into this one."

"Unless we find a way to beat him," Joe says.

Jilly reaches out a hand and touches Emma's knee.

"Did you make any notes?" she asks. "You say you stopped writing after Shannon passed, but there must have been times when you couldn't get everything she was telling you into the actual text."

"I don't know," Emma tells her. "I haven't looked at those files for a couple of years now."

"Why don't we go have a look?" Jilly says. She picks up the copy of her new book, helps Emma stand, and they head back to wherever Emma was looking for the manuscript earlier.

Gabi has resumed looking out the window, shoulders sagging. I cross the room and put an arm around her.

"I didn't think it would," she says, "but that really hurts. She's looking right at me and refuses to accept that I'm real. That I'm actually here."

"I know," I say. "Does it help that she's wrong?"

"Is she?"

I squeeze Gabi's shoulders. "She is as far as I'm concerned."

"She is as far as anyone's concerned," Joe says from behind us. "I know spirits and phantoms, Gabi, and you're a far cry from either. Trust me on this."

She turns to look at him. "You don't even know me."

He touches the side of his nose with a finger. "If you weren't real, you wouldn't have a scent."

"Hey, I had a shower this morning."

He smiles. "I'm canid on my mother's side. I've got their sense of smell."

"Canid?" I ask.

"Dog clan."

"Is that why Sonora and Bobo are always falling over themselves to get to you?"

He shrugs. "Like recognizes like. I'm corbae on my father's side, but that doesn't seem to bother them."

"Is that a Kickaha thing?" I ask. "Tribal clans?"

"They're literal. My old man was a crow, my mother a rez dog—not when I was being conceived, obviously."

This is going in a whole new direction of weird. Luckily, Jilly and Emma return at that moment.

"Find anything?" Joe asks.

Jilly holds up a thumb drive. "Everything Emma had on the last book is here. We'll look at it back home."

Joe nods. "So we're done here. That's good. I don't care for people who shirk all responsibility they have in hurting others." He looks right at Emma as he speaks.

"It's not all black and white," Jilly says.

"In my world it is," Joe replies. He puts a hand on my shoulder and beckons to Jilly. "Let's go."

Emma has a frightened look.

"Don't mind him," Jilly tells her. "He's just being protective. I hope your granddaughter enjoys the book."

Joe puts his other hand on Jilly's shoulder but he's looking at Emma.

"Jilly's wrong," he says. "You should mind me. You lost your daughter and I'm sorry about that. But a lot of other mothers are losing their daughters and sons, and that, lady, that's on you."

Then he steps us away.

~

I EXPECT us to appear on the mesa top again, but from that one step in Emma's condo Joe takes us right back to the greenhouse, where we startle Wendy with our sudden appearance.

"Gah!" she says as she jumps up and drops the pages she's reading.

The dogs start to bark but stop when they realize it's us.

Wendy puts a hand on her chest. "You're going to give me a heart attack."

Joe grins at her. "Sorry."

"Yeah, you don't look sorry at all." Wendy turns to us. "Did you have any luck?"

"Not much, but maybe some," I say.

Gabi and I bend down to help collect the pages. I'm not much use since Sonora throws herself at me and almost bowls me over. I end up sitting on the floor, the dog squirming happily in my lap, while Gabi does all the work.

"Turned out I was right that Emma wrote that manuscript," I say, pointing over Sonora's head at the pages on the floor. I proceed to give Wendy a brief rundown on the circumstances that led to drafting the novel.

"Wow, that's harsh," she says. "So is the story, at least what I've read of it."

"Yeah," I go on, "but what's frustrating is that she's not willing to help us by writing a better ending—and Joe says it probably wouldn't help anyway since she's lost her mojo—so that's a dead end. But we got a thumb drive with any notes Emma had on the book. Maybe something on it will prove useful."

Jilly is still cuddling on the floor with Bobo. Now she hands the thumb drive to the little dog. He takes it daintily in his teeth and brings it over to Wendy.

"What was she like?" Wendy asks as she accepts the drive.

"Emma?" Gabi says. "A sad coward and a—what 'ist' would you

use for someone who doesn't like a person just because they don't have a conventional origin?"

"A birthist?" Jilly tries. "Though I didn't get the sense that she didn't like you. It was more that she just shut down and wasn't willing to try to make anything better."

"Right. She was pretty much a cowardly dick," Gabi says.

Joe nods at the same time as Wendy says, "Well, that must have been disappointing."

"It was a challenging day for Emma on several fronts," Jilly says. "She's been through a lot, but in the end, Gabi's right. The humanitarian you sense in her books sure wasn't showing her face today."

"Your friend Cody," I say to Joe. "He's a bit of a dick, too. I mean, he helped us and everything, but he's so full of himself."

"That's kind of a tradition with him," Joe says.

"Sucky tradition."

"No question. But it goes back a long way, through a lot of lives. A lot of stories."

"I've never heard of him before."

"You might know him better as Coyote," Joe says.

"You mean *those* stories?"

Joe nods. I remember the second time we were on the mesa, when we took Emma there.

"So that dog we saw by the campfire when we went back…"

"Wasn't a dog. It was a coyote. The Coyote."

"He's still kind of a dick," I say.

Joe laughs. "I'll be sure to tell him that."

WENDY OFFERS to go through the thumb drive after she finishes the book, so we agree to meet up again here tomorrow. We commandeer Geordie to drive Christy's car out to Gabi's motel so that we can grab her stuff. Everything fits into a duffel bag, which I find sad. Geordie drops us off at my house. Jilly holds Bobo's paw up in a wave as they drive off.

"You did well for yourself," Gabi says, admiring the building.

It's one of those old brick Crowsea two-stories, the kind you used to see everywhere in the city, with a front and back yard, big oak trees on either side of the walk. A lot of them are being bought up and torn down for condos, but not in Lower Crowsea.

"It was my grandparents' house," I say. "Tam and I used to rent it out for the income, but when I came back it made more sense for both of us to live here since there's no mortgage and my residual cheques are enough to cover expenses."

She gives a little shake of her head. "I keep having to remind myself that you grew up here, not in Southern California."

Like Nora did.

"Come on in," I say. "We can make something for dinner and play catch up."

I unclip Sonora and she runs to the door, then stands there on the porch with a what's-taking-you-so-long look.

"I know everything's new for you," I tell Gabi, "but you're not alone. I've had so much thrown at me this week it feels like I'm starting over, too."

Gabi smiles, then asks, "Does Tam know about me?"

I shake my head. "And he doesn't have to unless you tell him. Though I do have to warn you, he's watched the show a lot."

"Because big sis was in it?"

"That's what he claims. But I think he got caught up in all the drama like the rest of our fans."

She sighs.

"Don't worry about it," I tell her. "He texted me to let me know that he's still hanging out with Lydia, this girl he reconnected with at FaerieFest. He won't be back home until later tomorrow."

8

TUESDAY

I come down in the morning to find something different about Gabi, but I can't put my finger on it. I think about it while I take Sonora out into the backyard. By the time she finishes her business I've figured it out. Most of Gabi's piercings are gone—the lip ring, nose stud, earrings, eyebrow studs. All that's left is the one in her right eyebrow and a couple of studs in her ears. She also had a go at my closet like I suggested, and instead of her usual black on black, she's wearing blue jeans and a rose-toned cotton cardigan over a white tee. The spiky hair hasn't changed.

"Coffee?" she asks.

"Please."

I feed Sonora before I join Gabi at the table.

"Well, this is a new look," I say.

She shifts self-consciously on the chair. "Are you sure it's okay to borrow this stuff? Do I look dumb?"

"It's all good. If I wasn't afraid you'd whack me, I'd say it softens you—in a good way," I add. "You still look strong."

"But does it make me look less like a character from an episode of Nora Constantine?"

"It does. But that's not a good reason to change things up."

"I think it is. It's past time I let go of Crescent Beach and the old Gabi. This world is my home now. For two years I've been skulking in the shadows, hanging on to the old Gabi. It was what kept me going while I looked for Nora and tried to stay off anybody's radar. But now that I can stay with you, it's like a weight has lifted and I get the chance to reinvent myself a little."

"Just make sure you're doing it for yourself, not for anybody else."

"I am," Gabi says. "Only don't get married to this look. I could change it tomorrow."

I smile. "Knock yourself out. But please don't dye your hair blond. This world's already got Allison in it."

"And maybe two Noras."

"Do you really think she's here?"

"I don't know anymore," Gabi says. "I thought she was. I counted on it. But now…"

I give her a sympathetic smile. "Let's go over to Jilly's. Maybe Wendy's found something or Jilly's had one of her brilliant ideas."

"In Crescent Beach, Nora was always the one who came up with the brilliant ideas."

"Except we're not in Crescent Beach anymore."

She nods. "I know. And you're not Nora."

"But I will try to be brilliant for you."

Only Sophie is up when we get to the house on Stanton Street. We find her in the greenhouse, slouched in a chair while she stares at the blank canvas on her easel. She perks up when we come in.

"How would you two like to be immortalized in a painting?" she says.

"That depends," I tell her. "Will you mind that people will think it's Nora Constantine fan art?"

She frowns. "I hadn't thought of that. I'm Sophie, by the way," she says to Gabi.

Gabi raises a hand in a half wave and introduces herself.

Sophie's eyes brighten with interest. "You're the girl from the parallel world version of Juniper's TV show. Jilly and Wendy were talking about you last night."

Gabi looks uncomfortable. "That's me. Hot topic."

"It was all complimentary," Sophie says with a smile. "How are you fitting in? Do you need anything?"

I watch as Sophie's kindness puts a smile on Gabi's face.

"I'm good," she says. "I've actually been here for a couple of years."

Sophie nods. "Great, but remember, if something comes up all you have to do is ask."

"Ask what?" Jilly says, coming into the room.

Bobo dashes out from behind her and races over to Sonora, dancing around in circles, bowing and licking at her face. Sonora is wonderfully tolerant with his antics.

Wendy follows Jilly into the room, carrying her laptop.

"I'm just making sure Gabi has everything she needs," Sophie says.

"Do you need something?" Jilly asks Gabi. "Anything?"

Gabi smiles. "You guys are too generous, but Juniper's got me covered. Literally," she adds, plucking at the sleeve of her sweater.

"That's a great colour on you," Wendy says.

Gabi blushes and looks over at the dogs. I can tell she'd rather not be the center of attention. It's weird, how I feel like I know her so much better than just as a character from the show. It's as though we really did grow up together in SoCal and have been friends all our lives.

"Were you able to track down who sold Ethan the book?" Gabi asks.

Wendy shakes her head. "I can't ID the email addy. Whoever sent it bounced from server to server all over the world until it got to Ethan. Do you want to give it a go?"

Gabi pulls her laptop out of her pack and the two of them take their computers over to one of the worktables. Moments later their heads are bent over the machines, talking to each other in what sounds like a foreign language, there's so much jargon.

Jilly and I sit on the sofa. Sophie leaves her easel and joins us.

"Wendy finished the book last night," Jilly says, "and didn't find anything new. But the thumb drive did have all sorts of notes, character sketches and plot points that go past the end of the manuscript."

"Anything about where Nora could be?" Joe asks.

Sophie and I both twitch at his sudden appearance, but Jilly just waves a casual hello and says, "Hey, Joe," like it's an everyday occurrence to have somebody just appear out of thin air. For her, it probably is.

He drops into a chair and stretches his legs out, looking instantly at home.

"So about Nora," Jilly says. "According to the notes, Emma and her daughter were playing with the idea that she'd been captured by Charlie Midnight and locked up in a cage in the library tower at the college. The reason he hadn't killed her yet was so that he could feed on her invigorating life essence. That's what's giving him his power to create monsters."

Gabi and Wendy have turned around to listen. There's a pained look in Gabi's eyes. I feel everything go still inside myself as I remember that series of dreams I had before Joe and Cassie gave me the no-dream pills. I was in a cage in one of them.

"Could that be where she is now?" Gabi asks.

Joe sits quietly rubbing his chin.

"Hard to say without actually having a look," he finally says. "Obviously, Rohlin and her daughter had a lot of mojo when they were writing the actual story. I just don't know that notes about ideas they had along the way would be as potent." He nods to Jilly. "What else have you got?"

"Is there anything about Ethan?" I add.

Jilly nods. "But just to finish up with Nora, it looks like they were considering having Carmen Hale be the one that finds and frees her."

"That cow Carmen," Gabi says. "She hates us."

"She's not that bad," I say.

Gabi scowls. "If we were dying, she'd pull up a chair and watch the show."

I shake my head. "I admit Carmen makes bad choices, especially when it comes to pushing your buttons, but I think there's a good person inside her. She's just too scared to let her out."

And then I realize I'm talking about someone I only know as a character from the TV show, where Carmen is Nora's frenemy, screwing things up for her as much as she helps. Gabi's going to have a whole different take from knowing her in the other Crescent Beach.

God, this is confusing.

"You know what?" I say. "I don't actually know her at all. We'll have to go with Gabi's take on Carmen." I look at Gabi. "Would she help Nora?"

"Only if she got something out of it."

"Well," Jilly says, "the notes only show that they were considering having Carmen help rescue Nora. There were no details."

"But we found something else," Wendy says, "possibly related to Ethan. There's a section in the file where Emma was clearly making notes about things she could use in another, regular, Nora Constantine story. And one of them is about a neuromuscular paralytic drug called…" She hits a few keys on her computer. "It's called Succinylcholine, or SUX for short, and it's used in anesthesiology, as part of surgery. It paralyzes all the muscles of the body, including the ones for breathing, so you need to be under the watch of an anesthetist or it will kill you."

She looks back at her screen. "It's given by injection and works very fast—within seconds to a minute. It's also very short acting because enzymes in the body begin to break it down almost immediately." She turns to us. "Which makes it tough for the crime lab since there's no drug left to test and if you do test for it the toxicology report comes back negative."

"That's a real thing?" Sophie asks.

Wendy nods. "I looked it up after we found the mention of it in the notes."

"So," Joe says. "A traceless poison, so to speak."

"Pretty much," Wendy says. "I've read that you can test for the breakdown products, which are called metabolites. That's often proved successful, but you have to know to look for them. It's not something that a crime lab would normally check for in a tox screen."

"Is it hard to get your hands on this stuff?" I ask.

"Not if you know an anesthetist who's willing to steal some from a hospital."

"We should pass this info on to the cops," Jilly says.

I nod. "But it still doesn't tell us who killed him or why. Ethan seemed to blame Charlie Midnight, but how's that even possible and why would he even bother? Midnight's in a whole other world."

I look at Joe. "And you would know if he made it over here, right?" Joe nods.

I turn to Wendy and Gabi. "Any luck on finding the seller of the manuscript?"

"Working on it," Gabi says, turning back to her computer.

"I need to go back to the Crescent Beach world," Joe says. "Check out this library tower."

I give him a puzzled look. "I thought you said we shouldn't pay attention to the notes because they wouldn't have enough mojo to make things happen there."

"It still needs to be checked—if only to eliminate it."

"Then I'm coming with you," I say.

He shakes his head. "That's not the best—"

"I'm coming too," Gabi says.

"What about finding this manuscript seller?" Joe asks.

Gabi shrugs, "It's proving a little thorny, but it can wait till we get back. I need to see what's happening over there."

"We should just get Saskia to find the seller," Jilly says. "I don't know why I didn't think of that before."

Gabi turns to her. "You guys have *two* hackers living here?"

"I'm not really a hacker," Wendy says. "I'm just good at fiddling with computers."

"Whereas Saskia is the internet," I say, which makes Jilly smile to hear me quoting her.

"Say what?" Gabi says.

"You'll see."

"Get her to have a look at it," Joe says, standing up. "But if you're coming along, we're leaving now."

Gabi shuts her notebook and sticks it in her backpack—I get the sense she never goes anywhere without it, just like on the show—and we walk over to where Joe's waiting. He has that look in his eye that sends a flicker of fear through me.

"Is this a trick you can teach," Gabi asks, "or is it something you're born with?"

"A little of both," he says. "But today's not the day to get into it."

He puts a hand on either of our shoulders. We take the step with him and we're somewhere else again.

～

THIS SOMEWHERE ELSE REMINDS ME of the hills of desert scrub behind L.A. except there's no sign of civilization here. Just the dirt underfoot, dried grass and weeds, cacti. Some big old oaks. When I turn to the west I can see the blue of the ocean a couple of miles away, clearly visible through a sky unsullied by smog.

"It's gone?" Gabi says, looking around herself. "The whole town?"

"We're not quite there yet," Joe says. "At the moment we're standing one thin layer away from the Crescent Beach world. If we crossed over from here, we'd be outside the perimeter that Midnight's followers have set up around the town. They weren't paying a lot of attention the last time I was here, but I'm good at keeping a low profile."

"So why the stop here?" I ask.

"I just want to make something clear. I can travel safely there because I'll be wearing a different shape. You two don't have that luxury. As soon as I cross you over, you're going to have targets on your backs."

"What do you mean you'll be wearing a different shape?" Gabi asks.

But I get it. I'm recalling the conversation we had in Emma's condo.

"When you told us your parents were a dog and a crow," I say, "you meant that literally? So you can take their shapes?"

He nods.

"Seriously?" Gabi says. "Because that is so cool."

"It has its advantages—advantages that neither of you have."

"So what are you saying?" I ask. "You have to sneak us through the perimeter Midnight's men have set up?"

"No, I can step you out right in the middle of town. I just want you to understand the risk you're taking. These creatures that Midnight's been making are fast and strong. I'm fast and strong too, but frankly, I'm pretty sure I'd have trouble handling more than a couple of them. Three or more come at us and I'll have a real problem."

"In the story," I say, "they're mostly nocturnal."

"And we can handle ourselves," Gabi says.

Joe frowns at her. "I don't care if you're cage fighters and can beat the crap out of a guy twice your size. These are supernatural creatures and against them a human doesn't have a chance."

"So you'd rather we wait here for you," Gabi says.

"That'd be the smart thing to do."

She exchanges a look with me then turns back to Joe. "We can play this on the down low," she tells him. "You go do your scouting. We just need a quick look around to see how bad it's gotten. We're not stupid. We won't take unnecessary risks."

Joe sighs. "Crossing over is an unnecessary risk all by itself," he says. But he grabs our shoulders and steps us away again. We come back out on the same landscape untouched by civilization, but this time we're right near the ocean.

"Wait here," he says.

He lets go of us and disappears. Around five minutes later he's back. He hands us both baseball caps and sunglasses.

"You," he tells me, "get all that red hair up under the ball cap. It's not much of a disguise, but somebody'd have to get a pretty close look to recognize you."

That makes sense. I do as he says. Gabi tucks her black hair under the other cap, then puts on the glasses.

She smiles at me. "This is like those dumb disguises you always had us wear when we were tailing somebody."

"They worked, didn't they?"

Gabi just raises her eyebrows.

After I put on my own shades, Joe gives us a critical look.

"Okay," he says. "I'm going to check out this college library. I'll be gone maybe half an hour. Keep a low profile and stay out of trouble."

He crosses us over and we find ourselves in Crescent Beach, half hidden between the adobe wall of a building and a jade hedge. Just the two of us. I felt his hand leave my shoulder as we crossed, and now I hear a crow cawing from the roofline above us. I look up to watch Joe circle a couple of times before he flies off in the direction of the community college.

Gabi peers out of the hedge then squeezes through the dense growth, motioning for me to follow her.

"Come on," she says. "Time to dive in."

I'm honestly thrown for a loop. I'm not sure what I was expecting, but I don't think it was quite this. We're really in Crescent Beach—not on one of the sets, and not in Santa Feliz or Long Beach, both of which stood in for various outdoor scenes and establishing shots. It's like we're in the middle of the damn show, the way it appeared on a TV screen.

When we step out onto the sidewalk, we're on Main Street where it runs down to the parking lot at the beach. The pier stretches out above the water, with Salty's Fish Fry at the far end. I can't tell you how many meals I've pretended to eat in there while we were filming. I look back up the sloping street, recognizing shops and restaurants that only existed in the show. The tang of ocean is sharp in the air and I realize I've missed that.

There are no people around like you'd expect on a beautiful day like this. Blue sky, sun almost overhead, the surf rolling in and crashing on the sand on the other side of the parking lot.

It takes me a moment to realize that there's more wrong than a lack of people. There are cars parked along Main Street and in the lot, but they're trashed. Windows broken, tires slashed, fenders, hoods and doors banged in, the finishes scratched and gouged. The buildings aren't in much better shape.

Kelly's Fashions and Souvenirs, right between Eddy's Surf Shop and the Dog'n'Burger, has its windows boarded up. It's not alone. As I look up the street I see three or four other storefronts all boarded up. Other shops have their windows smashed. A few have been burned and only charred walls lift out of the rubble.

"Jesus," Gabi says. "It's even worse than when I left."

I glance around us, feeling exposed. "Maybe we should have taken Joe's advice and stayed at the greenhouse."

"We'll be okay," Gabi says, though she doesn't sound convinced.

I take a deep breath and look up at the blue sky. "I guess. If Emma's manuscript holds, it means they're dormant right now, so we should be safe—or at least safer—as long as the sun is shining."

"Charlie Midnight's brood are like vampires."

I nod. "Except she called them 'bloods.' "

"Ignoring the fact that there's already a gang with that name."

"Stupid book," I say. We look at each other and both let out a nervous chuckle.

We can't see anybody but I feel a pinprick of—not exactly fear. It's more like a constant, low-level anxiety, as if we're mice out in an open field with the hawk circling above. Deer at a watering hole, knowing there are hungry wolves nearby in the woods.

"What did you want to do here, anyway?" I ask.

Gabi takes a moment to answer. "Um, it was to check for signs of Nora. But honestly? Now I regret coming. It's even more banal—and creepier than I remember."

"It's sure creepy," I agree.

"But we're here now," she says, "and Joe won't be back for a little while. Let's at least take a walk down to the pier. I think I see someone sitting there."

I shrug and let her lead the way but we make slow progress since I keep stopping, distracted by how everything looks like the Nora Constantine set—except it's real, if trashed. But we're only going two blocks so I'm not holding us up much.

We cross the parking lot and make our way to the closest end of the pier. At any other time there'd be people fishing from it. Kids hanging around. Tourists leaning on the rails, taking pictures of the surfers. But today there's only an old man sitting on one of the wooden benches bolted to the cement at the end of the pier. He's wearing a baseball cap, like us, a Grateful Dead T-shirt that looks like an original from the sixties, cargo shorts and flip-flops. Grizzled grey hair spills out from under the ball cap. His skin is brown from the sun and he's got a couple of days' worth of stubble.

"Got a death wish?" he shouts.

We stop and look at him.

"Yeah, you," he goes on. "I mean, yeah, you've at least got some cojones coming out here instead of hiding away in your house, but why waste your time walking around here? If I was your age, I'd be looking for a way out of this hellhole."

"Things are that bad?" I say as we approach and stop in front of him.

"Hello? Reality check. The world's gone to hell and we've been left here for the bloods to pick off one by one. Can't even count on the cops because Midnight's turned the whole police department into his monsters. But here you are, strolling around like everything's hunky dory."

I don't think I've ever heard anyone use that term in actual conversation.

"So, how would you get out?" Gabi asks.

"Nobody's getting out. We're all going to die here. You, me, anybody that's still left alive."

"But you're sitting here," I say.

"Yeah, why's that?" Gabi asks.

"I just don't give a good goddamn anymore."

This guy's almost more depressing than the wreck of this town.

I look down the boardwalk where it follows the beach. It's so strange to see it empty like this. Then I catch a glimpse of something dark in the sky. Moments later, I see that it's Joe in his crow shape, black feathers glistening in the sun. He does a slow swoop above our heads before he lands on the railing behind the old man.

"Get out of here, you dirty bird!" the old man yells.

He turns and takes a swipe at the bird.

Gabi grabs his arm. "Hey, leave him alone!"

"Fuck you," he tells her and jerks his arm out of her grip. "Those things eat carrion—you know what that is? The bits and pieces of us that the bloods throw out. Gristle and guts and whatever other shit's too gross even for them."

He leans over and spits on the pier.

"We should go," I say as the crow lifts off and heads back to where we entered this world.

Gabi nods. "I'd say it was nice talking to you," she tells the old man, "but I'd only be lying."

She walks away. I give the old man a what-can-you-do shrug.

"Fuck you, too," he says, giving me the middle finger salute.

Shaking my head, I hurry to catch up with Gabi.

Joe's waiting for us in human form when we squeeze back through the jade hedge.

"Find what you were looking for?" he asks.

"Well," Gabi says. "If you mean the complete lack of desire to ever come back, then yes. How about you?"

"There are cages in the library tower—like crates you might keep your dog in, only they're made of reinforced steel. I could only see into one from where I was. There was nothing in it except for a blanket in one corner. I could smell people though."

"And Charlie Midnight?" I ask. "Or the bloods?"

He shakes his head. "I didn't see any monsters, but their scent is all over the place. It's foul, even from the outside. I got the sense that there was a basement level, but you don't build underground in California, do you?"

"Not normally," I say.

"What do you mean, you got a sense?" Gabi asks.

He shrugs. "I've got a kind of sixth sense and I can usually tell if a place is inhabited or not. The library's pretty much open concept on all three floors, and I didn't see anybody through the windows, but I could feel their presence in there. If there's no basement, they're holed up somewhere."

"So what do we do now?" Gabi asks.

"Damned if I know. Go back to Bramleyhaugh, I guess, and regroup. Try to come up with some ideas."

"But if Nora's in there…"

"We'll be no help to her if we get killed or taken ourselves. We need a plan."

"What about tracking down Carmen?" I say.

Gabi pulls a face but she nods in agreement.

"And again, do what? If we come back, we should be geared up—body armour, some serious firepower. I wouldn't mind a few more hands on deck, and I'm not talking about Jilly and her gang, bless their hearts. We need people who can and are willing to pull a trigger, because the rescue mission isn't to find and help Nora, it's to help all those people trapped in this nightmare."

"That makes sense," I say.

Gabi glances at me, then looks back at Joe and says, "I agree, but I hope we get Nora out too."

"Of course," Joe says. "I'm not trying to take over here, but we need to play to our strengths. You know the lay of the land and you're good with computers. Juniper does her investigative legwork and talks to ghosts. Me, I'm the muscle here, the guy in the field who can put whatever plan we come up with into action."

"Sounds good," Gabi says.

"But I've got a question," I say.

Joe's gaze settles on me. "Shoot."

"The bloods aren't around during the day. Why don't the survivors just get the hell out of town? Why are they sticking around, hiding in their houses?"

"Maybe they don't have a choice," Gabi says.

Joe nods. "This is a pocket world. Head out of town in any direction and you'll find yourself right back here again. If we don't make something happen, everybody here is going to die."

I remember what the cranky old man told us at the pier.

"That's what the old guy told us," I say. "The one that was so pissed at you coming close to him."

Joe flashes us a grin. "I get that a lot, especially from cranky old farts." He winks at Gabi. "Thanks for having my back, kid."

Gabi just looks at him. "Right, like you needed me. I just didn't like his pissy attitude."

"That makes three of us," I say.

"Let's see what the others have come up with while we were gone," Joe says.

He steps us away, but instead of crossing back over to Jilly's house, we arrive in a small meadow surrounded by a pine and birch wood. After SoCal, the air feels almost moist. The salty tang is replaced with a deep earthy scent of leaves and what I can only call green—that smell you can only get in a summer field. The drone of insects, silenced for a moment by our appearance, starts up again.

"Where is this?" I ask.

"We're just on the other side of Jilly's backyard," Joe says. "I wanted to check a couple of things with you if we're really going to take a run at Charlie Midnight and his crew. Do either of you have weapons experience?"

"I do," I say. "I did a bunch of training for a movie where I played an assassin. The movie sucked, but our props guy was super competent and made sure everybody knew how to handle themselves. We spent a whole week taking apart guns and putting them back together, then practicing at a shooting range. I've kept up my chops."

"That's good. What about hand-to-hand?"

"We can handle ourselves," Gabi says.

I nod in agreement. "I've done a lot of action films and can't seem to stop the training when they're over."

Joe eyes us for a moment. "Okay. Come at me and don't hold back."

"What?"

Instead of answering, Joe takes a shot at me. I don't even think, I just react. I move my head and his fist goes by my ear. He catches my hand as I go for a body punch and it's like it's stuck in a vice until he lets me go.

"Good," he says. "Your reflexes are—"

He doesn't get to finish. Gabi swings her leg and sweeps his feet from under him. She drops, the point of her elbow coming down on his throat, but he rolls out of the way faster than should be possible and she hits the ground. She's on her feet immediately, ready to go at him again. But Joe's recovery is quicker. He stands a few feet back from us, the flats of his hands held out in front of him.

"Easy," he says.

"The fuck's the matter with you?" Gabi snarls at him.

I lay a hand on her arm. "He was just testing us."

"I'll test him."

I don't blame her for being pissed off. I'm a little pissed off myself. But I get what he was doing.

"Was that really necessary?" I ask.

He shrugs. "If I'm going into combat with somebody, I want to know that they can hold their own."

Gabi's calming down. "Combat?" she says.

"When we go back," Joe tells her, "it won't be to have afternoon tea with Charlie Midnight. We're going to war and they're fast. They're strong."

I think of Joe's speed and strength.

"Like you," I say.

He nods. "I was holding back just now, but they won't be, and by all accounts, they're better. I wanted to get a feel for what you can do because you can't always rely on a weapon when you're in the middle of a firefight."

"So you think we're going to be a liability," Gabi says.

"No. For humans, you did good. But when we go after the bloods, hit them from a distance. Body shots slow anything down and the torso makes for an easy target, but as soon as you get a chance, take the head shot."

I think of the weapons training I got for that crappy thriller and don't know that it'll be enough. For one thing, I've never fired a weapon at a real person and hoped I never would.

Joe gives us a feral grin, turning the full force of it on Gabi.

"So we're okay?" he asks, waving two fingers at both of us and himself.

"You're an asshole," she says, "but yeah."

"I've been called worse."

He slowly offers us each a hand—careful not to make any sudden moves around us after his little test—and crosses us over to the backyard of the Stanton Street house.

"I'm going to round up a few things," he says, "but I'll be back soon."

Then he's gone and it's just the two of us standing here. I look at the windows of the greenhouse. That was once a normal place where I'd hang with Jilly and the others. We'd paint, we'd gossip. We had fun. Now it feels like it's turned into command central.

"I'm not a hundred percent sure I can do this," I say without looking at Gabi.

"Nobody says you have to. I'm the one with the connection to Nora, not you. I have to do whatever I can because I know she'd do the same for me."

"I've never killed anybody before. I've never even hurt anybody. It's all been just playacting for film and TV."

"They're not people," she says. "They're monsters. I once saw a gang of them tear this guy apart like they were shredding a pillow. It's what made me follow Ethan over here. I told myself I was looking for Nora, but really, I just needed to get away. I was so scared."

"I get the being scared."

"Except now I believe Nora's still over there. It makes sense because I sure haven't been able to find her here. God knows what they've done to her, how they're treating her. I just can't leave her there without trying to do something."

"But we won't be going over to negotiate or sneak her out. You heard Joe. He was talking about body armour and guns. That means it's going to be a full-on assault."

Gabi touches my shoulder. "Really, I understand."

I finally look away from the greenhouse. "Just because I'm scared," I tell her, "doesn't mean I'm going to let you do this on your own. Besides, I played Nora for so long, she's kind of like a piece of myself."

"Juniper," she starts, but I grab her arm and pull her toward the side door of the greenhouse.

"Let's see what they've figured out while we wait for Joe to come back," I say.

Gabi lets me pull her along but she's shaking her head and smiling.

"Sometimes you are so Nora. She never backs off from anything either."

"Nora's got you," I say, "and you've got me. End of story."

WENDY AND SASKIA are sitting together on the sofa when we open the side door of the greenhouse and step inside. The two of them look up from the pad of paper that Wendy has on her lap and smile at us.

Once we've established that Jilly's off walking the dogs and Joe will be back in a while, Gabi drops into an empty chair. I sit on the edge of the coffee table and ask if they've had any luck.

"Saskia ID'd the guy who sold Ethan the book," she says. She looks down at the pad. "His name's Thomas Scott and he lives in Phoenix."

"He must be the guy who broke into Emma's place," I say.

"Or made it look like someone broke in," Wendy says. "Thomas Scott is Emma's son-in-law."

I look away. "Crap."

Wendy nods.

"Does he work in a hospital?" Gabi asks.

"No. Plus Saskia accessed a bunch of security cameras around the time that Ethan was killed. Thomas never left Phoenix."

"We still need to tell the police about the possibility of that drug," I say. I look at Wendy. "What did you call it?"

"SUX," she says. "Succinylcholine."

"Right, that. They need to look for a puncture mark—someplace that's not obvious."

"Like above the hairline," Wendy says. "Inside the nose, an ear, his mouth." She pulls a face. "Inside his anus. I'll get Christy to tell them since he's got the inside line through the Spook Squad."

I nod. But I'm still thinking of the implications. "To get that close to him," I say, "it had to have been somebody he knew and trusted."

"I love all you guys," Wendy says, "but I still wouldn't let any of you stick a needle into me in any of those places."

I turn to Saskia. "Can you get security footage of the park the night Ethan died?"

She shakes her head. "They don't have cameras there. I also checked any photos or videos that might have been uploaded in the same time frame, but there's nothing—or at least nothing that we can use."

Gabi is staring at Saskia. "Impressive! How long did that take you?"

"A few minutes."

"Say what? You have to tell me what kind of programs you're running."

"It's all in her head," I say, looking over at Saskia. "Isn't that right?"

Saskia smiles. "Not entirely. I only access the web. I don't actually hold it in my mind."

"You're the interface?" Gabi asks. "You're not using a computer of any kind?"

"None at all."

"Sweet. I'd love to learn how to do that."

Saskia shakes her head. "It's not something that…" Her voice trails off and she studies Gabi as though she's only just really seeing her.

"You know what?" she says. "It might be something that you can learn, considering your origins."

"My origins? What do you know about my origins?"

Saskia smiles. "I'm familiar with the collision of intent and binary coding that can create something tangible and new."

Gabi's still looking confused, but I understand what Saskia means.

"She's like you," I tell Gabi.

"Really?"

Saskia nods. "After a fashion."

"You have to wonder," Wendy says, bringing us back to the task at hand. "Why would Thomas steal that manuscript from his mother-in-law and then turn around and sell it?"

"It could be to pay off gambling debts," Saskia says. "He plays a lot of poker online and is constantly checking sports stats. I'm guessing that he's also been losing money offline to some bookie."

"Or he doesn't like Emma," I say, "and this is a way to hurt her."

"If that's the case," Gabi says, "I don't blame him. I don't much like the woman either."

Our last encounter with Emma Rohlin left me disappointed and conflicted, but I don't want to get into that right now.

"Whatever his reason for taking the manuscript," I say, "we still can't say for certain that he killed Ethan."

Wendy nods. "You should go talk to his ghost again."

"That would be a good idea, except I don't have the first clue how to find him."

"How did you find him before?" Saskia asks.

"I've only talked to him twice and both times I just kind of stumbled upon him. He doesn't seem at all like a ghost either, except the second time, when I poked him in the shoulder, my finger went right into him and he just sort of dissolved away."

"You probably have to be alone for him to come to you," Wendy says.

"I guess I'll try later."

We all look up at the sound of a small commotion erupting in the kitchen, then the dogs tear into the greenhouse, skidding on the floor. Sonora pretty much launches herself at me while Bobo races in mad circles from one end of the room to the other. I kneel on the floor so that I can hold Sonora. She wriggles as though she's trying to get right inside my shirt and pushes her muzzle into my neck.

"I missed you too," I tell her.

"We're ba-ack," Jilly sings, coming into the room.

Saskia laughs. "Really? We never would have known."

Jilly laughs and plunks down in a chair beside Gabi. "What have I missed?"

I get up from the floor to sit beside Saskia, Sonora lolling on her back with her head on my lap so that I can rub her belly. We all take turns telling Jilly what we know. She looks from me to Gabi when we're done, worry creasing her brow.

"You're not seriously going back, are you?" she says.

"We have to," Gabi tells her. "Or at least I do. If there's a chance that Charlie Midnight has Nora, how can I not?"

I shoot her a frown. "I? Are you forgetting me?"

"We have to go," she corrects herself. "But we're not stupid. We'll be careful. And Joe's coming."

"Where is Joe?" Jilly asks.

"He's gone to round up some help," I say.

Jilly shakes her head. "This has gotten way out of hand."

"It's really awful over there," I tell her. "And the same thing could happen here if Charlie Midnight comes looking for us."

"Why would he come looking for you?"

"I don't know. Ethan seemed to think there was a danger."

"You have to talk to him again," Wendy says.

"I'll try. But please don't hold your breath."

～

AFTER A WHILE, we start repeating ourselves. Wendy goes off to talk to Christy about contacting the police again. Sophie wanders in with a bemused expression and a mug of tea. She gives us all a wave, but it's easy to tell her mind's a million miles away as she goes to her easel where she picks up a piece of charcoal and starts sketching on her canvas. Saskia and Gabi get into a discussion about accessing the internet without using any mechanical means. When they take a breath, they look at Jilly and me. Seeing the incomprehension on our faces, they take their conversation upstairs to Saskia's room. Gabi's so caught up that she actually leaves her backpack behind. I haven't seen her without it since we met at O'Shaunessy's.

"You know, I'm really sorry about all of this," Jilly says when they leave.

I give her a puzzled look. "What do you have to be sorry about?"

"The way I pushed you to embrace this whole you can investigate as easily as Nora Constantine business. I didn't really think it through."

"Honestly, I think I needed a push of some kind. Sometimes you don't know you're treading water until it gets pointed out."

"But it's so dangerous."

"Crossing the street can be dangerous and at least this means something. If we pull this off, we're helping a lot of people."

"I suppose."

"Actually," I say, "if anybody should be apologizing, it's me to you."

Jilly blinks in surprise. "Whatever for?"

"You know I love you. You're like the sister I never had. You're good-natured and kind and silly and—I once thought—halfway mad. The way you're always going on about faeries and magic and people that can turn into animals was endearing, and it would make me smile, but sometimes it made me wonder. But I never said anything because I figured everybody else was just humouring you, and who was I to dump on the parade with a bucket of reality? I just went with the flow."

"That's a lot of water analogies," Jilly says with a wink.

I laugh. "Shut up. I'm trying to tell you that I'm sorry I didn't have enough faith in you."

"But nobody has to apologize for that," she says. "Magic has always had an elusive quality. It slips out of mind and memory like quicksilver. You have to make a bit of an effort to hold on to magical experiences and encounters."

"Nobody's going to forget crossing over into another world."

She smiles. "You'd be surprised what people can forget. They can utterly forget horrible things that happen to them and they can do the same for the most astonishing magical experiences. Our brains are—I was going to say 'wired,' but that's not right. Our brains are programmed to accept the"—she makes air quotes—"'World As It Is.'

That's what the Professor always called it. So anything that deviates gets explained away. Faeries and monsters, ghosts and alien invaders—interacting with anything like that, most people's brains are programmed to find a rational explanation rather than face the truth. Facing the truth puts everything in question and that makes a lot of people very uncomfortable."

"I guess." I rub my face with my hands and push my hair back. "It sure didn't happen with me. I was certainly startled, but after that—well, how do you deny what's right in front of your face?"

She pokes me in the shoulder. "That's because you, my dear, have an open mind and are willing to allow for there to be more to the world than what most people accept."

"I guess that's my superpower."

Jilly laughs. "No, I think your superpower is talking to ghosts."

"I'd rather be able to fly."

"Wouldn't we all."

"So do you have any tips on how to summon a ghost?" I ask.

"I don't think you necessarily have to summon them. Just find a quiet place and indicate that you'd like to have a conversation."

"Indicate how?"

She shrugs. "I don't know. Maybe it's just a matter of saying their name and inviting them to join you."

JILLY TRIES to get us to stay for dinner, but I beg off. I need another shower after grubbing about in the Crescent Beach world, and Gabi and I need to prepare for tomorrow. The whole way back to the house Gabi chatters about all the things she's learned from Saskia. I don't really understand it—there's too much jargon. All I know for sure is that Gabi can't seem to access the internet the same way Saskia does, even though Saskia says she should be able to do it.

"I'll just have to keep coming at it from different angles, I guess," she finally says.

"Yep. Giving up is for losers," I say.

"Exactly."

She helps me make dinner, including a mess of chicken, rice and vegetables to see Sonora through the next few days. I think Tam's home but I haven't seen him. I figure if he's hungry he'll come down for dinner, but I have the sense that he's sleeping off this past weekend. Whether Lydia is sleeping it off with him, I have no idea.

After dinner I go outside with Sonora and sit on the remains of the old wooden swing set in our backyard. It doesn't work anymore, but Tam and I put supports under the seats so we can still come and hang out here when it's a nice night. This evening certainly qualifies. There's a three-quarter moon peeking over the roof of the house next door and the stars are beginning to appear as the light drains from the sky. I can hear traffic but it seems a million miles away. Mostly I hear crickets and June bugs.

Sonora sits with me for a few moments before she gets bored and goes off to explore the garden.

Okay, I think. As Gabi would say, dive right in.

I clear my throat.

"So Ethan," I say. "Can we talk?"

I feel stupid as the words come out my mouth.

"About what?"

"Gah!"

I almost jump out of my skin because he's sitting directly across from me on the swing's other seat.

"God. Can't you give a girl a little notice like a normal person would instead of appearing out of nowhere and giving me a scare?"

"I'm not normal," he says. "I'm dead, remember? And you called me."

He looks so real. I'm half convinced he's not so much a ghost as that he has Joe's ability to step in and out of the otherworld. But I keep my hands to myself and resist leaning forward to poke him. Sonora trots over and regards him with suspicion until I tell her it's okay. I turn back to Ethan.

"Are you following me around?" I ask. "Because if you are, ew."

"I don't know where I was. I just heard my name and found myself here with you. What do you want?"

"Who killed you?"

He sighs. "You know, it's not surprising the show got cancelled after three seasons, because you seem to have totally lost any deductive ability."

"What's that supposed to mean?"

"I didn't even know I was dead until the last time we talked."

"Oh yeah."

"So how could I know who killed me?"

"But you seemed to blame Charlie Midnight, once you did find out."

"I can't think of anybody else who'd want me dead."

"What about the guy who sold you the manuscript?"

"Why would he want me dead?"

"I don't know. Why did you want me to find him?"

"I needed provenance for the manuscript, preferably notarized."

"So you could resell it?"

He nods.

"You didn't ask for that when you bought it?" I ask.

"I honestly didn't think of it."

"What did you pay for it?"

"Ten thousand dollars."

A low whistle escapes my lips.

"I know," he says. "I'm an idiot. But I got caught up in the whole idea of a new Nora book and kind of lost my head."

"Where would you even get that kind of money?"

"Buying and selling Nora memorabilia is surprisingly lucrative."

I had no idea. I mean, I knew the show still had a fairly avid fan base, and the money Greta could get me for appearances seemed stupidly high, but I never really thought about it the way Ethan did.

"Okay," I say. "Back to Charlie Midnight. Why would you think he's responsible? And why do you think he might go after Edward? And before you ask, I've arranged for protection for him."

Ethan's face lights up. "You did?" He seems both surprised and genuinely grateful.

"I did. Now tell me about Charlie Midnight."

"I've had horrible dreams about him," Ethan says. "Ever since I left Crescent Beach and came here. You know he feeds on a person's life essence, right?"

I nod. "It's in the book, but it's not clear how he does it."

"I don't know either. But I did find out before I left that he's particularly fixated on Nora and the people closest to her. In the dreams…sometimes I dreamt he was standing right at the foot of my bed. I couldn't see how he was doing it, but I knew he was pulling my life force out of me and I was too scared to do anything except lie there and wait for him to finish. In the morning I'd wake up and feel all tainted, plus stupid and sluggish for hours."

"So you think it was more than a dream."

"I didn't know what to think."

Something else has been niggling at me ever since Gabi told me she'd followed him here from the Crescent Beach world.

"How did you find your way here?" I ask him. "How did you even know there was a here?"

"Gavin told Nora about it. Well, not this world in particular, but that there are other worlds. He believed that Charlie Midnight came from this one and I guess in a way he was right."

"And Gavin is?"

"A very weird guy. He called himself an adventurer, but he was actually a cryptid hunter."

"Sorry—a *what* hunter?"

"Cryptids—a creature whose existence has been suggested by, you know, folklore or urban myth, but isn't documented by the scientific community."

"That's a Crescent Beach thing?"

He shakes his head. "It's a thing, period."

"Give me an example."

He shrugs. "The Loch Ness Monster. Bigfoot. The Jersey Devil. Werewolves and vampires."

"Wait a second. Gavin—he's the vampire hunter from the book, who tells Nora about the prophecy."

Ethan nods. "He said there are veils that hide the worlds from each other, but they're very thin and permeable in some places, particularly any kind of border."

At my blank look, he goes on. "Supposedly, magic works strongest where there's a natural threshold, or border. It can be at dusk—the border between day and night—or a riverbank, a seashore, the place where a meadow turns into forest. They're harder to find in the city, but he had some ideas. When I finally decided I needed to get away, I started looking in the places he mentioned and other places that I thought were likely candidates."

"And you found one."

"It took me a couple of weeks, but yeah," he says. "Just before I left, I broke into a jewellery store and grabbed a bunch of stuff. I got out before the cops showed up. I'm not even sure they came. By that point the bloods were starting to go after people and they had their hands full. I crossed over, then used the jewellery to buy myself a new life."

He sighs. "I guess I should be grateful. I got two years before my killer found me. Back there, I'd probably have been dead within two weeks."

With Gabi, I get confused about the memories that are real for her but I only remember from the show. The trouble is, the longer I spend in her company, the harder it is for me to tell the difference. But I don't have that connection with Ethan. Except for how he cares for Edward, he's a self-serving, pervy jerk. He just abandoned everybody in the Crescent Beach world and didn't look back. And his Nora-porn debased everything the character stood for. I don't owe him a thing.

I'm about to call Sonora and go inside when I remember how he and I first met, and I realize I can give him this much before I wash my hands of him.

"I tracked down who sold you the manuscript," I tell him.

"Seriously?"

I nod. "It was Emma Rohlin's son-in-law."

"Her son-in-law? Why would he do that?"

"We haven't figured out that part yet. Could be anything—greed, a gambling problem, might've owed the wrong people some money. Or maybe he just doesn't like his mother-in-law. You were right and wrong about the authorship of the newer books, by the way."

"How so?"

"Rohlin didn't write them—or at least she didn't write them on her own. They were collaborations with her daughter Shannon."

He shakes his head. "I didn't see that coming."

"Neither did I."

I stand up. As soon as I do, Sonora comes over from where she's been mooching around the shed at the back of the yard.

"I'll be seeing ya," I say.

"Wait. What am I supposed to do now?"

I honestly don't know what to say, so I settle with, "Whatever dead people do, I guess," and head for the house. I wait until I reach the door to look back. The swing is empty.

∾

GABI'S SITTING in the dining room with a newspaper spread out in front of her open at the comics page. She looks up when Sonora and I come in.

"Jilly just called with a message from Joe," Gabi says. "He wants us to meet at the greenhouse first thing in the morning."

"So we're really doing this," I say. "You had some serious regrets when we got there yesterday."

She gives me a rueful shrug. "I know. The shock of it really hit me. But I've been looking for Nora for two years and I'm not going to stop now. She'd never leave me hanging, either. I know what I'm getting into and, yeah, I'm going, though if you want to change your—"

I hold a hand up. "We've already had that conversation."

"Got it."

"Should we go see if there's anything useful in the stuff upstairs?" I ask.

"Sure."

Gabi helps me pull a couple of boxes out from the back of my closet. Inside are prop souvenirs from various movies and the Nora Constantine show. Most of them are fakes, but there's a pair of genuine Japanese swords—a katana and the shorter wakizashi—that we might be able to use since we've both practiced with bokken back in our martial arts days. I also find a long hunting knife that the props guy on *Dying in the Dark* gave me when the shoot was done. I guess he thought it was romantic. At the bottom of one of the boxes I find my old butterfly knife and I set it aside as well.

While we sort through the boxes, I replay my conversation with Ethan.

"I never knew Gavin was on the level," Gabi says. "I always thought he was kind of sketchy."

"Was he still around before you left? Because maybe we could enlist his help."

Gabi shakes her head. "Charlie Midnight had him beheaded in front of the town hall."

I feel the blood drain from my face. "Seriously?"

"Yeah, I heard it wasn't pretty. He killed the chief of police and Mayor Sanders at the same time."

I clashed with Chief Irvine on more than one occasion, and I never trusted Sanders, but I wouldn't have wished a death like that on anyone. Then I catch myself. That was on the show. Who knows what they were like in that other Crescent Beach.

"Do you think there's anyone left to save?" I find myself saying.

"You mean besides that foul-tempered man we met at the pier? God, I hope so."

We're both thinking of Nora. The Gabi from the show was never very social, so this Gabi probably didn't leave anybody else that she really cared about.

"I guess we'll find out tomorrow," she says.

We've just brought the swords and knives down to the dining room when the front door bangs open.

"Honey, I'm home!" Tam yells.

The silly fool.

I hear his backpack drop onto the floor. His guitar case he'll have set down much more carefully. Sonora bounces out to greet him and he fusses over her before stepping into the dining room. He gives Gabi a puzzled look.

"Hey, Allison," he says. "What are you doing in town? I thought Joon told me you were working on a pilot for Syfy out in Vancouver. And what's with the half-Gabi look?"

"What's a half-Gabi look?" I have to ask.

He looks at me like I'm off my rocker. "Come on. Gabi's always in black with, like, a million studs and face piercings."

He turns to Gabi and rolls his eyes. "How soon she forgets."

"This isn't Allison," I tell him.

"Yeah, right." He sits down and picks up the sheathed katana. "This is cool."

I sit down as well and take the katana from him. "Let me catch you up on what my life's been like since I last saw you on Sunday."

He takes it well. Better than maybe I would have if our roles were reversed. He does interrupt with a lot of "no ways" and "shut ups" as he tries to digest everything he's being told.

"No, no," he says when he hears what we're planning to do. "You're not the freaking Marines, Joon. This is not your fight."

"But it is mine," Gabi says.

He leans across the table to get a closer look at her.

"Seriously?" he says. "You're not Allison?"

I see Gabi bristle. "Do you have a problem with that?"

He sits back in his chair. "I have a million problems with it, starting with: what the fuck? How is something like this even possible?"

"Come on, Tam," I say. "We talked about some of this stuff before and you seemed to accept it."

"That was different."

"How was it different?"

"Now we're talking about other worlds and my sister's suddenly developed an action hero complex. If these monsters are real, you could end up dead."

I sigh and reach in both directions to squeeze each of them on the shoulder. This conversation could go around in circles, and Gabi and I need our rest.

"Let's sleep on it and talk again in the morning," I say.

9

WEDNESDAY

We get up early and are out of the house before Tam wakes, which saves us having to have the conversation with him before we leave.

By the time we arrive at the greenhouse studio, Joe's waiting in the backyard with a couple of other men. They're cut from the same cloth as Joe, handsome and rangy, with a slightly feral light in their eyes. He introduces them as Whiskey Jack and Nanabozho.

"Call me Bo," Nanabozho says.

They're dressed in jeans and cowboy boots. Joe and Jack are wearing T-shirts, Bo's in a flannel shirt. On the picnic table is a heap of body armour, a pair of police helmets, two riot shields and some serious weaponry. Automatic weapons. Shotguns. Handguns.

We're not going to need the swords and knives I brought.

"Where did you get all this stuff?" I ask.

"From the Spook Squad's weapons locker."

"What? They just lent it to you?"

Joe shakes his head. "No, we took it."

"Jesus, Joe."

"Don't worry about it. We'll either bring it all back before they ever know, or it won't make a difference to us."

He points two fingers at Gabi and me, then nods at the body armour. "Now suit up."

There are only two sets of body armour.

"What about you guys?" Gabi asks.

Joe shrugs. "Don't worry about us—we'll be fine."

I played a member of a SWAT team in *Blue Line of Valor,* so I know how the gear works. I help Gabi with hers then suit up myself.

Jilly stands by the door to the greenhouse, plainly unhappy with the turn her little adventure with me has taken. I walk over to her when I've finished buckling and strapping myself in.

"Stop worrying," I tell her. "We're not going to take any unnecessary chances."

"Besides going over there in the first place," she says, echoing Joe's concern the last time Gabi and I insisted we accompany him.

I'm not going to argue with her.

"So you'll take care of Sonora if—"

"Don't you even put that out into the universe!" she says. Then she gives me a hug made awkward by the bulk of the vest I'm wearing.

"Wisakedjak and Nanabozho," Gabi says by the table. "Those are names from Native American mythology."

Whiskey Jack gives her a grin. "Are they now?" He looks at Joe. "What are the odds on that?"

"Who's keeping an eye on Edward?" I ask.

"Some corbae who owe me a favour," Joe says.

He gives Gabi and me belts with a holstered Glock, taser and baton attached, waits while we buckle them on, then hands us each a machine gun on a strap. Gabi and I look at each other. If this business weren't so serious, the way we look would be hilarious, all bulked up and bristling with weapons. Instead, it's instantly sobering and I feel my chest go tight.

I close my eyes. Breathe, I remind myself, hearing the voice of every trainer I've ever worked with in my head.

"One last thing," Joe says, drawing our attention back to him. "The natural inclination in a confrontation of any kind is to try to use reason before action. Where we're going, that's only going to get you dead. The creatures Charlie Midnight's made aren't going to give you any quarter. They're going to strike harder and faster than you're expecting.

"If they were ever people, they're not people now. They've been changed into monsters and that change is final. It's like dealing with a

Windigo or a…zombie. You can't fix them. You can only take them down."

He looks from me to Gabi to see that we understand.

"Nice pep talk," Gabi says.

Bo laughs. I feel a delirious sense of giddiness rising, but Joe shoots us a frown and the moment passes. We're back to deadly serious as Joe begins to speak again.

"Jack, Bo and I will come at them from the front of the building. You two take the rear. When you hear that we've engaged with them, your job is to go in and find Nora and anybody else we need to get out. Bo, you take the sniper rifle. When you find some high ground with good sightlines, let us know. Jack, you're with me going in through the front."

Bo straps on a weapons belt and grabs the rifle. Joe and Jack arm up as well.

I glance over at Jilly. There's panic in her eyes so I go and give her another hug.

"Come back in one piece," she says.

"We will."

I join the others. Joe takes my hand, Bo takes Gabi's.

"Dive right in," Gabi says as they step us away into the Crescent Bay world.

～

GABI and I don't talk as we make our way to the rear of the library. It's early morning here, but still eerie to see the campus so deserted. There's no one around at all. It's so quiet we can hear the waves wash in to the shore, blocks away from where we've just hunkered down behind some shrubbery. The rear door is in clear sight from our position.

I resist the urge to touch the comm link in my ear. Joe warned us to keep exchanges to a minimum because we don't know who might be on the same channel. He wasn't even sure it would work in this world. But when we tested it on our arrival, I could hear everybody's voice in my ear. Since then we've all been silent.

It's making me antsy. I know what Joe said, but I can't help myself. It's talk or let my nerves take over.

"There was no basement on the show," I murmur to Gabi.

She looks worried. "I've never noticed one when I've been inside," she whispers.

"So I guess we're going up."

I take as deep a breath as I can with all this stuff on, scrunching up my shoulders and letting them fall, then regret it as my gear makes a metallic sound falling back into place.

We both go dead silent, listening for any sign that we've been heard. As the minutes crawl by, my jitters start back up.

I decide to distract myself by describing what I recall about the show. I keep my voice low. "I remember the library being three floors of open space with bookshelves and carousels, desks and sofas. The offices were in the middle on the second and third floors, kind of built into the staircases and around the elevator shaft. And there was the small amphitheater on the ground floor. Is that about right?"

Gabi nods in agreement. I'm wondering if she feels as awkward as I do in this body armour, the big helmet on my head, trying to figure out how to hold both the shield and the machine gun. I start to mention it to her when she suddenly lifts her head. Behind the Plexiglas of her visor I see her eyes go wide with shock.

"Holy crap," she says almost at normal volume.

I turn around, looking for what's startled her.

"What's going on?" Joe's voice asks in my earpiece.

"Hang on," I reply. "There's something happening to Gabi." I touch her sleeve. "What is it?" I ask her.

When I look back, her wide eyes meet my gaze, but I don't think she's seeing anything.

"What?" I repeat.

"It—it's like a switch just turned on. All I have to do is think of something and I can find it. Holy double crap. This is amazing."

I risk a peek over the bushes and I'm relieved to see it's still empty and quiet out there.

"Gabi," I murmur. "You're not making any sense and we need to be on top of our game here."

"Right, right. Hang on. I'm accessing blueprints for the library. Wait. They must have security cameras in there. Let me see if I can access them."

And then I get it. Whatever weird relationship Saskia has with the internet has just kicked in for Gabi.

"Oh man, I am so badass," she says. "I've got eyes on everything inside except for the offices. Makes sense that they wouldn't have cameras in there."

"Are you hearing this?" I ask for Joe's benefit. "Gabi's gone all Saskia on us."

"Should we pull back?" he says.

Gabi replies before I can say yes.

"Hell no," she says with a grin. "I'm on top of this."

"Copy that," Joe says.

I'm not so sure I buy it. It's so weird having her look at me and not really see me. She's seeing—I'm not sure what. A computer screen inside her head? All of the internet in some bewildering cyberspace chaos? Whatever it is, she sounds so matter-of-fact.

"Are you sure you're okay?" I ask.

"Never better."

"You're not…overloading or anything?"

"Seriously, I'm good. Saskia told me about this. She said when I did manage to connect, to treat my mind as a browser. I just shut everything out and focus on what I want to."

The far-off gaze behind her visor is starting to creep me out.

"So I guess the bloods are in the offices," she says. "I wish I could see inside them. What I need is a drone."

"What you need is to come back from wherever you are," I tell her. "This can't be good."

"That's where you're wrong. Whenever I'm not online I feel a little disconnected, but now for the first time I'm complete. This is every hacker's dream. Wetware that's an interface."

I don't like the sound of any of this.

"Can't you, I don't know, put it on hold for a minute?" I think about what I'm saying, then add, "Maybe reduce your connection so that it's just in a corner of your vision?"

"Good idea. I don't know if I can—wait. I've got it."

Her eyes snap into focus and for the first time in a few minutes, I feel like she can really see me again. She grins, ear to ear.

"Okay," she says. "This is very cool." She looks in the direction of the library. "I'm seeing the outside and the inside at the same time."

"It isn't dangerous, is it?" I ask.

"Don't know. Pretty sure I don't care. Dive right in, Nora. All the way to the core."

I don't bother to correct the slip of the name, but it adds to my worry.

Joe's voice comes over the comm link. "Our senses tell us there are bodies in there. Bo's still getting into position."

"Okay," I reply. "We'll wait to hear from you."

Except there's an exit door to our left, and Gabi gets up and trots toward it. I give the building a quick scan before I scramble to my feet and follow her. By the time I join her, she's trying the door.

"Locked," she says. Her eyes lose focus again. "Let's see. Okay it's got an electronic lock. I just need to find the program that controls it."

The fingers of the hand not holding her riot shield are moving at her side as though she's working a keyboard. I hear the lock disengage.

"And voila," she says. "Front and back doors are open."

When she reaches for the door's handle again I grab her arm to stop her. "Let's stick to the plan," I say. "Joe and his crew distract the bloods. We wait until they're drawn out before we go in."

She nods. I know she's only partially paying attention to me. Part of her is no doubt focused on the feeds from the security cameras inside.

Waiting brings my anxiety levels back up and I wonder again just what I'm doing out here in SWAT riot gear. This isn't a movie and I'm not a hero. I used to be an actor. Now all I want to be is an artist and a good mom to Sonora.

"Bo's in position," Joe's voice says in my ear, pulling me out of my own head. "We're good to go."

That's immediately followed by gunshots from the other side of the building.

"Heads up," Gabi says. "I've got movement. They're at the door in three…two…one…*now*."

"We see them," Joe says. "There's seven—no eight of them."

My knuckles are white on the strap of the riot shield. The machine gun weighs heavy from its strap on my shoulder. I put my fingers inside the trigger guard.

There's more gunfire from the front.

"You're up," Joe says.

"Okay," Gabi tells him. As she pushes down on the door handle she looks back at me and says, "We need to stay in serious stealth mode. Joe's crew has drawn them out, but there could be other bloods in there that aren't in range of the cameras."

I nod. She puts her shoulder to the library door and eases it open, quickly slipping in. I'm right behind her.

There are no lights on inside, but there are so many windows that it's easy to see. We duck behind the nearest bookcase while Gabi continues to monitor the camera feeds. Outside, the gunfire is sporadic.

Gabi looks at me. "Try the amphitheater first?"

She doesn't wait for my response. I catch up to her and we cross the main floor of the library, aiming for the double doors of the amphitheater. When we reach them, we hug the wall on either side of the doors.

"Everything's still clear," Gabi says.

We each grab a door handle and pull them open.

"Oh, shit," she says as a couple of dozen grotesque creatures turn their heads in our direction.

My first thought is body modification because I can't quite process that I'm seeing monsters. Live in L.A. for as long as I did and you end up seeing everything. People with implanted horns like those that protrude from the shaved heads of these creatures. Augmented noses, mouths and ears. Split tongues. Implanted fangs. Brow implants. Tattooed eyes, for God's sake.

I have a flash of panic. How certain are we that these are actually monsters? That they're not just people with a different preference of body aesthetics?

Registering our intrusion, they roar all at the same time, like some kind of hive mind is controlling them, and Gabi slams her door.

"Up!" she yells.

I slam my door and bolt up the stairs right behind her.

"We've got a problem, Joe," I say, hoping he can hear me above the gunfire. "We just stirred up a nest of bloods in the amphitheater."

"How many?" he replies.

"At least twenty," Gabi puts in.

We reach the second floor, but she takes us right up the next staircase.

"We're heading for the top floor," she adds for Joe's benefit. "We'll make them come at us just a couple at a time."

"Hang tight. We'll be inside as soon as we can."

My calves are aching and I'm panting for breath by the time we get to the third floor. I lean against the wall while Gabi peers back down the stairs, gun ready.

We both jump when a door opens down the hall. The blood that appears takes one look at us and charges in our direction. I drop my riot shield and bring up my machine gun, but suddenly I just freeze. I can't believe how fast he's moving. He's almost on me when Gabi lets loose a short burst of rounds. The thunder of the shots deafens me. His head explodes as the bullets hit, spraying blood and brain matter on the wall behind him. The body continues its forward motion, pushed by the momentum of its charge, and I shrink back against the wall. It goes by me and hits the railing where Gabi gives it an extra shove, sending it over the rail and down to the ground floor.

I drop to my knees, clawing my helmet off, and puke on the carpet.

"Don't bail on me!" Gabi yells.

The taste in my mouth makes me want to hurl again.

"I can't do this alone, Nora."

"I'm not fucking Nora!"

"You don't get your ass in gear, all we'll be is dead."

She turns away from me and fires a quick burst down the stairwell.

"Remember playing paintball?" she says. "Just think of it as that."

I don't know if she's referencing her memory or something from the show. But I've played paintball. I've also trained with this exact same gun I've got in my hands. I've just never fired it at another living being.

But Gabi's right. It's do or die. If I can't be confident, I can at least be competent.

I struggle to my feet and stand by the rail where I can see both the stairs and the hall. The blood Gabi shot is sprawled on the stairs. Two more scrabble over him, moving fast. Gabi and I both fire. At this range it's hard to miss, but half my shots go wild because I didn't compensate for the kickback on the gun.

The voice of my weapons trainer fills my head.

Squeeze the trigger, don't pull it.

Brace yourself for the kickback—use both hands.

Point the muzzle like you would a finger.

The next blood that comes over the growing stack of their dead gets two shots in the head when I fire. I shut away the panic. I taste bile and spit. Two more bloods come charging over the dead bodies that fill the stairs. Gabi and I stand shoulder to shoulder and we each take one, then I drop a third that's right behind them.

My ears are ringing with all this gunfire in the close confines of the stairwell.

"We could really use some help here, Joe," I say.

"We're on our way."

More bloods are climbing over their dead, but I hear something from behind me. The same door that spewed out the one monster at the start of this attack spits out two more. I get the first with a head shot, but miss the second. Before I can adjust to fire again he rams into me.

My body armour takes the brunt of the force but it still knocks the air out of me. He opens a mouth that's way too wide and filled with sharp teeth and bites at my unprotected head. Gabi slams the butt of her gun into his temple, but then she has to shoot down the stairs again and leave me to finish. Her help's enough of a break for me to jam the muzzle of my gun into the bottom of his jaw and blow away his head.

"Fuck," Gabi mutters.

I glance over to see that her magazine's empty. I rise up to take her place, giving her a chance to swap it out for a fresh one. Then I hear the *ping* of an elevator. Perfect. We're about to be attacked from both sides. I fire down the stairs and my gun runs out of ammunition.

Crap.

Gabi's still fumbling with her gun.

I swap in a fresh magazine, then shove my gun at Gabi and grab hers.

"Deal with the stairs," I tell her.

All those hours of taking weapons apart and putting them back together again serves me well. My trainer would be proud of how fast I get the job done. By the time the elevator doors open I'm standing in the hall, ready for whatever comes next.

Gabi fires behind me and we finally hear the welcome sound of more gunfire coming from below. The cavalry's here.

Three bloods step out into the hallway from the elevator. The front one is bigger than the others with far more ornate body modifications. Two rows of implanted horns run the length of his shaved head, with implanted metal spikes in between rising up like some bizarre Mohawk. Metal studs form a pattern on his face, surrounding his eyes and spiraling on his cheeks before running down in a zigzag across his bare chest. Spikes protrude from his shoulders, while more implants form ridges down both his arms.

He seems surprised to see me. His gaze darts to the room that the other bloods came out of and then back to me. He has no whites in his eyes. They're just a pair of bottomless pools, black as midnight. His gaze seems to lock on mine and I feel a sudden pressure in between my temples.

I want to lift my gun. My finger's in the trigger guard. But I can't seem to move any part of my body. I'm frozen again, except this time it's not from fear. It's something he's doing to me. Those midnight black eyes…

The realization hits hard.

It's Charlie freaking Midnight.

I didn't twig to it right away because all I've ever seen of him before was a vague Nosferatu shape in the shadows of a dream.

I can still hear the firefight down the stairs. It sounds like it's closer —maybe on the second floor. But that's not going to make any difference with me being paralyzed and Charlie Midnight walking towards me.

"I don't know how you got out of your cage," he says, "where you got that armour and gun, or who the rest of these assholes are, but you know what? I don't care. Nothing you do is ever going to make a lick of difference. So back in your cage you go because I own you, Nora Constantine, body and soul. Always have, always will."

He shouldn't have called me that.

Whatever hold he's got on me dissolves under a sudden flash of anger.

"I'm not Nora Constantine," I tell him as I raise the machine gun.

His black eyes go wide, then explode as I empty half a clip into his head. The two bloods behind him have the time to look stunned before I take them out as well. I hear something behind me and I turn, gun leveled, trigger finger ready to squeeze, but it's Gabi. I freeze.

She's holding her machine gun by her leg, muzzle pointed at the floor. The palm of her other hand comes up.

"Whoa," she says. "It's just me."

I lower the gun and look past her.

"You got the rest of them?" I ask.

She shakes her head. "No, the boys did. They've fanned out,

looking for stragglers. The stairwell's jammed, but we can take the elevator." She looks at the bodies in the hall. There's pretty much nothing left of their leader's head, but his body size and modifications are still evident.

Gabi looks like she might barf. "Was that...?"

"Charlie Midnight? Yeah. He called me Nora—pissed me off."

I look at Gabi, feeling this misplaced sense of crazy delirium.

She stares at me for a moment, then smiles and shakes her head. "Remind me never to do that again."

It's enough of a pressure release to let out a short laugh and gather my wits once more.

I take a deep breath. "I'm pretty sure he does have her in a cage somewhere around here."

"Nora?"

I nod. "I'm guessing she's in that room the bloods came out of."

I lead the way to the door. It's slightly ajar. I give Gabi a look and nod to the left, then we both hit the door hard. It's enough that it bounces off the wall but by that point we're both in the room on either side of the doorway, weapons ready.

But those three bloods must have been the only guards up here.

What we find is a row of cages, seven or eight of them. Half are empty. Two hold men I don't know. One holds a guy who looks just like Dean Farris, who played my on-and-off-again boyfriend, James Hearne, on the show. Nora's in the last one.

I stand there looking at her for a long moment, fascinated by her perfect resemblance to the woman I see when I'm in front of a mirror. The only difference is that right now she looks drawn and confused, her hair greasy, her eyes shadowed with dark hollows. I'm probably not looking so great myself, but she's suffering from who knows how many months of imprisonment.

"Who are you?" Nora asks.

"Well, I'm not Nora Constantine," I say.

Beside me, Gabi laughs.

I sling the strap of my gun over my head so that the weapon hangs at my back and cross the room to study the locks on the cages.

"Do you know where the keys are?" I ask Nora.

"In Charlie Midnight's pocket."

"Um, I'll get them," Gabi says, making a rueful face.

Nora's gaze goes to Gabi leaving the room, then returns to me.

"He's dead," I say before she can ask. "Again. I mean, if he's really Bret Palmer risen from the dead. Otherwise, he's just dead."

Gabi steps back in and tosses the keys to me. I open Nora's cage then move on to the others. Gabi helps her out. She can't stand up straight, but she won't sit down when Gabi tries to steer her to a chair.

"I need to see," she says.

I ignore the weird feeling of hearing somebody else with my voice as I open the last cage with someone in it, then help Gabi hobble Nora out into the hall. She stands over Charlie Midnight's ruined body for a long moment, then spits on it.

The elevator bell *pings*. Gabi steps in to support Nora and I swing my gun back into position, but it's only Joe and Jack. I don't see Bo.

"Where's Bo?" I ask, worry filling my chest.

"Relax," Jack says. "He's keeping an eye on things downstairs. Say hi, Bo."

"Hey Juniper," Bo's voice says in my earpiece. "You good up there?"

"I am now," I say.

Nora's leaning heavily on Gabi, studying the rest of us.

"Who are these people?" she asks Gabi.

"Friends."

Nora's gaze flicks back down to Charlie Midnight's body. "Yeah, I get that. But…"

"I'm Juniper," I say when her voice trails off. "And this is Joe and Jack."

"Why do you look exactly like me—except way more badass?"

Jack chuckles and I shoot him a dirty look.

"What?" I say. "I can't look badass?"

"No argument from me, darling," he says, reminding me a little of Cody, back in the red rock mountains.

But I guess they're all kind of related, in a way.

"It's a long story," I tell Nora.

Joe nods. "And why don't we let it ride until we get out of this place."

Dean and the other guys have crawled out of their cages, but they're not in much better shape than Nora. While Gabi takes Nora to the elevator, we help the rest of them. It's a tight fit, but no one wants to stay up here on their own, or make their way down the stairs over the bodies of the dead bloods.

Once we get to the ground floor, we pick our way through the battlefield until we're finally outside. Nora and her friends collapse on the grass.

"I knew you'd find me," Nora tells Gabi.

Gabi gets a pained look, but I can't help her there.

"So you've been there the whole two years?" I ask.

Nora looks shocked. "It's been two years?"

"Give or take," Gabi says.

"I don't get why the sheriff's office didn't do what we just did," I say.

"They tried," one of the guys says. "Midnight killed them all and turned them into bloods."

"I still can't figure out how five of you got the drop on them all," Nora says. "Or how you were able to fight off that mesmerizing thing Midnight does with his eyes."

"He pushed the wrong buttons with me," I say.

"Guys like him," Joe says, "don't do as well when the odds are more evenly matched."

"What does that mean?" Nora asks.

Joe only says, "Plus we had them outgunned."

"You didn't answer me inside," I say to Nora. "Was Charlie Midnight really Bret Palmer?"

She shrugs. "Who knows? But somebody definitely dug up Palmer's grave and Midnight showed up right after. If he was brought back to life, nobody knows how."

I do. Emma Rohlin did it, writing a book to connect with her dying daughter.

Jack and Bo have been gone for a little while. Now they come back with bottles of water and packages of jerky, which they hand around. My stomach does a little flip at the thought of eating anything, but I take the water gratefully.

"We should go," Joe says. "We've done our part but now it's up to the survivors to handle what they want to do next."

I nod. I kind of want to get to know Nora a little better and, at the same time, I want to get as far away from her as I can. It's too disconcerting to look at someone who looks exactly the same as me. Somebody who really is a part I only played on a TV show.

Nora still looks like a mess, but there's a bit of light in her eyes again.

"Who are you people?" she asks.

"Nobody important," I tell her.

Joe nods. "We just happened to be in the right place at the right time to help you out."

"You know I'll figure it out," she says. "I'm good at getting to the bottom of things, so you might as well tell me."

"There's nothing to tell," I say.

I'll leave it to Gabi to explain how much she wants. Speaking of whom.

"Gabi?" I say.

She meets my gaze and I see that I don't even have to ask the question; the answer's already in her eyes.

"This is my Nora," she says. "You've got all the support you need back home with your family of choice, but she's only got me."

"I get it."

"We're going to need that gear," Joe says.

Gabi takes off her body armour and adds it to the riot shields and helmets that Bo has already retrieved from inside the library. He makes a bundle of the weapons and protective gear and hefts it easily under his arm. He and Bo each grab one of the helmets.

"Thanks," Gabi says as she gives me a hug. "For everything."

I nod and hug her back.

When I step out of her arms, Joe takes my hand and we disappear from the Crescent Beach world, but not before I see the astonished look on Nora's face.

As soon as we're standing in the backyard of the greenhouse, it all hits me. I'm shaking so bad that Joe has to help me undo the fastenings to get the body armour off. I feel light-headed. He walks me to the picnic table, sits me down, sits beside me and puts an arm across my shoulders.

I bend down, face in my hands, overwhelmed by the enormity of what I've done. I want to throw up again but my stomach's empty. I want to cry but the tears won't come.

"I...I've killed people, Joe," I manage to get out.

Not pretend. Not in a film.

"No, you didn't," he says. "Those weren't people. I told you, once they've been turned they can't be changed back."

"I killed Charlie Midnight."

"Yeah. And he was never a person. He was always a monster. You erased a shadow and gave that world a chance to see a little bit of light."

"I've never killed anybody before."

"First time's a bitch," Jack says.

I open my eyes to see that he and Bo are sitting on their heels in front of me.

"And hopefully," Jack adds, "it's something you'll never have to do again. But Joe's right. You did good."

Beside him, Bo nods. "Yeah, I was doubtful about getting involved when Joe came to me—I mean, it's not really my business, right? But we did good. I feel good. You should, too."

"But those…they're all dead."

"They were already dead," Jack says. "We helped them rest in peace —they wouldn't have wanted to be walking around hurting people."

I straighten up a little, grateful for the steady support of Joe's arm around my shoulders. I might have fallen over otherwise. Now that the rush of action is over and the adrenalin's leaving my system, I feel the tenderness on my abdomen where the blood slammed into me. I'm going to have an unholy bruise there.

"You really believe that?" I ask Jack.

He makes the shape of a cross on his chest. "Hope to die, darling."

Joe gives me a light squeeze. "You need some rest," he says. "This kind of thing really catches up to you if you're not used to it."

"I don't think I can sleep. I'm afraid of dreaming it all over again."

"We'll guard your dreams," Bo says.

I want to ask how he can do that, but my mouth feels thick and I can't get the words out.

The last thing I remember is a wash of darkness coming over me.

10

THURSDAY

I wake in an unfamiliar bed in an unfamiliar room with the faint sound of dog laughter in my ears. I feel a confusing sense of uneasiness and contentment. I smell coffee and the distinctive aroma of bacon and eggs cooking. Resting on my leg there's a dog's head, which feels familiar. I reach down to feel the comforting bristle of Sonora's fur against my palm. She sighs at my touch. But it wasn't Sonora I heard laughing.

"Hey," a voice says.

I turn to see Jilly sitting in a chair by the side of the bed, mug in hand, Bobo snoozing contentedly on her lap. He lifts his head to look at me. That silly clown grin of his makes me smile.

"Did I faint?" I ask.

She nods and takes a sip of her coffee. "Joe said it was pretty rough over there. Saskia checked you out though. You're beat up but no breaks and no concussion. You were suffering from exhaustion and shock, so she said bed was the best remedy for you." She gives me a sympathetic smile.

Not remembering any of this is so unsettling I decide to ignore it. "I never faint."

"Oh, please," Tam says. "Girls always faint."

I turn my head to see him sitting on the other side of the bed.

"I'd give you such a whack if it didn't require moving."

He lays a hand on top of mine. "Just wanted to make sure you're my real sister and not some doppelgänger from another world."

"She'd give you a whack on the head, too."

"So you met Nora?" Jilly asks.

"Yeah, and wasn't that weird."

Now I remember dreaming last night that I saw her again. She seemed to be floating in the woods and I kept pushing through the branches to get closer, except when I finally did, it was only to find I'd been chasing my own reflection in a mirror set into the bark of a giant tree, as though it was growing there. I also remember feeling safe because sitting on either side of me were a pair of coyotes. They looked up at me. One said it was morning and I might as well get up. The other nodded, adding, yeah, we've got things to do.

Jack and Bo, keeping their promise. It was their laughter that woke me up.

"Earth to Joon," Tam says with a gentle tap on my hand.

I focus on him and we exchange smiles. "You actually met Nora Constantine?" he says.

"I did."

"How's that even possible?"

"You can ask that after meeting Gabi?"

"Where is Gabi?" Tam asks.

"She stayed behind to be with Nora."

Tam nods. "Of course she would."

"I think I want to get up," I say and give him a pointed look.

"Now you're being modest? Who do you think put you to bed?"

"Not him," Jilly says. "Joe carried you up. I have to tell you, I almost died when he carried you into the house and you were just lolling unconscious in his arms. Saskia and I put you to bed." She frowns. "That's quite the bruise you've got on your stomach."

I sit up and wince, feeling that bruise. I look around as Tam leaves the room, but I don't see my clothes. Jilly puts Bobo on the bed and goes over to a chest at the foot of the bed where she brings me my phone and some unfamiliar clothes.

"Yours were a mess," Jilly says as she lays them down on the bed. "They're in the laundry, so these'll have to do for now. They belong to Saskia, so they should fit."

"Thanks."

The sweatpants fit well. The top's a little roomy—Saskia is bigger up top than I am—but it'll be fine until I can get home.

"We sponged the worst of the blood and gore off," Jilly goes on, "but you're probably going to want a shower." She grimaces and sticks her tongue out.

I turn to the dresser and for a moment it seems like I'm seeing Nora reflected back, the way she looked when she'd just gotten out of that cage. My face is relatively clean, but I've got blood and God knows what else dried in my hair.

"I was tempted to just throw out your clothes," Jilly says, "because I don't know if all the stains will come out, but then I thought maybe you'd want some scruffy clothes for the next time you go adventuring."

I look over my shoulder to see if she's serious.

"Or not," she adds.

"What time is it?"

She shrugs. "Not sure. A little before noon, I think."

I pick up my phone to find out, and see that I've got a few texts. Most are from Tam, wondering where I am. The most recent is from Nick.

"What is it?" Jilly asks.

"There's a text from Nick."

"And you don't want to see him—or you do, but you need to recuperate, or…?"

She studies my face as she talks, trying to gauge what I'm feeling, but good luck with that, because I don't know what I'm feeling.

"I think I like him," I say, "and I'd like to see him, but I'm not ready for an actual date yet. I don't want the pressure of just one on one for a whole evening."

"So tell him we're all going bowling in a couple of days and would he like to come along?"

"Bowling?" I say.

"What? Who doesn't like bowling? Tell me you like bowling."

"I do. The whole cast and crew on the show used to go once a month and a lot of us kept getting together long after the show was over. It's just not something I've done since I left L.A."

"Oh, that's way too long." She frowns. "How come this never came up before?"

"Beats me. Where do you play?"

"Pop's Pins on Lee Street—up in Foxville. It's all ten-pin lanes and

I don't think it's changed much since it opened in the fifties. They even have the original soda fountain."

I give my belly a gentle press. The pain is immediate. "I don't know that I'll be able to bowl but I'd like to see the place. I'll text Nick to see if he wants to meet us there."

Jilly waits for me to send him the message, then gets me a towel from a linen closet and lets me take that blessed shower.

Maybe this whole going out thing will be too much, too soon, but I feel more myself once I'm clean, and I really need to make some positive memories to overwrite what happened in Crescent Beach. Not that I'm going to forget it any time soon. But I'm going to take a page from Jilly's book. She once told me that even when she's not feeling great she still puts on a cheerful face and half the time she ends up actually feeling better.

It's worth a try.

～

BY THE TIME I get to the kitchen I hear Tam playing music with Geordie in the backyard. Wendy and Jilly have decided to make me breakfast, starting with coffee, which I desperately need, and a bowl of yogurt and fresh fruit.

"Do you want pancakes or the eggs and bacon we had?" Jilly asks, leaning against the stove.

"Anything would be amazing. I'm starving."

"Eggs and bacon it is."

"You guys don't have to wait on me," I say.

Wendy smiles. "You're still looking a little peaked, and she's feeling guilty for getting you into the whole mess with Crescent Beach, so enjoy it while you can."

"Plus we never did find out how Ethan died," Jilly says.

"Yeah," Wendy adds. "The theory that someone injected him with SUX was a bust."

"Actually, I think I've figured it out," I tell them.

They both stop what they're doing and give me an expectant look.

"Well, don't leave us in suspense," Jilly finally says.

"I just need to confirm something first."

"No, no, no." Jilly shakes her head. "You can't leave us hanging. That's not how it works."

"Does Agatha Christie spill her guts," I ask, "or does she save it for a big reveal?"

That seems to mollify her. "Are we gathering all the suspects together in one room?"

I shake my head. She keeps trying to cadge an answer out of me —"Just give us the tiniest of hints!"—but I stick to my guns. I do have a last thing to confirm, but mostly, I'm just having fun teasing her.

LATER, I sit on the front steps and look out at Stanton Street, Sonora leaning against me and nudging my hand whenever she needs another pat. The oak trees are full of crows, as usual, and I find myself wondering how many of them are crows and how many are magical beings that can take the shape of people.

"So, Ethan Law," I finally say.

I say his full name with intent, willing him to come. He appears on a lower step and looks back at me.

"How do you do that?" he asks.

"Do what?"

"I'm—I don't know what or where I am, but suddenly I'm here with you."

"All I did was say your name."

"Well, stop it."

"I will. But first we need a last talk."

He sighs theatrically.

"I've figured out how you died," I say.

"I know how I died. Charlie Midnight came into my dreams and…"

His voice trails off when he sees me shaking my head.

"Then what?" he asks.

I've been thinking about this a lot. Whatever else Ethan was—and let's face it, we would never have been friends—he still cared about Edward, cared enough to want to protect Edward any way he could. So when he thought Midnight might be able to step through his dreams as a way into this world he did the only thing he could think of to keep Edward safe.

"You gave up your borrowed life," I say. "You abandoned it and let it go."

"What are you talking about?"

"You were afraid that Midnight would be able to come after Edward through you, so you disappeared out of his life. You crawled away under those bushes and tried to let yourself go the same way you left Crescent Beach. I guess you felt or saw something in the bushes?"

He gives a slow nod. "There was a kind of pull…"

"There was no gateway there, so all you did was step out of your body and with your spirit gone, it stopped living."

There's a faraway look in his eyes but he's still nodding. "I remember…"

"I know what it was like," I say. "Midnight got into my head. He was haunting my dreams and Gabi's too. I don't know about her, but if he'd upped the pressure and I couldn't have gotten him out, I'd have been just as desperate as you were."

"How did you beat him?"

"He got sloppy and I got lucky. Plus I had a gun. It's hard to put the mojo on somebody once your head's been blown off."

The words come out casually, but I can't suppress a shiver. I don't want to ever experience something like that again. Right now I hope I never have another gun in my hand.

Ethan just sits there, not saying anything.

"I'm sorry," I say.

"About what?"

"That it worked out the way it did. That you couldn't go back to the Crescent Beach world and you can't go back to Edward and your life here."

His shoulders droop. I hear the crows chattering in the trees, but they seem very far away from this pool of silence that lies between Ethan and me on the steps. Someone nearby must have cut their lawn today because the smell of grass is strong in the air.

"I hate him so much," Ethan says.

"Who? Midnight?"

Ethan nods.

"The only comfort I can offer," I tell him, "is that he's never going to hurt anybody again."

"Why do you say that?"

"Because he's dead. I killed him yesterday."

"You killed him before."

"That was Bret Palmer."

I almost add, "and that wasn't even real," but in the Crescent Beach world, it was. And I didn't kill him. Nora did.

"How do you know he won't just come back again?"

"Whatever power it was that allowed Emma and her daughter to bring that all to life doesn't exist anymore."

"So I died for nothing."

"You were protecting Edward—that's something. You were selfless and brave."

I'm laying it on a little thick, but he did care about Edward, and it doesn't hurt me to let him go away thinking he did something that mattered.

"But he doesn't know," Ethan says.

And there we go. Here's the Ethan who, if he can't be alive at least wants credit for the sacrifice he made. But I'll give him that.

"I can make sure he knows," I say.

Ethan sighs and then surprises me. "No," he says. "It's probably better this way. I don't want him to have to carry the burden of knowing I died trying to protect him."

Except that doesn't feel right either.

"So it's better that he thinks you abandoned him?" I ask. "That you just disappeared from his life and he never gets to know why?"

"I'd rather he was mad than sad."

"He's going to be both if he never learns the whole story."

Ethan's been staring out into the street. Now he looks at me again.

"If it was you," he says, "would you rather know?"

"Absolutely."

"So tell him. But don't make me out to be some kind of hero. If I were a hero, I'd have confronted Midnight the way you did."

"I had help. A lot of help."

"But still…"

I nod. That doesn't change the fact that he's dead.

He stands up.

"I guess I owe you a million dollars," he says.

I get up as well, eliciting a groan from Sonora because she's just lost the pillow of my thigh for her head.

"I guess you do," I say.

He holds a hand out to me.

"Thanks, Juniper," he says.

I lift an eyebrow.

He smiles. It's a good effort, even if it doesn't reach his eyes.

"I always knew who you were," he says.

I go to shake his hand, but as soon as I touch him he fades away. Even in the broad daylight, it's still eerie.

I don't know how long I've been sitting on the stairs with Sonora when Jilly comes out of the house and plunks down beside me. I tell her what I told Ethan and she gives a slow nod of her head.

"How did he take it?" she asks.

"Pretty well, all things considered. He's worried about Edward, of course."

"We should look in on him."

"Tomorrow," I say.

She nods. It's a really nice day, the kind we don't always pay enough attention to when they're actually happening. I lean back on my elbows and look up through the oaks to the blue sky beyond. After a few moments I turn to look at Jilly.

"How did the professor die?" I find myself asking.

Nobody in the house ever talks about it.

Jilly gives me a surprised look. "What makes you think he's dead?"

I sit up. "He's not? But he left you and Sophie his house."

"He did. And then he moved to Mabon."

"Which is…?"

"In the otherworld."

"Of course it is. You told me that before. That's where Sophie goes when she dreams."

11

SATURDAY

I go to the gym. I do some cardio, a few weights, work on the bag. My stomach hurts and the bruise is ugly but arnica is already doing wonders for my healing. What went down in Crescent Beach was brutal but I've had similar injuries filming action scenes that I insisted on doing rather than bring in a stunt double. I'm trying to process Crescent Beach like it was one of those.

Pearse comes out of his office just as I'm finishing up. Sonora lies on a towel by the bench along the wall and I sit beside her. I wipe my face with another towel and drape it across my shoulders. Pearse sits on his heels and pats Sonora before he joins me on the bench.

"Did you get your problem worked out?" he asks.

"Pretty much. The bad guys are dead and the survivors are going to try to put their lives back together."

He nods. "Gabi?"

"She stayed over there."

He nods again. "I liked her."

"Me too."

Sonora pushes her nose against his leg and he gives her a scratch behind the ear.

"And how's Juniper doing?" he asks.

"Better, now that I've had the chance to punch something."

We sit there a little longer while I give him an abbreviated version of what happened in the Crescent Beach world.

"Working the bag," he says when I'm done. "That's not going to be enough to make what happened go away."

"I know that. But it helps. The repetition clears my head."

"You should talk to somebody. Don't bottle it up."

"I'm talking to you."

"Except I'm a trainer, not a shrink."

"Yeah? What do you do when you're trying to deal with your feelings?"

He shrugs. "I work the bag."

"Asshole."

"Nice. Is that any way to talk to your elders?"

I laugh and leave him with Sonora while I go grab a shower.

"Make sure you wash that mouth of yours while you're at it," he calls after me.

I give him a one-finger salute.

~

POP'S PINS has exactly the vintage vibe that Jilly promised. I feel like I'm stepping back through time as I come through the door. Polished wooden floors and vinyl seats, eight ten-pin lanes, mood lighting, but the lanes are bright, a jukebox pumping out Buddy Holly. Everything about the place immediately puts me in a great mood, so much so that when I see Nick waiting for us I give him a big hug.

It's a good thing Wendy reserved us a couple of lanes because pretty much the whole gang from Bramleyhaugh has come along, except for Izzy and Kathy, that odd pair of girls who live in the attic, and Lyle, who offered to stay home with the dogs. The place is hopping but our lanes are waiting for us.

We rent shoes, choose our balls, order drinks from the bar with half of us going for beer, the rest opting for the soda fountain.

I sip a cola float as I wait my turn to play. "I haven't had one of these in forever," I say.

Jilly beams. "I have one every time I come—this or a root beer float."

We're not the most orderly group in the alley tonight. There are a lot of laughs, gutter balls, screams of delight when someone actually makes a strike. I'm so rusty I can't even make a spare. Plus I'm still stiff and a little sore. But it doesn't take very long to realize that Nick and I seem to really click. Maybe it's when I give him a short version of what happened to Ethan, and he doesn't think I'm crazy. Maybe it's just that I like his sense of humour and his form when he's bowling.

Actually, everything would feel pretty much perfect, except earlier in the evening I noticed this girl leaning against the shoe rental counter by the hall to the bathrooms. She's medium height, brown hair, dressed like a sixties librarian. The kind of girl who's not particularly memorable, but I notice her because throughout the evening I keep feeling her looking at me. Whenever I turn in her direction, she quickly looks away.

I set my second cola float on the table by our bench.

"I'm off to the ladies' room," I say.

I get up quickly before anyone can accompany me and walk over to where the girl is standing. She straightens up at my approach and pushes a lock of hair behind her ear.

"Do I know you?" I ask.

She gives me a small smile. She doesn't seem to know what to do with her hands, so she holds them in front of her, fingers entangled. "No," she says. "But I know you."

I stifle a groan. This is exactly how it started with Ethan.

Except then she adds, "You're Juniper Wiles—the detective who helps ghosts."

"I'm Juniper," I tell her, "but I'm not really a detect—"

"I need your help."

She says it just like that, cutting me off, her gaze earnest. I don't want to be rude and I have to admit I'm a little curious.

"Help with what?" I find myself saying.

~

"Why were you standing over there talking to yourself?" Mona asks when I get back to my party.

Everybody's lounging around the little area we've commandeered except for Sophie and Geordie, who are up next in their respective lanes. "This Is England" by The Clash comes on the jukebox for the third time in the past hour. Wendy has developed a huge interest in the band, this song in particular.

"You didn't see her?" I say.

I look around, but no one knows what I mean.

"I was talking to a ghost," I say.

Everybody looks in the direction of where the girl was standing, then back at me. I hold Jilly's gaze.

"And it looks like we have another case," I add.

She grins, then turns serious. "It's not going to be dangerous, is it?" she asks.

I shake my head. "She just wants us to find her wedding ring so that her husband can hold it in his hand when he passes. She thinks it'll make it easier for him to find her."

"Is that a real thing?" Saskia asks.

"You're the internet," I say. "You tell me."

Nick has a teasing look in his eyes. "If I didn't know differently from all I've heard tonight, I'd say your claiming to talk to ghosts is a cry for help."

That earns him a nudge in the side before I return my attention to Jilly.

"You know this is just a one-off," I say. "You up for it?"

Jilly gives me a shocked, "I can't believe you have to even ask" look, then grins.

"We'll need a name to go by," she says.

I shake my head. "We don't, actually, because we're not really detectives."

"I've got it," Mona pipes. "You could call yourselves The J-Girls Detective Agency."

"Not helping," I tell her.

Even Nick has to get in on it. "No, it needs to be classier than that. How about Coppercorn & Wiles, Private Investigators."

"Oh, I like that," Jilly says.

I smile. "Only because your name comes first."

"No, it just makes better phonetic sense. Otherwise it sounds like a wily coppercorn which—admit it—makes no sense at all."

"Nothing about this makes sense," I tell her.

"All the more reason to at least try to instill some seriousness in the name of our firm." She thinks for a moment. "I wonder how hard it is to get a private investigator's license."

"That's an excellent question," I say, "for anybody who actually wants to be one."

Geordie comes from the lane, having bowled a spare, and plunks himself down beside me on the bench.

"You know arguing is pointless," he says.

"I have to try."

He smiles. "Of course you do, but the problem is she's always had this fascination with detecting, and finding clues, and whatever else it is that private eyes do. Plus she rocks a trench coat."

"I do," Jilly says. "But I wouldn't wear one unless you did too."

"You know," I say, "it's not all fun and games for the people who are asking for help."

I know from the solemn look in her eyes that she gets what I'm saying.

"I would never forget that," she tells me.

And I know she won't.

"Coppercorn & Wiles actually sounds pretty good," I say.

ACKNOWLEDGMENTS

Thanks as always to MaryAnn, who lent her ever astute and discerning editorial eye to the story you've just read, and to first readers Julie Bartel-Thomas and Alice Vachss, and also to my most patient agent Russ Galen.

Also very special thanks to Rodger Turner, Kin Jee, Cynthia A. Taylor, Jack Johnson, Denise Cardos, Alan Allinger, Kim Miller, Samuel Beard Jr., Aaron Daniels, River Lark Madison, Lizz Huerta, Kath Sargent, Valérie Giese, Kelly Beaudoin, Michael Babinski, Beth Moore and Leslie Howle. I'm so grateful for the time and effort they all put into the going through the manuscript. Reading is fun. Critiquing and proofing is harder work, but they were willing to put in the time.

And thanks as well to my loyal readers who wait for books with great patience and are so supportive of our indie publishing endeavours.

2020-2021 has been such a crappy time. I hope this story has allowed you to step away from it for just a little while.

Ottawa, Winter 2021

ABOUT THE AUTHOR

Charles de Lint is a Canadian author with more than eighty published adult, young adult and children's books. Widely recognized in his field, he has won the World Fantasy, Aurora, Sunburst, and White Pine awards, among others. He has been inducted into the Canadian SF & Fantasy Association Hall of Fame and received a Lifetime Achievement Award from the World Fantasy Organization. De Lint is also a poet, musician, songwriter, performer and folklorist, and writes a monthly book review column for The Magazine of Fantasy & Science Fiction. He makes his home in Ottawa, Ontario. For more information, visit his website at www.charlesdelint.com.

Made in the USA
Middletown, DE
24 May 2021